I0451218

Murder Most
NOTORIOUS

LESLIE HACHTEL

Murder Most Notorious, Copyright © 2021 Leslie Hachtel

Cover Art by Jena Brignola

Layout by www.formatting4U.com

This is a work of fiction. Names, characters, places and incidents are products of the author's imagination or are used fictitiously and are not to be construed as real. Any resemblance to actual events, locales, organizations, or persons, living or dead, is entirely coincidental.

All rights reserved. No part of this book may be used or reproduced electronically or in print without written permission, except in the case of brief quotations embodied in reviews.

LeslieHachtel.com

Also Available from Leslie Hachtel

Contemporary/Historical Crossover
Stay With Me

Romantic Suspense
Texas Summer
Payback
Once Upon a Tablecloth
Memories Never Die

The Dance Series
The Dream Dancer
Emma's Dance
The Jester's Dance
A Dance in Time

The Morocco Series
Bound to Morocco
Tied to Morocco
Freed from Morocco

Historical
The Defiant Bride
Captain's Captive
Hannah's War

Acknowledgments

Thanks to Nikki Brock who helped make this book so much better and to Bob, my patient husband, for his support and wonderful attention to detail.

And to Judi Fennell who saves me every time.

Table of Contents

"Crack'd in pieces by malignant Death"

Richard III

Chapter One

Gruesome wasn't anything new to Detective Laura Chandler, but butchery always pressed its way in and burned itself on her retinas. From the preliminary description of the crime, she expected the latter and she wasn't looking forward to getting to the crime scene.

It had started out as such a lovely sunrise. Pinks and blues and golds painted across the blue sky. A thirty-minute bike ride on the Greenline, the straight, shaded pathway on the edge of the city, that had cleared her head, as it always did. She always hated to cut her ride short, since the tree-lined strip was so easy to maneuver and a soft breeze whisked away the exertion. But she never wanted to be late and start her day with a jammed up workload. Returning home to a freshly perked cup of coffee and a warm shower, it had promised, at first, to be an easy morning. She catalogued what needed to be done: a call to set up a meeting with the D.A. about a prior case and some follow-up paperwork. No major drama. Until her phone rang.

Pulling up to the scene in her unmarked Chevy, the rainbow flashing lights from the ambulance and squad cars screaming for attention, Laura took a deep breath. Swallowing her last sip of lukewarm coffee, she tied her shoulder-length auburn hair back at the nape of her neck to keep it out of her way and reduce the chance of adding DNA to the scene.

Exiting the car, she looked around and assessed the area. She grabbed some PPE from her trunk and approached the house. This was a very nice middle class neighborhood, with attractive homes, well-maintained. All the lawns were bright green in the sun, which already beat down relentlessly, even though it was only nine in the morning. Laura shook her head. Even the tall maple trees couldn't manage to ease the heat bearing down. Would she ever acclimate to the choking mugginess of a Memphis summer? Probably not since she'd been here all her life. A confirming sheen of perspiration coated her upper lip and a slick of moisture slipped down her back.

An ambulance was edged into a spot in front, its back door wide. Seated on the edge, an older woman was being treated by an EMT. She was slightly bent over and wrapped in a blanket, although the temperature even this early had to be over eighty and the humidity was through the roof. An oxygen mask covered her face.

The paramedic glanced up and Laura flashed her badge.

"Hysteria," he mouthed.

A uniform walked over to her. "She's a neighbor," he stated flatly, indicating the woman. "Discovered the bodies." Civilians generally got pretty upset when they stumbled onto dead people.

The officer stepped back, showing no interest in accompanying Laura into the house. Although that was unusual behavior, since most cops wanted to be part of the assessment, it didn't fully alert Laura to what she would find inside. A few of the other uniforms on scene huddled and whispered by the front door. She overheard one of them saying "What a way to start the week," but still that didn't give adequate warning. She shot them a look and they separated, getting busy with various tasks.

Two large oak trees flanked the front walkway, whispering of the peace of nature, and beds of multi-colored pansies along the path offered cheer which, in this case, proved misleading since the tension was thick enough to taint the atmosphere.

Stopping at the entrance, she donned her booties and gloves. Then, moving through the black and white marble foyer and into the living room, understanding punched her. Two people, a man and a woman, were tangled together on the floor in a mix of blood and severed limbs. Bits of bones caught the glint of the light coming through the window and peeked out from a cocoon of muscle and gore. One arm looked as if it was about to up and leave the body entirely. Laura couldn't tell if it belonged to the man or the woman. Both were Caucasian, late forties or early fifty-something years old, from what she could tell. Laura had seen rough in her career, but this topped anything to date. Good thing she had a stomach of iron.

One of the uniforms, this one also wearing booties, angled next to her, carefully keeping his gaze averted from the carnage. The metal stench of drying blood reached up Laura's nostrils, coating the back of her throat, and the unmistakable scent of the dead took front and center until Laura controlled it away. With a finely developed sense of smell, Laura had learned long ago to breathe through her mouth when confronted with

3

death. Too bad she hadn't brought some Vicks. Nothing masked the smell like that stuff.

She turned to face the officer, a good-looking man in his late twenties. Two unnatural spots of pink painted his cheeks, but his set jaw indicated he was going to treat this as a professional.

"I'm Officer Sanchez. I was first on the scene and the neighbor out there, a Mrs. Barbara Cassis, threw herself into my arms. I came in and assessed the victims, then called for the coroner. I tried to comfort her while we waited for the EMT's and she just spouted out a bunch of information. I wrote it all down as fast as I could." He ran his fingers through his thick dark hair and then cleared his throat, seemingly embarrassed.

"Great," Laura replied. Sanchez dropped his gaze and Laura could only guess that other detectives had not been happy to get information from a mere officer. She wasn't picky. Any knowledge was good for her. "Go ahead," she encouraged.

He read to her from his notes. "Nora and Evan Whiting. According to Mrs. Cassis, they've lived here for twenty years or so. One daughter, Alexandra, who lives in the next town over. The witness wasn't sure where exactly, but she thinks near the university where she works. These were quiet people. They went to church every Sunday. The neighbor said she saw them coming home last night around nine and was surprised to see their front door open wide this morning about seven, so she came over. When she walked in and saw them, she just started screaming and one of the other neighbors called 911. She wasn't sure who since no one came over." So much for caring neighbors. At least someone called for help.

Well, that clearly established the time of death sometime between nine p.m. and seven this morning. Was the killer waiting for the vics when they returned home? Laura held up her hand, and stepped back out into the foyer to check for a keypad, indicating an alarm system. It was flashing green. She motioned Sanchez over.

"Was the alarm going off when you got here?" she asked.

"No, ma'am. Mrs. Cassis said she didn't hear anything."

So the vics either knew their assailant or they didn't set it before the attack. Or had the perp managed to disarm it?

"Thank you." Laura said, recording the information in her own notebook. "Has anyone touched anything?"

"No ma'am. I was the only one who came inside after Mrs. Cassis described..." He lifted his chin to indicate the victims. "When I saw them, I didn't bother checking for pulses."

Laura closed her eyes in agreement.

"Then I went back out and we waited for you and the crime scene people. We knew not to mess with anything."

"Good job, Sanchez."

Sanchez snapped a nod and moved away as Laura turned back to the slaughter.

The woman was on the bottom, the man draped on top of her in a bizarre tableau of protection. They had been dressed for bed, he in light-colored pajamas, she in an old cotton nightgown. The carpet beneath the couple might have had a pattern at one time, but it was just drying pools of thick crimson now. The woman's expression was frozen into a rictus of horror and disbelief. Laura stared at the two and indulged terrible sadness for a brief moment. Then, the clinical stepped up and pushed emotions aside.

Massaging the knot forming in her neck, the sound of retching caught her attention. Sighing, she turned to one of the several uniforms who had wandered into the foyer.

"Please take the rookie outside and get him some water," she called to no one in particular. Her tone was not unkind. This scene could turn the stomach of the most seasoned.

Her attention back on the victims, Laura laser-focused in. The ultimate betrayal was when someone you knew, trusted, brought an axe to the party.

The offending weapon lay nestled next to the work it had wrought. Laura knelt down next to it and cocked her head, then pulled out her phone and measured it. The handle was eighteen inches, bathed in gore, but the patterns on the wood were smooth. The killer must have worn gloves, which would confirm premeditation. A single blade, it was probably readily available in lots of stores. CSI would collect it and attempt to gather any fingerprints, but she doubted they would find any.

Sanchez walked up next to her and she turned to him.

"If it helps, it looks to be a Hudson Bay Camp Axe. I used to have one when I went camping with my family. They're about two pounds."

"Easy to get?" she asked.

"Any camping store, sporting goods, so yes," he answered, confirming her supposition.

"Thank you, Officer Sanchez. You saved me a lot of Google time."

He smiled and strode away.

Laura stood, took a few steps back and surveyed the room. A table lamp had been knocked to the ground, its base shattered, chunks of colored glass scattered about, not even bothering to glitter in dismay. Behind the bodies, the coffee table was knocked askew, its granite top streaked with blood. Splatter, like someone gone wild with red paint, was on the walls, the furniture, and the knick-knacks, attesting to the hideous violence of the crime. A single, smeared, bare footprint next to the corpses led nowhere.

A pathetic bowl had scattered its contents of popcorn and two glasses of what appeared to be some kind of soda angled next to each other on the floor. So the vics were about to settle in and watch TV when they were interrupted.

She pulled out her cell phone and started snapping pictures from every angle. It helped her to a have a visual record of the crime scene.

Laura followed a hallway to the master suite, then into the master bathroom. Streaks of watery blood left a trail down the shower walls. There was no doubt the killer would have been soaked in the blood of his victims and knew leaving the scene so conspicuously decorated would have someone calling 911. The perp had thoughtfully left the towel on the floor. Now why would a killer who had been so careful as to wear gloves have been equally careless with a towel, which most certainly had hairs or other possible DNA?

Laura returned to the actual scene. Knowing without looking that her partner, John Resciniti, had stepped up behind her, Laura was grateful he was canny enough to keep his mouth shut. Certainly, his boy-next-door good looks had opened a lot of doors, but he took nothing for granted. He had only been a detective for a few months and was anxious to improve on his skills. And they immediately connected as partners, which made her life easier.

Laura pointed to the area. "What do you see?" she asked, ignoring the crime scene photographer who had appeared and was clicking away next to them. Letting John make his own initial assessments and then discovering if he was right or wrong would teach him more than lecturing.

John heaved a breath and walked further away so he was facing the corpses at an angle. "The two vics were standing next to each other. The assailant was here." Pretending to grasp a murder weapon, he swung his arms in a wide arc. "He swung at the woman first and the man tried to jump in front of her as she went down. And he continued his work until he had finished them both." He swallowed hard. "And then some." Looking at Laura for a reaction, she could tell he was pleased when she nodded.

"Wait," Laura responded. "You said 'he'. Why couldn't it be a woman?"

John frowned, considering her words, then shook his head. "I guess it could. But she'd have to be pretty strong."

Laura shrugged. "Wanna arm wrestle?" she asked, raising her eyebrows.

"No. You're already smarter and prettier. You don't have to completely humiliate me."

Ignoring the compliment, she continued. "Look at

the footprint. It would have to be a woman or a very small man."

John dropped his chin a notch. "Point taken. No more jumping to conclusions."

Laura turned at the sound of footsteps coming into the room. Dr. Marian Vanhouten, the medical examiner, strode in, her comfortable shoes scraping the floor. Laura wondered if she ever picked her feet up when she walked. But Marian was very good at her job. Not for the first time, Laura wondered what she did after work. Marian was only forty something, but her hair was the steel gray of someone older. She was lean and her movements were efficient, wasting nothing. Did she have a life other than death? Marian approached the bodies, walked in a circle around them and looked at Laura.

"Well, saves me re-sharpening my bone saw. And I certainly don't have to guess at the murder weapon." Staring down, she shook her head. "Haven't seen anything like this before, and I've been at this more than twenty years." She whistled a tune Laura recognized but couldn't place.

"What is that song?"

Marian smiled. "Lizzie Borden took an axe…"

Shaking her head in feigned disgust, Laura stepped away to wander around the rest of the house, John at her heels. There were no footprints leading away from the bodies, and only the one bare imprint, so the perp must have removed her shoes before the crime, then covered her feet after, which more than suggested premeditation.

This was a single story house, in apparently good shape, three bedrooms, two and a half baths, with a roomy, modern, and efficient kitchen, no dirty dishes in the sink. The house was clean but not obsessively so. A sweater flung over a chair in the bedroom, a pair of socks on the floor.

The only other pieces out of place in the master bedroom were two framed pictures that had been knocked to the floor face down. Laura picked up the first one. The glass was cracked in several places, the photograph missing. It was the same with the other.

"Family photos?" John suggested.

"Possibly. But this certainly suggests the murders were even more personal."

"Yeah," he agreed.

"I want you to go through this place. Look in drawers, cupboards, cabinets, closets," she stated. "Tell me what you're looking for."

"I guess I won't know unless I find it. But I will pay attention."

"Good. You're looking for anything that might give us some insight into the vics or their assailant."

Something about this case rippled through Laura like a windy day over water. It wasn't her first murder case and she was certain it wouldn't be her last, but she was certain it would end up tattooed on her soul like no other.

Chapter Two

Laura left Captain Donner's office after briefing him, and angled her way through the squad room to her corner desk. She was grateful he never tried to micromanage her, unlike his predecessor who thought women should be barefoot and pregnant. Donner trusted her to get the job done.

Glamorous was not a term that would apply here. The furniture was old and scarred and the floor worn down from a thousand pairs of feet in and out over the years. The only thing new was the coffee maker and that was only because the captain insisted. Thank heavens.

This was Memphis, so the room always held the scent remnants of barbeque from late nights and long hours. It was comforting compensation for the work.

She had no sooner sat in her non-ergonomic wooden chair with the worn seat when Ella, the station receptionist ran over, her young face pink with excitement. The girl was nearly bouncing from foot to foot, sending her ponytail into a frenzy. "Have you seen him?"

"Who?" Laura asked, not really interested. Returning from the crime scene had her thoughts elsewhere. Usually, Ella was amusing, but today Laura's sense of humor was lacking.

"The new cold case guy," Ella stage whispered, as if this was information too important to be shared. "He just transferred here after we opened the department. He's a detective." She was almost swooning.

Laura was only half listening. "What about him?" Laura was vaguely aware there was a new detective in the department, but right now she had more important things to think about.

"Movie star!" Ella leaned in conspiratorially. "You need to make an effort to check him out." She looked up at the ceiling and hugged herself. "Yummy!"

"Okay, sure," Laura responded. Ella was one of those people who despised silence and needed to fill it with any idle chatter that occurred to her. She was sweet enough and good at her job when she wasn't yattering. Luckily, she was called away and Laura sighed. Ella got so excited over so little. She probably didn't realize cold case cops were usually tired and ready to just sit back and review paperwork and do research. Not Laura's idea of stimulating. Her thoughts immediately returned to the murders. Capital crimes were certainly not a phenomenon around here, but these were particularly outstanding in their brutality. Either they were looking at a completely deranged killer or this was personal. Which didn't exclude completely deranged.

She picked up her notes from the morning and again her work was interrupted by the chiming of her phone.

"Hey, Cara," Laura said, irritated at the interruption, but relieved it was her best friend.

"Hey. You up for a drink tonight?"

Recently divorced, Cara was always ready to socialize and scout for her next ex-husband. Her work in real estate was perfectly suited to her outgoing personality and so different than Laura's everyday dealings with the dark side. Talking to Cara always made Laura feel better.

Laura tried not to let the disappointment get to her. She would have loved to have a drink and just visit with her friend. "I would be, but I can't."

"Don't tell me. Another yucky murder?"

"Yep."

"You know, you're going to have to stop letting work interfere with your social life."

"Well, as soon as I win the lottery…"

"Oh, I know you. You would still work. I'll forgive you this time, but dinner soon? There's a new place I want to try and…"

"I know," Laura interrupted, laughing. "New being the key word here. New faces, new possibilities."

"Exactly."

Laura hung up and couldn't help but smile. Cara always had hope for the next best romance, but Laura's short-lived marriage had done it for her. Other than the occasional casual date, she spent her time focused on her career. Relationships were not her strong suit. She had never had a role model for that kind of thing and she felt perfectly content without a man in her life. Realizing her thoughts were drifting, she forced herself to focus.

A quick Google search and Laura confirmed what the neighbor had said. The Whitings had one child, a daughter, Alexandra, twenty-six and working as an admissions advisor at the nearby university. She found the daughter's address and scribbled it in her notebook. Laura was not looking forward to giving the notification. There was no easy way to break this kind of news.

Deciding she needed some caffeine to fully concentrate, Laura headed to the break room. She hadn't slept well lately and it was beginning to tell. Maybe it was the portent of things to come—like this day. When the first part of your day had been an axe murder massacre, she could only wish it might improve. But Laura also knew that putting the puzzle pieces together that would lead to the perp—that was why she was here. It was something she was good at. In fact, she had the best solve record in the department. Getting the bad guys. That's what had motivated her from the very first and it made her feel...

Happy to stall a few more minutes before the unenviable task of seeing the daughter, she reached for a cup and rinsed it out. The dark stains were embedded, but at least she wouldn't catch anything. She was just pouring the steaming liquid into her cup and adding creamer when she heard footsteps. Raising her gaze, her breath caught in her throat. Ella had not been exaggerating. He was so handsome. Scratch that. She now knew the meaning of drop dead gorgeous. Thankfully, her heart continued to beat, only much faster than a moment ago. And she managed not to actually drool.

Tall, at least six feet two, with a dark brown gaze that dove directly into her soul. He was bald and his skin was the color of the coffee she had stopped stirring. And no ring on his left hand. Her girl parts woke up and kicked her. That was a shock, since that happened in?... she couldn't remember the last time.

"Hello," he said, moving a little closer and holding out his hand. His voice was like thick lotion poured over dry bared skin. "I'm Devin Andrews."

The name was familiar somehow and she wracked her brain to remember. Cocking her head, it came to her. He was the one whose partner OD'd a year ago. Pain shot through her chest, imagining what it had been like for him.

Shaking off the knowledge, Laura grasped his outstretched hand, cautioning herself not to hold on too long. "Laura. Laura Chandler." She cleared her suddenly tight throat. "Detective Laura Chandler." Speaking the title made her feel more in control.

"Heard you had an interesting morning," he said, lifting an eyebrow.

"Yeah," she scoffed. "Interesting. So you must be the new cold case guy."

"That's me. Paperwork is now my middle name."

"Why cold cases?" It was the first question that popped into her head after 'can I jump your bones right here?', then realized it might be an uncomfortable question. No doubt the death of his partner contributed and she wanted to kick herself for her insensitivity. But she was off-balance. He was so not what she had expected, but Ella had warned her. Weren't cold case guys supposed to be near retirement or something? Of course, she was certainly not complaining.

His eyes narrowed slightly, his expression very serious. "Because the victims and their families deserve more."

Laura dropped her gaze. "Yes. Yes they do."

Then, he smiled. "But if I can help you at all, please don't hesitate."

That smile. The room vibrated with it. "Thanks. I might just take you up on that." *Or something else.* Behave, she admonished herself. But he was so damned hot. Now, she was beginning to sound like Cara. Heaven forbid!

***

She is one beautiful woman, Devin thought as he walked down the steps to his basement office. All that dark hair curling to her shoulders with red highlights, those amazing green eyes and a body that—wow. Just wow. He stopped on the third step. He'd forgotten his coffee. He would look like an idiot if he went back now. And the very last thing he wanted to do in front of Laura Chandler, Detective, was look foolish.

Devin knew she was smart and her reputation had preceded her, but he didn't expect her to be so heart-stoppingly sexy. His Google search of Detective Chandler hadn't revealed too much. Divorced, no kids. Graduating from the Academy eight years ago, she had put in her time as a street cop and worked her way up to detective four years ago. Of course, fighting crime in this city was like killing a hydra: cut off one head and three more appear, so if you worked hard and you were smart, there were definite opportunities for advancement.

Definitely out of his league, right? His mother would disagree, but then she thought he hung the moon. He did love his mother.

It had taken a while to get over Jillian. Doubting himself after she left, he had sought counseling and then when Jim died, he had to fight hard against the demons that threatened. He was winning most of the time, and he honestly believed he was ready to move on.

He was going to at least give it a try. It would take some thought and taking it slow, he decided. Rushing in and acting like the fool would not impress this woman. And right now, he definitely wanted to impress her. And what could go wrong? Another broken heart? Besides, out of his league or not, he was not a quitter.

He heaved a sigh, and thoughts about the pile of files on his desk brought him back as he stepped into his office. Compact, which was a nice word for claustrophobically small, it had been sectioned off from the evidence corral and reminded him of a holding cell. Even when it was new, it was probably hideous, with dark grey concrete walls and a scuffed linoleum floor, but people didn't come here for the décor.

His chair, the cracked leather on the seat faded to a sort of green-gray, groaned aloud as he sat and perused the stack in front of him. The files had been dumped in no particular order, which suited Devin. No case would be more important than the one he was working on until it was solved. He opened the one on top.

August 2008-RaeAnn Smalley, 47 years old. White female. Body was found buried in a shallow grave in the middle of one of the city's parks. Don and Nancy Pariss, local residents, made the discovery while out walking. Their dog apparently dug up the remains and the couple notified police. Coroner determined COD to be blunt force trauma to the skull. Smalley had been dead approximately 6-8 months. She was divorced and her ex-husband, Burt Smalley, had remarried. He and his family had moved to Eastern Tennessee three months prior to the time of death, alibi verified. Two children: Amy, age 9 and Randy, age 12. Full custody of both children had been transferred to father in the divorce proceedings. No known enemies, no life insurance.

17

Damn, and it was almost always the husband, Devin snorted. How good was that alibi anyway, he asked himself. But if it checked out, as the file reported, he wondered why he couldn't have picked a more difficult one? He knew the drill. One step at a time. Check everything and check it again. Take nothing for granted. Taking a deep breath and sitting forward, he opened his laptop and started to type some notes.

***

Trees canopied the sidewalk along the campus walk, easing some of the mid-day oppression from the sun although the humidity wouldn't relinquish its hold even when the day gave up. Laura made her way slowly to the building housing the university offices. The air was like walking through a wet blanket.

The administration building still maintained an air of the regal glory from an earlier age. Brick steps led up to the entrance. Opening the heavy, carved wooden door, she stepped into the dark cool interior and breathed a sigh of relief. The building exuded age and purpose. A quick glance around and she headed to the door marked "Admissions" and stepped inside. A long reception desk stood guard over the offices behind it. An obviously very disinterested young woman, with multiple piercings and a tattoo up the side of her neck, managed to pull her eyes away from her phone and give Laura a questioning glance.

"I'm here to see Alexandra Whiting."

The woman angled her head behind and to the left and went back to her phone.

Don't let me disturb you.

Alexandra's door was open, revealing an office cluttered with papers, burying the surface of the desk and the two chairs in front of it. A pile of files reached about a foot high next to the computer as she tapped away at the keys. Her gaze lifted from her work when Laura rapped on the doorframe.

"Yes?"

Laura slipped into the room, pushed aside her jacket to show her badge, and closed the door. All the color drained from Alexandra's face and her body visibly stiffened. It was obvious her expectation was not of something pleasant.

"Can I help you?" she ventured. She raised her hands to her face, then dropped them to her lap. It seemed anyone with a badge was no longer automatically considered a friend and a visit from one of them never brought good news.

Laura moved some of the papers back from the nearest chair and perched on its edge as she assessed the Whiting's daughter. Alexandra was pretty in an unspectacular kind of way, slender with shoulder-length blonde hair and brown eyes. Her suit was a soft shade of teal, well-tailored and accented with a lace blouse. The outfit screamed designer, bought in Beverly Hills or on Fifth Avenue. It seemed a little over done, but then Laura was so used to dressing in her sensible blouses and skirts or pants, she had little interest in expensive clothes.

Alexandra inhaled, blew it out and tightened her muscles, as if expecting bad news, then visibly relaxed. "How can I help you?" she repeated. The words were more cordial than the tone, which was flat. Oddly, her reaction seemed a little theatrical, forced even. Most people were apprehensive or surprised, but this woman's response seemed as overdone as her outfit. Laura filed that and focused on her purpose for being here.

She had found that ripping off the band-aid was the best policy. "Ms. Whiting, I am so sorry to inform you your parents are dead."

For a moment, the woman didn't move. Then, her eyes widened. "What?" She blinked several times and dropped her head, pressing her palms against her cheeks. She lifted her gaze and tilted her head to the side, looking at Laura as if she were some new species she hadn't encountered before.

"They were found this morning. They were murdered."

Alexandra swallowed loudly. She tilted her head in the other direction now, as if Laura were speaking a foreign language. "What do you mean?"

Laura had to assume this was shock, but she was determined to have the other woman understand what she was saying. "They were killed sometime between last night and this morning."

Alexandra's mouth dropped open. "But… that can't be. My parents? No. You must be mistaken. I spoke to my mother yesterday morning." The frozen expression suddenly morphed into one of pure horror. Sobs choked off her words and tears streaked down her face, dripping on the papers on the desk.

"I'm afraid not." Laura pulled her notebook out of her bag, then raised her gaze and paused, giving the other woman a moment. "Again, I apologize, but I have a few questions I need to ask."

"Now?" The words were strangled in sobs.

"Yes, I'm sorry. But the more information we have, the sooner we can find out who did this."

Alexandra nodded and wiped away the moisture with the back of her hand, then reached for a box of tissues in her top drawer. "Okay."

"Did your parents have any enemies, anyone who might want to hurt them?"

Suddenly, like flipping a switch, Alexandra was alert and very calm. The change in her was startling. "God, no. They weren't very social, but they did get involved with their church. Everyone loved them. They wouldn't hurt anyone and no one would want to hurt them." A tear that had hovered on her cheek dripped onto some paper.

"And what church is that?" Laura promoted.

"The First Baptist. They loved the Lord." Alexandra sniffed and coughed, then shook her head, again in denial of her loss.

"And I have to ask you where you were last night and before you came to work."

Her eyes widened again. "You're joking, right?"

This was a more normal response, and Laura remained quiet, waiting for Alexandra to answer the question.

"Am I a suspect?" Disbelief mixed with anger filled her tone.

"Just trying to eliminate anyone we can connect to the… your parents." Laura's voice was soft and Alexandra's shoulders slumped.

"I was working until about seven last night. And then I went home." Another sob tore through Alexandra's body. "They were being killed and I was going on with my life as if nothing was wrong."

"I am so sorry," Laura repeated, then hesitated, giving the other woman another moment. "Did you stop anywhere on the way home? And can anyone verify what you just told me?"

Alexandra closed her eyes and audibly exhaled. "The security guard was here when I left and I stopped by the McDonalds on the way home. My boyfriend was there and we ate the food and watched TV. Then we went to bed. This morning, I woke up, got dressed and came to work."

"Can I have your boyfriend's name and address?"

"Sure. His name is Jeff Hines. And we live together."

"Do you know where I can find him now?"

"Probably in class or in his office. He's a professor of biology here."

"And how about your relatives? Aunts, uncles, cousins?" Laura pressed.

Alexandra shook her head. "There's no one else."

Laura frowned. "Really? No other relatives? On either side?"

"Well, my mother had a sister, a twin, but I never met her and my mother never spoke about her. But then Mom wasn't close to her parents, either." Another tear trickled down. "I'm pretty sure they died." She stared off into space for a moment. "My father's parents were killed in a car accident before I was born and he was an only child."

"Do you know why your mother wasn't close to your grandparents?"

"My mother did something they didn't like right after she graduated from high school and they never forgave her. They threw her out and she was only eighteen or so."

"Do you know what that was?"

"I think it was because she had me," Alexandra replied, then shrugged. "Before Mom and Dad were married. Apparently he didn't know about me until after I was born and then they got married."

"Why do you think your maternal grandparents have passed away?" Laura pressed.

Alexandra shrugged. "My mother mentioned something about it a while ago. She was sad she wasn't able to make it right, I think."

"And your aunt? Do you know if she's still living?"

"I wouldn't have any way of knowing. I guess I always wondered why she didn't contact my mother after their parents died, but I don't even know her name."

"How about your parents' friends?" Laura asked.

"You should check at their church. I think that was the sum total of their social life."

"We will, thanks. Oh, and we need to collect a DNA sample from you. And get your fingerprints."

Alexandra's jaw dropped. "Why?" Her voice had risen.

"Standard procedure. Your DNA and your prints are certainly all over your parents' house, so it will help us eliminate you in our search there."

"You don't need my fingerprints. They're already in your database since I work for a school."

"Humor me. I'm sure you aren't in the criminal database."

Laura took out a collection kit and swabbed the inside of Alexandra's cheek. Then she held out the fingerprint kit. Once both tests completed and wrapped in plastic, Laura slipped them into her bag.

"Thank you." Laura passed Alexandra a business card. "I'll be in touch and if you think of anything that might help, please don't hesitate to call me. And again, I am so sorry for your loss." Laura hesitated at the door. "One more question. There were some framed pictures in the bedroom."

"Yes. What about them?" Angling her head, it was clear Alexandra was puzzled by the question.

"What were they pictures of?"

She frowned in thought. "Oh, well, one was of my parents and me when I was little and we went to an amusement park. One of our rare outings. And the other was the three of us when I graduated college. Why do you ask?"

"They're missing."

Alexandra let out a little gasp. "Do you think whoever hurt my parents..." She swallowed audibly. "Do you think they might be coming after me, too?"

"There's no real evidence to indicate that, but just be careful. If you get nervous, or see anyone suspicious, don't hesitate to let me know."

But would the perp target Alexandra next? Laura wouldn't have thought so under other circumstances, but the missing pictures and the means of death made these murders very personal. She opened her cell to call the local sheriff's office and ask them to keep an eye out.

After getting directions, Laura then headed across the campus to the biology department.

Housed in an older building, the dark corridors and worn floors declared upgrades were not a priority here.

Locating Jeff Hines' office was easy, and the door stood open. No one was inside, so Laura leaned against the wall to wait. A few minutes later, a man of about thirty came strolling down the hallway and caught her eye. He was tall and slim, but wiry. His horned-rimmed glasses seemed appropriate. He was not handsome, but also not unappealing, with brown hair and eyes. He looked like the prototype biology professor.

"Can I help you?"

"Are you Jeff Hines?" Laura asked.

"I am."

She flashed her badge and Jeff ushered her into his office and indicated the guest chair.

When he was seated, he looked directly at her. "I know why you're here. Alex just called me. It's so terrible. I'll help in any way I can."

Although he seemed sincere, Laura still had that niggling feeling he wasn't quite as he appeared. "Can you tell me where you were last night?"

"Of course, I got home about six and waited for Alex. She showed up around an hour or so later with food. We ate and went to bed."

"Did you know the Whitings?"

"I'd met them a few times. Alex said they wouldn't approve of our living together, so we never invited them to our house."

"Did you like them?" Laura asked nonchalantly.

Jeff shrugged. "I didn't really know them. They were a little uptight, if you know what I mean. Although I don't think people use that expression anymore."

"Uptight how?"

"Rigid in their views. Alex was raised with a lot of rules." He clamped his mouth shut, as if he'd said too much. Then, dropping his shoulders and sitting back, he continued. "She loved her parents and this is quite a shock. I was on my way to see her, but I had to stop by my office to lock the door."

"I need a DNA sample from you and your fingerprints. Just to eliminate you." She dug into her bag for a collection vial and fingerprint kit.

Jeff stared at her as she stood and had him open his mouth to swab his cheek and then slipped the test into the container. As with Alexandra, she had him hold a card and then placed that in plastic.

"Thank you." Laura then handed him a business card. "Please call me if you think of anything that might help."

He stood, tapping the desk with his fingers. "Of course. Now, if you'll excuse me, I need to see Alex."

They parted ways and again Laura had an uneasy feeling about him. But he didn't strike her as the type to wield an axe. He was more the con man type. Which was an odd impression since he was a professor of biology.

Chapter Three

Afternoon waning light gave an eerie glow to the house next door to the crime scene as Laura approached, but after this morning, she thought the ghostly appearance appropriate. She glanced over at the Whitings, yellow tape glaring in vivid relief against the background of the house, and wished the building could talk. It would save so much time. But then, she wouldn't have a job.

This home was smaller and the yard could definitely use some attention. Weeds and knee-high bits of grass were liberally sprinkled across the lawn. An old, withered wreath of dried flowers decorated the front door, which was badly in need of some fresh paint. The concrete steps up to the porch were cracked in places and crying out to be swept free of the dead leaves, probably still hanging out since last autumn.

Barbara Cassis opened the door slightly at Laura's knock. The wrinkled hand resting on the frame was trembling, her face drained of all color, except for the red rims of her eyes which evidenced her recent tears. Laura flashed her badge.

"I'm Detective Chandler. Do you remember me?" She kept her voice low and her tone soft.

"From the Whitings?" she sniffed, opening the door a little wider. "So horrible." She pressed her other hand to her throat.

"Yes. May I come in?" Laura asked with quiet respect.

The woman nodded, grey hair escaping from the tight bun at the nape of her neck. Dropping her head, she led the way into the living room, leaving a trail of cloying, too sweet perfume. The house itself carried the scent of older homes, a cross between musty and slightly sour with an undertone of Lysol. A well-worn couch covered in a faded floral fabric sat in the center of the room. A coffee table made from an old trunk squatted in front of it, flanked by two petite striped chairs. Fidgeting with her skirt, Barbara perched on the edge of the sofa, and Laura sat across from her.

"I am so sorry, Mrs. Cassis. I know this must be very difficult for you. But I do want to hear what happened while it's still fresh in your mind."

"Barbara, please." The woman nodded. "I already told that other policeman who was there. Such a nice young man. So kind to me."

"Yes," Laura encouraged. "Please tell me again what you told him."

"I live alone since my husband, my dear Mort, passed. I do miss him so much. Well, I usually mind my own business, but it was so strange. Evan and Nora, the Whitings. I mean, weren't exactly friendly. But they were good neighbors. Quiet." She hesitated, then leaned slightly forward. "Does their daughter know?"

"Yes, I informed her a little while ago."

Barbara pressed her lips together. "So terrible, so terrible." She lifted her watery gaze. "I will never forget what I saw. Never.' She licked her dry lips. "How could someone do that? It was like a horror movie. And I'll have to pretend that's all it was or I'll never be able to close my eyes and sleep again." She sniffed again. "This is… was… such a safe neighborhood."

Laura shook her head. "I can't imagine you're in any danger. But I would make sure to lock my door if I were you."

Barbara twisted her hands in her lap. "Oh, you needn't worry about that. And I have that Life Alert service." For emphasis, she held up the button she wore around her neck. "They'll call for help for me."

"Good. That's good." Laura sat back.

"Can I get you something? Some tea or … I'm sorry I don't have any cookies. I don't bake anymore. Not since Mort passed."

"I'm fine, thanks. Now, you were telling me how you discovered the Whitings." She was careful not to use words like corpses or bodies.

"Right. Well, I usually go for an early morning walk. The doctor says it will help with my backaches. I get terrible backaches. I do hope it's not that terrible arthritis or a slipped disc or something. Maybe it's my mattress. I think it might be time to get a new one. I must go back to the doctor one of these days, but I'm afraid of what he'll tell me. Getting old isn't for cowards."

Laura closed her eyes for a moment. *Patience. She's obviously lonely so let her tell it in her own way.* "You were saying you were going for your walk."

"That's right. So, I was passing by their house. The Whitings I mean, and I noticed their front door was wide open. That had never happened before. I was worried something was wrong, so I walked up to see if everything was all right. And of course it wasn't." A tear tracked down her cheek. "I walked inside and…

I'm pretty certain I started to scream. I don't remember much after that."

"Did you see anyone coming or going any time since yesterday? Anything or anyone that was suspicious?" Laura pressed. "Someone in the neighborhood you didn't recognize?"

"No. The only unusual thing was the wide open front door this morning. That'll teach me to mind my own business."

As if, Laura thought, but not unkindly. "Mrs. Cassis, I know how difficult this has been for you," she repeated. "I appreciate your time." She reached into her bag and withdrew her business card. "I want you to call me right away if you think of anything else. Day or night."

***

It was early the next morning when Resciniti slid into the chair next to Laura's desk and waited patiently for her to talk. She closed her laptop and gave him her attention.

"Just doing some background," she said, shaking her head. "Not sure if it will help. My guess is there aren't going to be any surprises from the coroner, so let's focus on victimology. I want to know everything about the vics, from where they worked and played to what they had for breakfast. Did you find anything at the house?"

"No. Nothing out of the ordinary. Other than the actual crime scene, nothing appeared disturbed except those pictures in the bedroom. Nothing had been ransacked, no closet doors opened, and all the jewelry appeared to still be in a case on the dresser, along with his wallet containing about two hundred and fifty dollars and various credit cards."

"So, robbery doesn't seem to be a motive," Laura affirmed. "Not that I thought it would be. Robbers don't usually break into houses carrying an axe. Murderers do that."

"True. Unless they had some secret safe with millions we couldn't locate and the axe was incentive for the combination? Maybe the daughter can tell us if that's the case." He huffed a sigh. "I know that's farfetched. I was just hoping to find something."

"Well, that would be too easy, wouldn't it?" Laura returned. "We need to concentrate on neighbors, relatives, friends and anyone who might have hated them enough to do what they did."

"Okay, where shall we start?"

"Alexandra mentioned an aunt. She said the woman was her only living relative. Apparently the aunt wasn't in contact with the Whitings and Alexandra never met her. There might be something there. She also said her mother didn't have any contact with her parents who are listed as deceased."

"You thinking some family drama?" He raised an eyebrow.

"It would have to be pretty serious for such brutal killings. But you never know where the trail will lead."

"What do you have so far?" he asked.

"The mother's maiden name was Kessler. Background didn't have much on her parents, since they were apparently pretty law-abiding. The father was an investment banker and the mother was society, involved in fund raising, that kind of thing. According to records, there were two daughters: Nora and Natalie. They were identical twins. But, according to Alexandra, Natalie was estranged from the family. I want to know why. I can't find any paper trail for her, so we'll have to dig deeper. She's the first one I want to talk to after the neighbors."

"So Nora Whiting came from money. Interesting, since their home didn't reflect that. But if she had nothing to do with her family…" He dropped his gaze in thought, then raised it again. "Unless twins are separated at birth, aren't they usually pretty close?"

Laura tilted her head. "I would think so. But obviously not in this case."

She pushed her hair back and rubbed that constant knot in her neck again. "Meanwhile, when you interview the neighbors, don't forget to ask if there are any cameras in the neighborhood. Wouldn't it be nice if we could catch the killer on film."

"Yeah. You got it." Resciniti nodded and stood. Hesitating, he turned back to her. "So much rage," he said quietly, shaking his head.

Laura made her way to the break room, craving more caffeine. She shook her head in disgust that whoever had poured the last cup hadn't even bothered to rinse out the pot. As the water ran, her thoughts drifted. If the daughter's alibi checked out, that would presumably eliminate her boyfriend as a suspect, too, since they were together at the time designated for the killings. No other family but the aunt, no enemies… well, someone hated them.

She tried to clear her mind as she focused on the hot liquid dripping into the pot. The aroma of fresh coffee always made her smile. It was, like bacon, one of those foods whose smell was even better than its taste.

Pouring a steaming cup, she wondered what delicious new cold-case guy Devin was doing about now. Maybe he needed a pick-me-up too and would walk in any minute. She glanced at the empty doorway. Or maybe he was the jerk who took the last cup. No. He wasn't the type. He struck her as thoughtful and considerate. Or maybe she was just projecting, since he was so damn gorgeous.

Making her way back to her desk and picking up her pile of sticky notes, Laura headed to a larger office in the far corner next to the captain's that served as a makeshift conference room. It was empty except for a seen-better-days long wooden table, some mismatched office chairs, and a whiteboard against the back wall. Stepping over to the board, Laura placed the slips of paper with names scrawled on them in an order that made sense. The Whitings, their only child and the girl's boyfriend, and now Aunt Natalie. All Laura needed to solve this was motive, opportunity. The means was left bloody at the scene. Oh, yes, it might also help to have a viable suspect to begin with. She doubted 'the butler did it with an axe in the library'.

Reassuring herself that every investigation started this way, waiting for clues to come trickling in with agonizing slowness, she still hoped for a miracle to make life easier. No one wanted an axe-wielding maniac out on the streets.

Hearing footsteps and expecting to see Resciniti looking for her, Laura was pleasantly surprised to see instead the smiling face of Devin, standing in the door, leaning casually against the frame.

"Hey," he greeted her.

"Hey. How's it going?" Her pulse kicked up a

notch and she tried to ignore her reaction to him. He definitely didn't seem a one-night-stand type and she wasn't interested or ready for anything more. Her emotional bank account was already overdrawn, what with her divorce and—well, if it's not one thing, it's your mother… at least in her case.

"I was just about to ask you the same question."

"What is the old song, 'We've Only Just Begun'?" she replied, unconsciously taking a step closer to him. Her female parts were making their presence known.

"Umm, listen, I was wondering…" He angled his head and inhaled.

Never patient, Laura counseled herself to shut up and wait. Not easy.

"Not to sound cliché, but life is short, and I was wondering…" he started again, shifting from foot to foot. Odd to see a big, strong man who had initially appeared so confident, seem unnerved.

Laura couldn't stand it, so she decided to cut to the chase. "That would be nice."

His smile lit his handsome face and he whooshed out a breath. "Yes?"

She waited another long minute. "We could have coffee. It must be hard being the new guy."

His big brown eyes sparkled with amusement. "Great. That's great. Thanks for ending my agony."

"A little dramatic, don't you think?" she countered.

"Nope. Give me a vicious killer armed to the teeth and I'm in my element, but social stuff… well…"

She laughed. "How about tomorrow afternoon?" She had just started an investigation and probably shouldn't take the time, but she could always use a cup of coffee, right? And she had to wait for the forensics and the autopsy report. This was definitely one autopsy she had no desire to attend. And besides, he'd be a great sounding board. Not that anything would ever come of it. She had no interest in a long-term anything, except the one with her job. But he sure was pretty.

"Perfect." He handed her a card with his phone number. "Just let me know what time and where. And thanks."

As he stepped out of the room, she inched closer to the door and watched him walk away. *Nice butt. He is definitely appealing. And he smells so good. Like citrus and ocean and man.* She took a deep breath. *Okay, party is over. Let's solve some hideous murders.*

***

She was even more attractive close up that he had initially thought. When she wasn't at her desk after they had met earlier, he was disappointed, but then he saw someone moving around in the conference room. It might be obvious he was seeking her out, but what the hell?

All she had to do was look at him and the electric current went straight to his groin. And when she turned to see him, she smiled and his world turned a whole different shade of happy. Tomorrow was going to be a hundred years away.

He strutted back into his tiny office and sat. He hadn't been this attracted to a woman since—Jillian. Of course, that ended so badly, he hadn't wanted any kind of long-term relationship for years afterward. But this woman, Laura, revived some of those long-buried and bruised emotions. It wasn't just the waves of lust clouding his brain. There was something about her that—what? Made him wax poetic? Well, maybe she wouldn't be quite so appealing after spending more time with her. But he secretly hoped the spell continued. He was ready.

Forcing his thoughts back to work, he reviewed what he had on the case. Middle-aged

female, apparently amicable divorce, no known enemies. Found buried in a park, COD blunt force trauma. It was such a frustrating dead end so far, as they all were, but that just piqued his curiosity. There was no challenge in solving the obvious ones. Of course, the obvious ones didn't land on his desk.

In cases like this, the spouse was the obvious first choice, followed by anyone who had to gain by removing the victim. But the ex-husband was out of consideration due to an ironclad alibi. The chances of finding the murder weapon were slim to none. Blunt force could be anything from a brick to a bat to a frozen leg-of-lamb. Yeah, he had read that once. The wife offed her husband by hitting him with an icy piece of meat and then cooked the thing and ate it. Talk about cold. No pun.

He drove home, banishing all thoughts of brutal murders and replacing those images with all sorts of scenarios with the luscious Laura Chandler. Most of them revolved around sex, but he did take a moment or two to picture quiet dinners and long walks. He prided himself on not being a total savage.

His house felt different tonight. Emptier. He poured himself a scotch and walked around the living room, admiring the newest acquisition to his collection of local artists. This one was a palm tree on a dark background. The fronds were lifted by an invisible breeze and the sense of peace was absolute. But also very lonely.

His thoughts drifted to Jillian and he inhaled through his nose. The beautiful Jillian who had simply walked away one day with his diamond engagement ring on her finger and a good-bye text. *This just isn't working for me. Sorry.* Cold as ice. The shock had cracked his chest open, leaving him with a sense of unreality that yielded to crushing pain. He had thought she was his soul-mate, the love of his life and had been certain she felt the same. His world dissolved like one of those graphics in movies where the screen moves inward to black.

He forced all his emotions into a block of ice, feeling nothing, responding only when required.

Counseling helped and after two long, dry years, his heart had suddenly begun to thaw. One look at Laura and his insides were actually warm. Even if things didn't work with Laura, even if she wasn't the woman of his dreams, at least he could take solace in the ability to actually feel something again. Since Jillian left and his partner Jim died, he had wondered if he was even alive anymore or merely going through the motions. He went to work, he went home. He visited with his family. Sometimes he went to art shows, spending his money on expressive, emotional work that shielded him from any real feelings of his own. Until now.

It was not unlike when one of your limbs fell asleep and the feeling came back in fits and starts. Uncomfortable but absolutely necessary to prevent total atrophy. Clinically interesting, personally unsettling and a little scary.

The next morning, he woke with a sense of excitement. That usually meant he was onto something with whatever he was working on, which was the only thing to elicit any real response for a very long time. Racking his brain, he couldn't think of anything new on the case. But he had faith it would come to him. He just had to be patient. But this morning was different and he knew the real reason for his good mood.

He was thinking about later today when he would be having coffee with Laura Chandler. Detective Laura Chandler. He kind of felt like a teenager, all nervous and excited. If he ran into her before their date, he wanted to come off as confident and strong. He chose his favorite blue shirt and a blue striped tie. At least he would look the part. Maybe he would ask her to dinner after the coffee. Or to come home with him. He splashed on a little extra cologne.

This afternoon couldn't come soon enough.

***

The autopsy had taken a little longer than usual, since Marian was short-handed, as always. Apparently assistant to the coroner wasn't on the list of things kids wanted to be when they grew up. And this case was more challenging than most. The limbs of the victims weren't just tightly intertwined by accident. They had almost been woven together. The killer had taken the time to do this and it must have taken a while, even if lifeless limbs were more cooperative, at least temporarily.

In fact, when they were transported here, Marian had seen to it they were moved together. The one loose arm seemed to be the result of limited flexibility. It had nearly broken off. Laura hadn't thought there was any need to come to the autopsy. She trusted Marian and her reports were always very complete. But Marian had called and asked her to reconsider since this was very unusual. Staging one body was one thing, but intertwining two together was unique.

Laura berated herself that she hadn't noticed how intentionally the bodies had been set at the crime scene, and she should have. But she reminded herself, it wasn't that easy to distinguish who was who in that carnage. It was clear now the perp had taken time to arrange the victims purposefully and carefully. As if to communicate the two were one. But one what? Of one mind? Together? Yes they were married, but this was more than that. That was what Marian had wanted Laura to see since it seemed to be a message of some kind. So the killer had chopped them up and then rearranged their bodies. Apparently the violent rage had been dissipated after striking all the blows that killed the vics and then the perp had taken more time to place the severed limbs in a way that made sense to him or her. In this case, Laura was convinced it was a woman. Females could be just as vicious as males, more so sometimes.

The coroner's office was in the basement of the old city hall. Some offices still held court there, but most had been shifted to the new building with better wiring and WiFi. No matter the location, there was always an inevitable chill in the air.

Laura walked down the steps, the unmistakable smell of formaldehyde announcing her destination. A door to the left opened onto the autopsy room, with Marian's office tucked behind it. The space was always so *Twilight Zone* bright and conjured images of horror movies. Laura wondered how Marian stood it every day. But then, she supposed anyone could get used to anything if they did it long enough.

Two of the stainless steel tables had been pushed together to accommodate the victims. Just as Marian had described, they formed a hideous tableau, one Laura would never again unsee.

The cause of death was just as repugnant as she feared. Somehow the perp had managed to overcome them and Laura was guessing it was the element of surprise. They were obviously unable to defend themselves, and then tortured.

The vics had died slowly, helplessly and in excruciating pain watching their parts hacked away. They had both bled out, but it was not quick since no arteries were severed. Whoever the perp was, they had a working knowledge of human anatomy. Their daughter, Alexandra, lived with a professor of biology. And, since they were each other's alibis, they could have planned this together. Except, Alexandra seemed genuinely shocked at the news of her parents demise. Of course, if criminals looked and reacted like criminals, life would be so much safer. And Laura made it a point to never begin with preconceived notions.

The time of death was set between nine p.m. and two a.m. One of the other neighbors might have noticed a visitor coming or going at that time of night. But Laura doubted the perp would have just strolled out into the night afterward, as if hacking people to pieces was something normal. Then again, hiding in plain sight wasn't a new concept.

John checked out Alexandra's alibi and had called it in to Laura an hour ago. The university had cameras that verified when she left her office and the McDonalds' camera time and date stamped her driving through and getting her food at the time she said. But since the TOD was a five-hour window after she was last recorded on tape, she would have had time to get home, eat, drive to her parents' house, kill them and get back to bed with her boyfriend. Laura still wasn't convinced she was the perp. But she wasn't convinced she wasn't, either. Instincts had served her well over the years and she was waiting for them to kick in on this one.

She had just come back from the coroner and glanced at the clock when John sidled up to her desk and she looked up hopefully.

"Tell me you have something."

He shook his head. "I wish. I talked to all the other neighbors. They all had the same story. The Whitings were quiet people, went to church, always ready to offer help if someone needed it. Boring." He sighed. "You?"

"They were both squeaky Not so much as a parking ticket and they lived within their means. There was a ten-thousand dollar life insurance policy provided by his old employer naming the daughter as the beneficiary, but really, that'll only cover the funeral expenses. So there goes the money motive, even though I really never considered it a real possibility."

"How about the autopsy?"

"The autopsy was…" She exhaled. "The vics were intertwined, on purpose, like a message. And they died slowly. Whoever did this, must have really hated them. Which makes no sense."

"Anything else?" John asked.

"Mr. Whiting was a retired homeowner's insurance assessor. Worked at the same company for thirty-two years. He was four years older than his wife. She was a part-time substitute elementary school teacher, but she stopped working when he did. Before that, she worked in Nashville at the Tennessee Department of Vital Records as a file clerk."

"So exciting," John said sarcastically.

"The only interesting thing I found was they were married when Alexandra was two. Which verified what she told me. Apparently, when Evan found out about the baby, he married Nora so they could be a family."

"So, when they married they moved to Memphis?" John asked.

"Well, she did. He was already here and working."

"I checked. It's his name on the birth certificate," John responded.

"So, still, nothing to suggest nefarious motives. Or secret boyfriends." She couldn't hide her disappointment.

"Were you hoping for retired CIA? Or accountant to the mob?" John teased.

She rolled her eyes. "Feel like going to church?" Laura asked him.

"That's a loaded question," he lobbed back.

***

The First Baptist Church should have been built in the most pastoral of settings instead of above the parkway, which was always teaming with traffic. It spread its hefty wings over a large plot of land, as if to make up for sitting in the middle of the city. Surrounded by well-kept lawns and large trees, it did manage to convey a sense of peace and solitude.

The entrance was dark and hushed, lit in this early

afternoon with shards of color from the beautiful stained glass windows on both sides. They walked inside and were greeted by the pastor, a young man looking more like a surfer than a man of the cloth, with his blonde hair and lean build, but he had a sincerity that impressed Laura. They introduced themselves and he shook his head. "I'm sure you're here about Evan and Nora. I just spoke to their daughter about a memorial service. I still can't believe it. Who would want to hurt them?"

"Will there be a burial?" Laura asked. Many times the killer would show up at the funeral, especially at the cemetery where he or she could better blend in.

"No. Just a service here. She's having them cremated as soon as she can. Apparently, a viewing is out of the question." A green cast colored his cheeks as he said this last.

"Pastor Michael, how well did you know them? The Whitings?" Laura asked.

"Pretty well. I came here about five years ago and they were some of my most staunch supporters. I know I don't exactly look the part, and I got a lot of skepticism, but they defended me and were always the first to sign up for or lead any activities. Eventually, the rest of the congregation accepted me. And I have them to thank." He shook his head and raised his shoulders as if to ward off the specter of death "Had, I guess. Had them to thank." He inhaled roughly, pressing down the rising emotions. "I can't believe they're gone."

"Do you have any idea who might have wanted to hurt them?" John pressed.

"No. Everyone loved and respected them. They never had a mean word to say about anyone and no one ever said anything negative about them. As I said, they were the first in line when it came to helping their neighbors or supporting the church."

"Did it ever occur to you they felt guilty?" Laura suggested. She wasn't sure where that thought had come from. Maybe she spent too much time listening to murder podcasts?

The pastor raised his eyebrows. "Guilty?"

"Well, sometimes people who feel remorseful about something go out of their way to be more helpful to others, if you get my meaning," Laura continued.

The pastor shook his head again. "I can't imagine those people ever did anything wrong."

"What can you tell us about their daughter?" John ventured. "Have you ever met her in person?"

"Yes. A lovely girl. When she was in town, she would come to church with her parents." He leaned in and lowered his voice. "She lives with her boyfriend and I think she knew her parents wouldn't approve."

"She told you that?" Laura asked.

"She was explaining why she wasn't here more often, I think."

"We'll need a list of your parishioners. Someone might know something useful."

"Of course. I'll email it over to you if that's okay."

"Perfect, thanks. And please let us know when the memorial service is."

"Of course."

Laura handed him her card. "If you think of anything else that might help, please don't hesitate to contact me. And thanks for your time."

"I hope you catch whoever did this, Detectives."

Laura smiled. "We will," she stated with a confidence she didn't feel at the moment.

Chapter Four

The coffee shop was set back between a karate studio and a fancy boutique. It was small and intimate, with little groupings of chairs and tables. The lighting was soft and the walls a cool shade of blue. Striking her as ironic, a fireplace sat in the middle of the room, thankfully not lit today since the temperature outside was flirting with ninety. The occasional grunting heard from the karate studio and the quiet chatter of the customers were the only sounds.

The main counter, on the far left wall, boasted a myriad of coffee and tea choices and tempting pastries. Sitting at one of the tables and trying not to tap his foot with impatience, Devin considered ordering for Laura. He hesitated, worried it might be too presumptuous. Glancing at his watch, he sipped his second mug of coffee. She wasn't late; anticipation had gotten the better of him so he was embarrassingly early. And continuing to slug down caffeine wasn't helping his nerves. But he had to do something to keep his hands busy.

His heart bumped at the tinkling of the little bell over the door. Not her. He focused again on not tapping his foot. Maybe she wouldn't show? Before that thought could take root and pull him down, she was there, smiling at him. Suddenly, he was warm and cold at the same time. He stood and she slipped into the chair across from him. He did have the chance to notice her skirt hugged her curves and her blouse dipped just enough in the front to promise. She wore a thin gold chain around her neck and the charm dangled provocatively down. Temptation, thy name is Laura Chandler, Detective Laura Chandler.

"Hi." *Lame, Devin. What happened to that famous Andrews confidence? Oh, yeah. Jillian.*

"Hi," she returned. "Am I late?"

"No, I was early." He stood, inwardly shaking his head at the admission. "What can I get you?" He was trying not to stare but the glimpse of her cleavage was almost too much to resist. Her skirt was tight and he was grateful it fell to her knees. If it had been shorter, he might have lost it.

She licked her lips and he thought he would just lay down and die right there.

"Coffee, with some cream please."

He raised an eyebrow. "Pastry?" He angled his head toward the case full of scrumptious calories. "They look good."

She licked her lips again and his groin tightened dangerously, so he angled his body away from her.

"I did skip lunch. Maybe a cookie? Any kind."

He ordered two coffees and carefully chose an assortment of pastries. When he came back to the table, she looked at him with a mixture of pleasure and confusion.

"This is too much," she stated, licking her lips at the cookies, cupcakes and muffins.

"You said you were hungry." He shrugged, smiling.

"Well, thank you. I guess I will have a bite or two." She picked up a chocolate chip cookie and nibbled it and he found himself staring at her mouth. He needed to think of other things, and quick.

"How's your case going?" *Could he be more banal?*

"Still just starting. You know how that goes. You?"

"Same." Devin realized he was a little nervous and wondered what to say next. "Why did you decide to be a cop?" It was a standard getting to know you question and he had hoped to dazzle her with brilliance, but it was all he could think of. She was very distracting.

"Swimming," she stated.

"Swimming?" He leaned in, totally confused.

She inhaled. "Not just splashing around. One summer I took a job doing water exercise with severely damaged children at a special facility. Some were born with problems. Like Elizabeth. She had suffered asphyxiation during birth. Her parents were ashamed, so they hid her in a back room for twelve years. No sunlight, no fresh air. They told everyone she died. Until there was a neighborhood fire and the firemen discovered her."

Devin's mouth dropped open. "Seriously?"

"And Patrick. He apparently wouldn't stop crying one day so the mother's boyfriend shook him until he quit. Shaken baby syndrome." She choked, swallowed and continued. "I decided then and there I had to do something to try and protect all those who couldn't fight for themselves. I may not be able to stop criminals before they do things like that, but I sure as hell can see 'em arrested."

47

"Wow," he breathed. "Were the parents all charged?"

"Elizabeth's were charged with child endangerment and abuse. The mother's boyfriend in Patrick's case served three years. Not nearly enough."

"Agreed." He shook his head.

"I understand the draw of cold cases. It's pretty terrible to imagine murderers and abusers getting away with it. And the survivors getting no closure. But what made you choose police work to begin with?"

"Blue through and through. Father, uncles, brother. No escaping it in my family."

They reached for the chocolate cupcake at the same time and a current of fire ran from his hand directly to his chest and then turned south. Startled by the contact, he lifted his eyes to hers and the intensity in her gaze was electric.

She cleared her throat and they both laughed, breaking the tension.

"Is it rude or premature if I say I want to know more"—at least he stopped himself from saying 'everything' even though he wanted to—"about you?" he asked. "I am a detective, you know."

"That's the rumor," she countered. "Only if you return the favor."

"Done. Ladies first."

She glanced at her watch. "I think it might take too long and I have to get back." She finished her coffee and eased out of the chair.

"Dinner?" He held out his hand to her and she sat back down.

She chewed her lower lip and inhaled.

"Devin, I don't know about this. Do you think going out with a co-worker is maybe a bad idea?"

"No, no I don't. We aren't partners, we don't work on the same cases, we even have completely separate offices. I don't see a conflict."

She leaned over toward him and toyed with the cupcake wrapper. The view of her cleavage stopped his heart for a minute.

"It's just I've never dated a fellow cop before. I'm not trying to jump the gun here—so to speak—it's just I don't want it to get awkward."

"I understand, so I'll make you a deal. If it goes badly, which I doubt, but if it does, I will give up coffee." He nodded to affirm the statement.

She was clearly baffled. "What?"

He snorted. "That way I won't have any excuse to go to the break room and walk past your desk."

She laughed and shook her head. "Do you always have all the answers?"

"Hardly. I'm a guy."

"Point taken." She hesitated, thinking. "Dinner when?"

***

The memory of her afternoon with Devin and the anticipation of spending more time with him in the future eased the anxiety that always built before she had to visit 'the home'. But she had promised herself she would at least stop by once a week. Otherwise, her conscience would nag relentlessly. But she definitely didn't look forward to it. She visualized the rips in her ego, like sharp fingernails, going deeper with each visit.

The time was coming when she had to make a decision. Her mother was declining into dementia and she would need to be transferred to another section of the facility soon. Laura had planned for this when she moved her mother here, which was why she chose this place. It was divided into assisted care, dementia/Alzheimer's care, and severe mental health issues care. She worried that her decision might be premature since there were days when Clair was perfectly lucid. Of course, then she would slip away, but the meanness remained. The change would mean more confinement and less privacy since it was impossible to have locks on the individual doors and keep track of the patients. But it would also be safer. Laura knew she wouldn't be able to live with herself if her mother suffered any kind of neglect. She might not have affection for the woman, but Clair was still entitled to her dignity.

The sky was decorated with pinks and greys and oranges as the sun began its decline. Timing was everything. Soon it would be dinnertime and that was always the perfect excuse to leave. Never get between these people and their next meal. Most of them had nothing else to look forward to, which was very sad.

The home, or residence as the sign on the door said, looked like an older, very large and stately house. High white columns stood sentry at the front and it was surrounded by flowering plants and tall trees, offering color and shade. A few of the residents sat on the front porch, in white wicker chairs with bright cushions, soaking up the less than generous breeze, watching the world go by.

The front doors were locked, accessible only with a code for both entering and leaving. Laura stepped through the front doors, nodding to the receptionist who ignored her, and made her way down a very white corridor scented with bleach, urine, and old age. Coughing and the occasional groan filled the hallway, along with the faint beeping of machines doing their best to fulfill need. In the distance, the clacking of plates and silverware heralded the upcoming meal. Her mother's room was the second door on the right and she stepped inside, trying to paste a smile on her face. The sound of snoring vibrated the air. Grateful that her mother slept, Laura cocked her head and watched the woman's chest evenly rise and fall. So peaceful, so quiet. So pleasant. And a happy respite.

"Hey, Laura," a voice greeted her softly from behind.

Laura turned to face the nurse. "Hey, Jocelyn. How is she?" Laura's favorite caregiver would never sugarcoat. Jocelyn was about Laura's age and very pretty. She would have looked better without the bluish stains under her eyes, testament to a lack of sleep and the obvious stress of her job. The woman seemed to be there all hours and Laura wondered if it was dedication or the need for more income.

"Meaner than a snake," Jocelyn whispered back, grinning. "As ever."

"You'd think she'd mellow," Laura sighed.

"I've always wanted to ask you—was she like this when you were growing up?"

Laura snorted. "So much worse."

Jocelyn tilted her head. "I'm sorry. But you seem so devoted."

"Devoted? No. Just building up my good karma. And, besides, as next of kin, someone has to make the decisions."

"You're a good person," Jocelyn said, reaching out to pat Laura's hand.

51

"No. Children are supposed to love their mothers, aren't they? But she makes it very hard." Laura rubbed the ever-present knot in her neck. "Does she need anything?"

"Well, you might want a word with the head nurse. The doctor is still prescribing calcium and vitamins and your mother hates the pills. Especially the big, hard-to-swallow ones."

"Just another reason for her to complain."

"Yes, but it is unfair to make her take so many when she really doesn't need them. But you didn't hear it from me."

"I agree. Thanks, Jocelyn." She hesitated. "If, I mean when, I have her moved to dementia care, will you still be able to take care of her? Not that it's your fondest dream."

"No, but there are other nurses over there that will do a good job. Don't worry."

"I wasn't. I just look forward to seeing you when I come visit. Maybe you and my friend Cara and I could go for a drink sometime."

Jocelyn smiled, clearly pleased. "I'd love that."

With that, Laura strode down the corridor to the head nurse's office. Angela Johnson was a mad-at-the-world woman who never seemed to grasp the concept of 'care' in caregiver. Laura tapped on the doorframe and stepped up to the woman's desk. It was so organized, it screamed attention to detail. Even the paper clips were in a neat row. As Laura entered, she saw the flash of distaste in the other woman's expression, which she immediately managed to cover with a half-smile.

"Ms. Chandler," Angela said, with a tiny modicum

of warmth. "Good to see you." Laura was impressed how well the other woman managed to conceal her irritation.

I'll bet. Laura was one of the family members who complained and that was never welcome here. "That's Detective Chandler and I want to make sure you understand that my mother is to have only her pain meds and no supplements unless there is a compelling reason. Please communicate that to the doctor. I thought I was clear that I have medical power-of-attorney."

The woman lost some of her color. "Oh, well, we thought some calcium and vitamins might be nice."

"Calcium? My mother is bedridden. What are you afraid of? Osteoporosis? Or were the charges too low?" Laura didn't bother to hide her sarcasm and the other woman's cheeks now turned a bright pink. Before she could respond, Laura held up her hand. "Pain meds only. Unless there's an infection or something that requires medical intervention. Thank you." She pivoted on her heel and stalked back to her mother's room. Peeking in, she assured herself all was clean and in good order and, satisfied, she beat a hasty retreat, her obligation met.

***

Laura stepped into her house, the cool air from the overworked air conditioner washing over her. Happy to be home, she flipped off her shoes and plopped down on the dark blue leather couch, one of her few extravagances after she bought the house. Hungry and wondering what she should eat, her gaze drifted around the living room. It was functional, with a TV and coffee table, with the look of someone who doesn't spend much time at home.

There were no family pictures and only one photograph of her with Cara when they went to the beach together years ago. Cara, as always, had been man shopping while Laura was finalizing her divorce— definitely reason to celebrate.

Maybe she should get some pictures for the walls or some decorative pieces to brighten the room? Well, not today.

She stood and walked into the kitchen. An opened bottle of red wine sat on the counter and she poured herself a glass, sipping as she glanced into the refrigerator. It struck her that she might seem pretty cold-blooded right now to someone who didn't know her. A vicious murder scene and mangled corpses and she was thinking about food. What would Devin think? No, he was a detective. He would understand. If she couldn't compartmentalize, she was risking starvation. Her work was the brutal side of life and her job was not to take it personally.

She picked up the phone to call the Chinese restaurant that delivered this late.

***

Laura was getting ready to leave the station two days later, neck in knots and eyes burning. The entire day had been spent on the histories of both Evan and Nora Whiting. She had discovered very little that helped her case. She needed a bike ride, but with this case, she hadn't had time. And if she slept badly before, this case had made rest so much more elusive. Unable to let it go, even for a few minutes, she went over what she had so far.

Evan had graduated from a small community college with a degree in business. He found a job as a real estate assessor and stayed at the same company for thirty-eight years until he retired. He married Nora when he was twenty-four, which they already knew was two years after Alexandra was born.

As for Nora, there was one interesting thing: gaps in her history. Between the time she graduated from high school and the year before she started working at the state offices and then later before she married Evan, there was nothing. She had quit her job, had no bank account, no car, no apartment rented in her name. According to Alexandra, she hadn't lived at home. So, how and where had she lived during those times? Maybe the key was even deeper in her history, since his was as exciting as day-old oatmeal. So where did she go? Someone must have helped her. Maybe Evan sent her money and she stayed with friends? Of course, twenty-five odd years ago, people didn't leave a paper trail the way they did these days. The internet and social media were suffering from their own birth pains back then. So it was possible to fly under the radar. Or hide under it. And then there was the aunt.

Laura had just stuffed her phone in her bag when it rang. She hoped it wasn't Devin calling to cancel their dinner date, since that was the only thing that had kept her going these days, but the caller i.d. wasn't one she recognized.

"Detective Chandler?" the older woman asked tentatively.

"Yes."

"It's Barbara Cassis. The Whitings' neighbor."

"Yes, Mrs. Cassis."

"Well, you said I could call you if I thought of anything and I did."

Laura's heartbeat kicked up a notch. "Of course. What is it?"

"Could you stop by? I don't know that I should mention it on the phone."

The older woman was no doubt lonely, but luckily her house was not too far from Laura's, so it wouldn't be out of the way. If she was delayed, she could call Devin and have him meet her at her home. No, that was tempting fate since her attraction to him was way up there on the charts. And she had no intention of letting her clothes fall off tonight. But she should be okay on time if she could just get the woman to stick to the point. And since there had been no real leads so far, maybe Mrs. Cassis could help.

"Of course. I'll be there in ten minutes or so."

Laura made it in seven. The older woman opened the door wide, smiling broadly. "Thank you so much for coming, Detective. Please," she said, waving her hand for Laura to enter.

Laura stepped into the living room and turned to the other woman expectantly. Barbara looked better today, her eyes bright and her demeanor more cheerful. Unlike just after her grisly discovery, she now exuded an air of suppressed excitement, like she had a secret that she was busting to share.

"You said you remembered something," Laura encouraged, trying not to sound pressed for time.

"Yes, yes. Please sit." She motioned Laura to the couch. Instead of sitting immediately, Barbara paced back and forth as if trying to find the right words. "Tea? Coffee? I also have a little brandy." She said this last like it was a shameful little vice she rarely shared.

"No, thank you. You said you thought of something," Laura repeated, controlling her impatience.

"Yes, well, it might be just the silly thoughts of an old woman." She fluttered her fingers in the air. "But, I was thinking about their daughter, Alexandra. You know, I never had any children, but I do love them. Mort and I just weren't able. We did entertain adoption."

Laura pressed her lips together, forcing slow breaths in and out.

"You were telling me about the Whitings' daughter, Alexandra?" she reminded Barbara, hoping to get her back on track.

"Oh, yes. Well, I have seen her on occasion in the neighborhood." Barbara sat on one of the chairs across from Laura, crossed her arms over her generous bosom and sighed contentedly, as if she had just imparted the secrets of the universe.

Laura was confused. Alexandra's parents lived next door, so what could be nefarious about seeing her? "But Mrs. Cassis, she visited her parents often." Laura narrowed her eyes, trying to discern the special significance of this.

"Oh, yes, but I don't mean those times." She waved her hand in dismissal. "Other times."

"I don't understand."

"Well, I didn't concern myself with it. I mean, I did wonder if it was odd, but you know how some people are."

"No. How are they?"

Barbara grinned slyly. "You know. They act strangely sometimes. Like Alexandra. Well, lately, once in a while, she would come up to the house and just look in the window. Or sit in her car across the street. At least

I think it was her car. Now mind you, this wasn't often. Just a few times and, as I said, just lately."

Laura leaned forward in her seat. "When exactly. And how many times?"

Having captured Laura's full attention, Barbara preened. "Oh, yes, well, the last month or so. And I would say three or four visits. That is, that I saw her. But I am certain she didn't know I was watching. I'm like a cat, you know." She lifted a shoulder proudly.

"No doubt. And when did this happen. What days and times?" Laura prodded, reaching into her bag for a pad and pen.

"Mostly at night. Definitely during the week. Which is why I noticed. I know Alexandra works during the week. But the university isn't that far away. Do you have any idea why she would do that? I mean, her parents were not exactly exciting. No parties or anything. Do you think she was spying on them because there was something illicit going on?" She pressed her lips together in obvious anticipation of something juicy.

"So, do you know why she would do that?" she asked again.

Intrigued by this information, Laura was nonetheless afraid her brain might explode from the woman's non-stop chatter. "No, no I don't, but I will definitely try and find out." She stood.

"Is there anything else you remember?"

"Did I help? It's very exciting to be able to assist with a murder investigation. Mort used to say I watched too much crime on TV, but I knew it would come in handy one day. It did, didn't it?"

Laura eased her way to the front door. "Yes, and I

thank you very much. Again, if you remember something else, please don't hesitate."

Laura managed to make it outside before the woman went on any more. Relief washed over her and she drank in the quiet of the early evening. The question nagged. Why would a daughter stop by surreptitiously and spy on her parents? What was she hoping to see? Was she trying to summon the nerve to confess about living with her boyfriend? Maybe. Laura couldn't really think of a reason that would hold water. The Whitings were not exciting, not involved in anything even interesting that Laura could find. So why watch them? It made no sense.

Glancing at her watch, she would just have enough time to change clothes and make it to the restaurant. Maybe Devin would have some insight, because right now Laura didn't have any answers for Alexandra's strange behavior.

***

Walking into the bar and grill, Laura was pleased at Devin's choice. It was casual and comfortable, but managed to be intimate, even on a Friday night. They served meals that didn't entail messy barbeque or corn on the cob. Good! The bar was filled with people, but somehow the acoustics managed to keep the noise down to a dull roar. The energy was high and men and women were drinking and laughing and enjoying the night.

She passed by the crowd and looked into the dining area. Taking a moment to admire him sitting in a corner table, she couldn't help but smile. He was indecently attractive and when he looked up, there was no missing his interest in her. Laura's pulse increased. *You cannot*

59

sleep with him tonight. Are you listening? the inner voice demanded. *Was she listening?*

She approached him slowly, his strong jaw and well defined features highlighted by candlelight. There was no denying he was very appealing. But she had to work with the guy. Well, not with him, but in the same department, and she definitely did not want to come off first-night easy. It had been a long time for her. Months. And this was the first man that had incited a hot flash like—ever. And she wasn't even near menopause.

He stood when she approached the table and held the chair, then moved to his own across from her. "I ordered some white wine. I hope that's okay."

"I'm off duty, so yes. That sounds nice." So much better than stale brandy with a non- stop talker. Even though Mrs. Cassis meant well and did provide an unusual clue.

The waiter, either new at the job or ill-suited for it, approached with two glasses and an open bottle of pinot grigio. In a very un-sommelier manner, he plopped the open bottle of wine on the table, handed each of them a glass and took out his notebook. "Ready to order?" he asked, clearly distracted by the pretty young girl at the next table.

Devin cut his eyes to the waiter. "Could you give us a few minutes?"

"Sure, uh yeah." Shoving his order pad back into his apron, he nearly collided into another waiter as he left their table. Both Devin and Laura tried not to laugh out loud.

Devin poured them each a glass, then held his up for a toast, the pale liquid glittering in the candlelight. "What should we drink to?" he asked.

"How about to success. And catching the bad guys."

They clinked glasses and each took a drink. It was very satisfying and much needed. Fighting frustration, Laura wanted to focus on the man across from her. But the murders plopped down right in the middle of the table, distracting her. She hated this part of a case when there was nothing concrete yet and no clues strong enough to follow. Her meeting with Barbara was rattling around in her head. Talking about this with Devin might help her clarify her thoughts and also keep her mind off his hands. He had beautiful hands. *You are not sleeping with him tonight!*

Laura sat back. "You don't mind if I pick your brain, do you? It's just that something is bothering me." Work thoughts always grounded her and right now she was desperate to stop thinking about his hands.

"Of course not." His direct gaze nearly unraveled her concentration.

She leaned in. "Why would a daughter who regularly visited her parents secretly spy on them?"

Devin set down his glass, frowning in thought. "She suspected them of something?" he ventured.

"That's the logical assumption. But these people were boring with a capital 'B'. Retired, no debt except their reverse mortgage, went to church every Sunday and participated in church activities. And... they had a nosy neighbor who would have noticed if one of them kept odd hours or if they led separate lives. And would have taken great pleasure in reporting it."

He stroked his chin and she noticed his hands again. She was a sucker for long fingers and well-kept cuticles on a man. She tried not to imagine how those hands would feel against her skin. *What is wrong with you? Since when do thoughts of sex take precedence over solving a case?* But she knew the answer. Since Devin.

She shook her head to send those illicit thoughts flying and tried to listen to what he was saying.

"Maybe the daughter knew something and wanted confirmation. You should ask her."

"Oh, absolutely, but I was hoping to go in with some idea. I mean, it doesn't make much sense. Does it?"

"No. But we know there's always a reason for actions, always an answer. We just have to find it."

As they sipped their wine and nibbled on the basket of bread, they talked about his case.

"Twelve years is a long time. I can't imagine trying to investigate without a hot crime scene, witnesses who may be dead or moved away. Do you have anything new?"

"The vic was local, so I'm guessing she was killed here in town somewhere and dumped in the park. The burial was hurried and shallow. Not very professional."

"The husband?"

"Yeah, always the first choice. But he had already moved away and was remarried with a solid alibi. They apparently were amicable after the divorce, but I need to interview the two kids to verify that."

"Is it possible to have an amicable divorce?" she asked, agitation stirring her blood and seeping into her voice.

"Wow, you make that sound like personal experience," he returned, raising an eyebrow.

"Sorry. Bitter? Me? Well, maybe a little. My ex tried to get me for alimony and child support."

"Oh, you have kids?" His tone was neutral. Would it matter to him?

"No. His kids. He said they had a better life because of my income, so I was responsible to maintain it for them."

Devin's eyes widened. "He didn't get away with that, did he?"

"No. His record of cheating was undeniable and he had already bankrupted our accounts. And there was that little problem of the pathological lying. Oh, and we were only married eight months before I filed. He was a piece of work. But it did make me question my judgment."

"I know it's none of my business, but why did you marry him?"

Laura chewed the inside of her cheek. "I've wondered that myself. I think it's because I wanted to prove I could be normal. You know, white picket fence, two point five kids. SUV in the driveway." She dropped her gaze, holding in a gasp. She'd never admitted that to anyone before, not even herself. "I'm also just mad at myself for being conned. I'm a detective. I should have seen what he was." She inhaled, calming herself. She knew she said way too much on a first date.

Devin took a deep breath and reached his hand across the table, touching her fingertips. "It happens to all of us, I think. Questioning our judgment. And 'normal' is fine, but I don't think it's for either one of us."

Laura tilted her head. "No aspirations for a wife and kids?"

"I didn't say that. But I do happen to hate SUVs."

Her insides were turning to warm caramel and she leaned closer to him just as the waiter reappeared.

"Ready?" the kid inquired, oblivious to his bad timing.

Devin glared at him again and he took a step back. "Okay, a few more minutes." And he quickly retreated.

Laura smothered her smile

Devin refilled their glasses and held his up again. "Here's to solving crimes and having better life experiences."

"I'll drink to that."

"Now where is that damn waiter?"

Chapter Five

Dinner had been delicious and the conversation flowed as if they had known each other for years. Devin and Laura walked outside and a breeze lifted her hair, wafting her nearly irresistible scent of flowers and musk toward him. Their cars were parked down the block. Night had eased the heat of the day and the humidity was reduced to bearable. To the left, a service alley beckoned. Devin led her into the opening and took hold of her hands. Only the moonlight pooled nearby, relieving the total darkness.

He had never hungered for a woman like this. His entire being was consumed with need. But it was more than lust. It was a total awareness of her scent, her form, her very breath. And the desperate desire to incorporate that into his life. Devin didn't want to consume her, but rather join with her as a partner in every way. And he wanted to make love to her more than he had ever wanted anything in his life. His blood sang through his veins at the thought of touching her.

He gently pressed her back against the stone wall and took a deep breath, inching his mouth to hers, until their breath mingled. Their lips were a millimeter apart and all he could focus on was he wanted to devour her mouth, explore with his tongue, discover every part of her body. The world blurred. He was totally aware only of the two of them and the electric current sparking between them.

He knew she felt it, too. The heat, the voltage, the power of desire. He also knew he needed to control his raging longing. He would not pressure her. Entice her, maybe. But she had to be the one to close the tiny vibrating space between them. A quiet moan in the back of her throat weakened his resolve, but he knew what was right. He held his ground as, ever so slowly, she moved her head forward. Her mouth pressed his and every nerve ending in his body was alight. His erection pressed against his zipper, desperately searching for release. Closing his eyes, he now took the lead. His fingers reached into her thick curls, his nails gently scratching her scalp. Inch by agonizing inch, he moved his body closer into hers, melting into a maelstrom of such pleasure, it took his breath. His tongue sought the sweet inner sanctum, tasting, teasing, demanding and she met him with equal enthusiasm. There was that moan again, and he thought he would lose his mind. As if on their own accord, his fingers slid up along her ribs, lifting higher to stroke the sides of her full breasts, aching to stroke her nipples and feel them harden in response under his fingers.

His hands moved downward and, without breaking the contact of their lips, she held his fingers in place.

Angling her head slightly, she inhaled, gasping for air. "Not here," she whispered.

"No. Not here," he affirmed. "I just couldn't wait another minute to taste you." Reluctantly, as if pulling back from a force of life, he took a step back. Taking hold of her hand, he led them to his car and opened the passenger side. She hesitated for the briefest of seconds and he thought his life had ended. To his relief, she slipped into the seat.

***

Laura didn't remember the ride to his house, couldn't recall anything until they were flesh on flesh. Her body was an inferno of desperation and he was the only cure.

Sensation enveloped her, pushing aside her thoughts until all that remained was her awareness of his muscles, his flesh, his scent, him. She let go and then grabbed on as they lifted higher than she ever thought possible. Those beautiful hands of his played her body like a Stradivarius, unleashing all her secrets. Stroking her fevered body, he took his time. His tongue drew a molten path down her belly until finally, he was between her legs. Her core throbbed, pulsed, driving her to the brink until her entire being was totally focused on release.

The sound of the foil tearing reassured her and somewhere in the back of her mind, she was grateful that he had the presence of mind to be careful. And then, mercifully, he was inside her. Of their own accord, her legs wrapped around his hips and pulled him deeper as the inferno was ignited yet again. They moved together, into a fever pitch until, once more, she shattered just as his muscles tensed.

He had managed to defeat gravity for her and his weight was the only thing keeping her on the earth.

Slowly, in small increments, her brain started to function again. Laura closed her eyes to make the world stop for just a few minutes more.

Easing over onto his side, his kiss this time was soft. Neither spoke. It was her laughter that broke the silence. He tensed and she stroked his cheek.

"Oh my God," she breathed.

Relaxing, his laughter joined hers.

"Where did you learn to do that?" she asked.

"I was just about to ask you the same thing."

"But I didn't do anything," she said, confused.

"Well, then I think I should be afraid of when you do *something*. I might not recover."

Laura snuggled back into the pillows. "Is this your house?"

He grinned at her. "I hope so. Otherwise the owner would probably be pretty upset if he came home and found us like this."

She chewed her lower lip. "I meant, do you have a roommate?

"No. All mine. Do you like it?"

She laughed. "Well, I didn't really get a chance to look at it before we... ." She inhaled. "This has never happened to me before."

He narrowed his eyes. "Which part?"

She laughed again. "Oh, I wasn't trying to say I was a virgin or anything. But that's what it felt like."

"Thank you," he grinned.

"I meant I don't just do this, especially not on a first date." She could feel the blush on her cheeks.

"Laura, I wanted you from the first moment I laid eyes on you. I'm impressed with myself that I exercised great self-control."

"Really?"

"Well, I thought about it in the coffee shop, but the tables were too small."

Laura twisted and lifted her head, resting it on her palm. "Well thanks for that. If they'd called the police, we'd never have lived it down." She pushed back the covers and started looking for her clothes.

"What are you doing?" He sounded hurt.

"Getting dressed. Going home." She hesitated. "Oh, I don't have my car here." Embarrassed to her toes, she busied herself gathering her bra and panties.

"I can drive you back, but I want you to know something." His tone was so serious, she stopped fastening her bra and looked at him. A ray of moonlight illuminated his features and she could see the concern in his expression.

"Okay." She had no idea what he was going to say, but she steeled herself in case it wasn't what she wanted to hear.

"I don't do this either. And I don't want you to go. I'd be happy if you'd stay with me tonight." Before she could reply, he rushed on. "We can get up early and I can get you to your car so you can get home and change before... are you planning on going to work? Because if you do, I will, too."

A tenderness unlike anything she had ever felt suffused her. Laura didn't believe in love at first sight, but she was suddenly nonplussed and the foreign emotions coursing through her were unsettling at best. She wasn't comfortable with soft feelings and always tried to maintain control, but he was making it very difficult. One of Devin's remarks came back to her. 'Give me a vicious killer armed to the teeth and I'm in my element, but social stuff... well... ' She was experiencing the same emotions. This was new and exciting and terrifying.

A part of her whispered it was too soon, she didn't know this man, he could have instinctively known what buttons to push to get her in bed. Reluctantly, she had to admit she wanted him as much as he seemed to want her. And where was the harm? They enjoyed each other. It didn't have to go any further. It didn't have to get out of control. *It's already out of control,* that nasty voice in her head whispered. How she hated that voice. Reminding her she was short of the mark. Her mother's voice. But the vulnerability she was experiencing was so new. She had never really known the emotional high that making love evoked. It touched her core, her bones and was so exhilarating and so terrifying, all at once.

Mind made up, she slipped back into bed and snuggled her bottom into him. His arms wrapped around her and she drifted off. What felt like five minutes later, she awoke with a start. Grabbing her phone, she relaxed when she saw it was only five a.m. The sound of water running signaled Devin was already awake and in the shower. She plucked his shirt off the floor and put it on, then ambled to the kitchen, following the enticing aroma of coffee. He was shaping up to be the perfect man so far. Of course, he probably had a corpse in the basement freezer or some weird fetish he hadn't revealed yet. Laura had to ask herself if that would make her feel better, but the answer was a resounding 'no'.

His home was orderly and neat. The furniture was tasteful, a leather couch facing a big screen TV and a recliner off to the side. A well-worn coffee table squatted in front of the sofa. Family photos graced the bookcase on the back wall and the overall feeling was homey and warm. But the surprise was the eclectic art on all of the walls. Several canvases with colors and shapes and interesting patterns, a beautiful nude and a serene landscape. Everywhere she looked, there was an enticing image to hold her attention. So much so she forget about getting coffee.

His voice behind her startled her.

"Oh, sorry. I didn't mean to scare you." His gaze went to the walls. "Do you like it?" he asked. He nestled his head into her shoulder, his skin still warm and damp. "My gallery of local artists."

"Amazing. Who would have guessed?" She turned in his arms and smiled. Secretly, she had always dreamed of painting on canvas, but she never felt she was talented enough. That was why she so appreciated those that were.

"Did you think I was just a dumb cop?" He lifted an eyebrow.

"Hardly." She turned in his arms. "But I didn't expect an art connoisseur. These works are gorgeous."

"There is so much virtually undiscovered genius out there. Most of these came from local craft shows."

"Maybe I can go with you sometime," she suggested, then choked. They had an amazing night, but this was a little presumptive. She needed to change the subject. "Can I tell you something? It's very important."

His eyes darkened and narrowed in anticipation. "Okay."

"If I don't get some of that coffee soon…"

He grinned at her and led the way to the kitchen. A towel hung around his narrow hips and she couldn't help but notice his butt, sending her thoughts back to bed. He poured two cups and handed her one.

"Oh my God," she exclaimed. "This is so good."

He laughed with pleasure at the compliment.

"I don't think we should advertise this at work." She waved her hand between them.

"Are you ashamed of me?" he teased.

"Heavens no. I just don't want to be anyone's excuse for prying looks or gossip."

He nodded. "Makes sense," he replied, sounding unconvinced.

***

An hour later, Laura was poring over the reports left on her desk. It was taking longer than usual since memories of the night before kept her squirming in her chair every now and again. *Concentrate!* Devin passed by and smiled at her, but kept walking just as John appeared and slipped into the chair next to her desk. He watched Devin's retreat and sucked in his cheeks.

"Good morning," he greeted her, grinning like the cat that just swallowed the canary. "Happy Saturday? Or should I ask—happy Friday night?"

Laura pretended not to notice, but she could feel the color rising in her cheeks.

"So, how are you this morning?" His tone was teasing and she glared at him, but she was sure he had noticed the blush when Devin went by. John was incredibly observant.

"Are you here to work or get on my nerves?" She tried to sound harsh, but John wasn't impressed.

Smothering a grin, he cleared his throat. "Since the husband was the father or, at least, his is the name listed, it makes you wonder why the delay? Twenty odd years ago, an unwed mother was not exactly acceptable.

Maybe he got cold feet in the beginning, then decided to marry her. Or maybe he didn't think the baby was his. Or maybe he didn't find out about the baby until a couple of years later."

Good points," she responded. "So there was no one else in her life romantically?" It wasn't really a question.

"Not that I could find. Of course, there is that time gap."

"Which means she was a single mother for the first two years," Laura assessed. "And from what I could find, no income or place to live? That makes no sense, especially with a baby."

"What about her family?"

Laura at least had a little something here. "The aunt Natalie. I finally was able to find her—in a residential home. It took some digging, but her address finally turned up. And it turns out it's the same one my mother lives in"

John frowned. "Seriously?"

"But apparently she's in a different section. I say let's go check it out today."

John nodded.

"I'm hoping the aunt knows something." Laura had run into dead ends before, but this was one wall after another.

"You find anything else?" John asked.

"Not yet. The labs came back on the bodies and no surprises. And the DNA won't be back for a while." Then she filled him in on her visit with Barbara Cassis. She had asked about the CCTV cameras in the neighborhood. "Did you get anything on the daughter watching her parents?"

"No. There are no cameras. Funny, because there are some prop ones over a few doors, but none of them are connected."

"So, we can't verify Barbara's story. Damn." Laura was hoping for something concrete.

"But, even if we saw the daughter watching them, what would it tell us?" he asked.

"I have no idea. It's just strange."

"What's with you and the new guy?" John asked. angling his head toward where Devin had been.

"I believe we were talking about a case here," she admonished him.

John shrugged innocently. "Come on, you can tell me."

"Do I ask about your private life?" She sucked in her cheeks. She shouldn't have said that and she knew it. John was very guarded about the fact he was gay and she had no intention of embarrassing him.

He dropped his gaze and some of the color drained from his face. "No," he whispered.

She instantly changed the subject. "Let's go talk to Aunt Natalie."

***

Laura and John flashed their badges and the receptionist sprang to her feet. A twenty-something girl, she had bad skin and purple hair. A pierced nose and eyebrow completed the less than professional picture. She didn't seem to recognize Laura, but then she was never particularly attentive when Laura visited. If you knew the door code, you weren't worth her time. Laura could only wonder if today she was feeling guilty about something or just so bored that a visit from the cops was big excitement.

"We'd like to see Natalie Kessler," Laura stated.

The receptionist giggled. "What'd she do, rob a bank?" When both Laura and John glared at her, she sobered and glanced at the clock. "I have to check with the manager."

Laura and John waited while she picked up the phone and dialed, spoke for a minute and hung up. "Mrs. Merriweather would like to accompany you. She'll be right out."

An older woman in her fifties dressed in a dark business suit stepped in the lobby and held out her hand. "Allison Merriweather." She looked at Laura. "Don't I know you?"

"Yes, my mother lives here. We met when I checked her in a year ago. But we need to speak to another of your residents."

"You want to speak to Natalie Kessler?"

"We do. Is that a problem?"

"No. It's just that she hasn't had visitors..." she turned to the receptionist. "Has Natalie ever had visitors?"

"Not that I can remember."

Laura wondered if the girl would ever recall a visitor, since she obviously couldn't care less about the comings and goings here.

"How long has Ms. Kessler been here?" Laura asked.

"Let's go into my office, shall we?" Allison led the way down a corridor and into an office decorated in pinks and white. Framed pictures of flowers decorated the walls and the chairs were covered in a pale pink striped fabric. Laura resisted the urge to shudder. She remembered this office from a year ago. It reminded her of a Pepto-Bismol bottle. Allison took her place behind the desk and John and Laura sat in the chairs in front.

"You were asking how long Natalie had been here. About fourteen years. She was one of our first residents." She lifted her chin. "Can I ask what this is about?"

"Her sister and her sister's husband were murdered and we wanted to ask her a few questions," Laura replied.

Allison paled. "Murdered?"

Laura nodded.

"You can't tell her that. She won't be able to deal with it."

"Why exactly is she here?" John asked.

"Well, I'm not really at liberty to discuss that with you, but let's just say she isn't the most stable of people and she needs more than full-time care, if you know what I mean."

"No. What do you mean?" Laura prodded.

"Supervision at all times. Most of our residents, like your mother, require care for the basic needs. But some, like Natalie Kessler, cannot be left alone. Ever."

"Why?" John asked.

Allison inhaled. "She can get—agitated—sometimes."

"Is she dangerous?" Laura asked.

Allison's smile was slow. "Not as long as she has someone nearby and available."

"Someone with access to chemical restraint?" Laura pressed. They didn't hold back on the use of drugs that calmed here.

Allison straightened. "We take care of our charges. We see they are safe and well cared for." She glared at Laura. "Do you have any complaints about your mother's care and safety here?"

"No. None that I can't deal with myself."

"Who pays for it?" John asked bluntly. "All that special care for Natalie."

"There is a trust account. I believe her parents set it up for her."

"And they never came to visit?" Laura asked.

"Not that I know of. Apparently they were people who had a hard time accepting that their daughter was— in need of help."

"Did you know she had a twin?" Laura asked. "The sister that was murdered."

Allison's eyebrows nearly disappeared into her hairline. "No. I had no idea."

"So her sister never came to see her either."

"No."

"May we visit with her?" Laura asked.

Allison bit her lip. "You cannot say anything that might upset her. As I said, she has a tendency to be— difficult—if she gets upset." Allison hesitated. "Do you really need to talk to her? It's not as if she could be a suspect."

"Ms. Merriweather, Natalie's twin sister and her husband were brutally murdered and any information will help us. We have no desire to shock or disturb her. But we were hoping to learn about her family life before she came here. It might give us some necessary insights," Laura explained patiently, pressing her lips together to control her dislike for this woman.

Allison stood and led them back to the hallway and

down the corridor. To the left, it opened into a large room filled with tables and bright with sunlight. She pointed to a chair in the corner and both Laura and John nearly gasped. Natalie Kessler was dressed in a clean robe with her hair pulled back and the resemblance to her late sister was startling. Next to her was a young man dressed in scrubs talking to her softly.

"I'm going to stay, if that's all right," Allison said, but it was definitely not a question.

Allison caught the attention of the orderly, who nodded and left the table, presumably to make arrangements in case Natalie became—difficult. The three then approached Natalie, who looked up with wide eyes filled with suspicion. "No!" she screamed, attracting the attention of the other occupants of the room. Allison quickly went behind her and placed her hands on Natalie's shoulders. "They won't hurt you. They're my friends. They just want to talk to you." Her voice soothed Natalie, who visibly relaxed. "Isn't it lovely to have some visitors?"

"Okay. If you say so." But her hands had tightened into fists.

"Hello, Natalie. My name is Laura and this is John. We just came to see you because we always like talking to twins."

Allison nodded her approval, so Laura went on. "Can you tell me what it was like growing up with a twin sister?"

Natalie smiled, but her gaze was distant. "We played with our dolls. They matched, too."

John took a step forward, but Natalie glared at him, so he moved back.

"My mommy and daddy said we should be just like

those dolls. Perfect." Natalie's expression clouded. "But Nora was better. Until she wasn't." She broke into a fit of giggles and then suddenly calmed. "Have you seen my mommy?"

"No, I'm sorry I haven't, but I'm sure she loves you," Laura ventured.

"No," A tear slipped down her cheek. "I was always bad. She had to punish me. But she always said she tried to love me. But when I hit her, she sent me away. Then I came here. I like it better here." Laura noticed Natalie's fists had opened partway.

"Thank you for talking to us, Natalie," Laura said gently.

"Are you going to visit me again?" She looked up at Laura, a pleading look in her eyes.

"Yes, we will."

"Pinky swear?" Natalie asked, holding out the finger. Laura looped it with her own and then Natalie's gaze took her somewhere else again.

They walked out with Allison, who led them back to her office.

"Apparently, based on what she just said, she was in another home before she came here," Allison said without preamble. "That would mean she's been cared for most of her life. I never knew that. But I can't say it's a surprise."

"It wasn't in her history?" John asked.

"She was here long before I got here. I was told her diagnosis and that she was long term. I'm not a psychiatrist, so how much more did I need? Take care of her and sedate her when she gets anxious."

"Is she violent?" John asked.

Allison pressed her lips together. "I wouldn't

classify her behavior as violent. More as I told you before—difficult. But only if she's agitated, which isn't very often." She huffed a breath. "Detectives, we can't take the chance she might... accidently... hurt someone. We are paid to do a job and I believe we do a good one."

"Well, thank you for your time." Laura turned to the door, then back. "Just out of curiosity. There's no way she could get out, right?"

"You're asking if she might have sneaked out to kill her sister?" Allison snorted. "You've seen her. She isn't capable of the simplest tasks half the time. But, to answer your question—no—every door is locked and there is always someone stationed by the exits. A code in and a code out." Her tone was patronizing.

As they walked to the car, John scratched his head. "Could Natalie be faking?"

"I doubt it. I guess it's possible, and we need to check it out, but she's apparently been locked up for years. If she wasn't crazy before, that would do it for me."

"Yeah, me, too."

"She did say something interesting, though."

"Yeah, I caught it. About Nora being good until she wasn't," John said, nodding.

"Let's follow up on that." She grinned. "I also have a friend at the home. A nurse that cares for my mother. She might be able to give us some more insights.

"Good."

She picked up her cell.

"Hey, Jocelyn, it's Laura. How's it going?"

"Just another day in paradise."

"So, I have a question."

"Okay. Is that your professional voice?" Jocelyn asked.

"Pretty astute. Yes. There's a patient in another part of the home that I was wondering about."

Laura could visualize Jocelyn raising an eyebrow. "Go on."

"Her name is Natalie Kessler and she's been there for years."

"Yeah, I know her. Everyone knows her. Powder keg Kessler."

"That bad?" Laura asked.

"Not all the time. But over the years, she has made a spectacle of herself by tearing down the halls screaming. And hitting people."

"Did you know she had a twin sister?" Laura pressed.

"No, but I hope her sister is a polar opposite. Natalie is a very sad case. She was abandoned here. I'm sure I'd be pretty crazy if my family did that to me."

"Do you know how she got here in the first place?"

"No. But if you like, I can try and ask around. I can't give you specifics without a warrant. Sorry. But I can give you a summary of the rumors if that would help."

"It might. Her sister and her sister's husband were murdered and I was hoping to get whatever insight I could as to victimology."

"I'll see what I can do."

"Thanks. And thanks for putting up with my mother."

"That's why they pay me the big bucks."

Chapter Six

Laura's eyes ached and, although she hated to admit it, she missed Devin. They hadn't spent any time together, aside from work, since Saturday morning. He did text her every few hours, but here it was already Monday and hell, she wanted to spend some quality—meaning sexy?— time with him. She had run into him earlier and he said something about dinner tomorrow night. Definitely something to look forward to.

As if on cue, her phone rang. Cara.

"Hey, can we meet for a drink tonight?" Laura blurted before even saying hello.

"Read my mind. You okay?"

"Yes and no. How about Charlie's at six," Laura suggested.

"Sure. Sounds serious. In a good way?"

"See you later."

"I will probably die of curiosity before that."

"Be brave," Laura teased and hung up. She needed to talk about this Devin thing. It was definitely throwing her off balance which was not a place she was used to being. Talking to Cara always helped her focus. She pushed the conflicting emotions into the vault and went back to the list of potential witnesses.

At ten fifteen, she called John.

"Where are you?"

"Right behind you," he laughed as she reacted to hearing his voice in stereo.

"Let's go."

They headed to her car and drove to the First Baptist Church where people were assembling for the Whitings' memorial service. The place was standing room only. Laura scanned the list of parishioners Pastor Michael had sent over. It seemed the entire congregation had turned out to honor the deceased.

John and Laura stood at the back, watching all the attendees, hoping for something. At the front of the room, Alexandra sat next to her boyfriend, the occasional sob vibrating her back. Jeff reached over several times and patted her hand.

The pastor spoke and prayed with the congregation, then invited Alexandra up to speak. On shaky legs, she made her way up to the pulpit and leaned on it for support.

"Thank you all for coming. My parents…" A heaving of her chest interrupted, but she quickly regained her composure. "Well, you all know what wonderful people they were. I remember…"

Alexandra droned on for several minutes, regaling the crowd with sweet childhood memories, while Laura and John scanned the gathering. Nothing appeared out of the ordinary. People reacted to the humor in Alexandra's stories, some just cried silent tears. No one leaned forward, no one had any unusual reaction. Laura was certain this was a wild goose chase, but it was always worth a try. Many times a perp would show up to gloat or re-live the scenario of death.

Finally, it was over and John and Laura filed out

with the mourners. They stopped to say thank you to the pastor and to offer condolences to Alexandra and Jeff, her boyfriend. Alexandra didn't question their presence there and Laura was happy she didn't have to come up with the standard excuse they were just paying respects. Of course, that was better than saying they were attending to assess if any of the friends and neighbors was a cold-blooded killer.

They drove back to the station and went over what they had, which was not much. John was going to get a warrant for the couple's financial records and Laura would build the profile of victimology, but with so few relatives and friends, other than those at the church, this was going to be a long haul.

At twenty minutes to six, Laura stood up and stretched. Organized for tomorrow, she picked up her purse and headed for the door. Charlie's was only a short walk and she wanted to clear her head before she met Cara. It had been a hell of a day with nothing positive to recommend it. Looking around, she had to admit she was hoping to run into Devin, but chances were he had already left. And they were having dinner tomorrow. *Stop acting like a lovesick teenager,* she admonished herself.

Charlie's was dark and cool, the long bar stretching the length of the place. It catered to regulars who preferred talk over football blaring from the walls.

Cara was sitting at one of the small tables on the wall opposite the bar. A waiter was just delivering two glasses of white wine and Laura smiled. Nothing like a bestie who knew what you needed.

Laura slipped into the chair opposite and Cara leaned in. "So, what's his name?"

"Devin," she responded.

"And how did Devin appear in your life?"

"He's the new cold case guy." Just talking about him increased her blood flow.

Cara sucked in air through her teeth. "Sounds like you're in trouble. And so fast?"

"Here's the thing. I just started with a case. A particularly brutal one. I need to concentrate on solving it, not spending time worrying over..." Laura took a gulp of her wine.

"Wow. That bad, huh?"

Sheepishly, Laura nodded.

"Have you slept with him?"

"You know when you read those romance novels about the sky opening up and the world exploding?"

Cara's eyes widened and she grinned. "You're joking, right? That only happens in the vivid imagination of some writer."

Laura shrugged.

"I have to meet this guy."

Inhaling, Laura took another sip of wine. "I want you to meet him. I do. But first I have to figure out what's going on with me."

"It sounds like that movie—you know—you were hit by the thunderbolt. I am so jealous."

"What should I do?" This was uncharted territory.

Cara shrugged. "Enjoy it. Do your work during the day and have some fun at night. You're entitled. All you've had for so long is the work and the misery. Speaking of—how is your mother?"

Laura rolled her eyes. "Charming as ever."

"You know you're a hero for taking care of her."

"Conscience is a cruel mistress." She hesitated. "Her mind is going. She thinks she's having lunch with my uncle and my grandmother. And both have been dead for years."

"I'm sorry. What are you going to do?"

"Have her transferred to memory care. It's just—there's no privacy there and she complains so much as it is. But I don't see I have another choice."

Cara shook her head in sympathy. "You'll do the right thing. You always do." Cara reached over and patted her on the hand. "Let's eat something and talk about my social life."

"Really? Your social life? As in someone new?" Laura was certain she would have heard if a new man was on the horizon.

"No, not really. But look over at that guy. What do you think? Potential?"

Laura glanced in the direction Cara indicated. "Looks perfect except for the wedding band."

"Yeah, well, isn't the devil always in the details?"

***

Laura tossed and turned until four. Between the case and Devin, her mind was clacking away like an old typewriter. Reluctantly giving in to the white noise in her brain, and the persistent annoyance of her body, she got up, showered, dressed and made herself some coffee. Which reminded her of Devin.

She sat at her kitchen table and pulled her list for the day out of her bag. In a murder case, the first order was to interview anyone and everyone who knew or had any history or contact with the victim, or in this case victims. It was a spiral starting in the center and moving outward.

Usually, this was an extensive list. People had associates at work, in their social circles, through family. But these people had no family but their daughter and the aunt in a home, they were retired and their entire social circle seemed to consist of mingling at church. She considered interviewing the parishioners, but there were nearly three hundred of them and Laura had a feeling it would be a total waste of time. They might have to do that in the future, but for now she was hoping to turn up something more relevant in the victimology.

Wanting to find out as much as she could about Nora's history, Laura was convinced there was something there. Luckily, these days, there was no secret the internet couldn't uncover if you just kept digging.

Her thoughts again drifted to Devin as she sipped her coffee. Cara had said she should enjoy it, but that was foreign to her. Her mother was only kind when there was an ulterior motive and her ex taught her to be more than wary. There really hadn't been any good relationships in her life and until now, her work had kept her thoughts on problem solving and had filled her days. She worked herself to exhaustion most of the time and when she was off duty, she was too tired to pursue anything other than a casual encounter. Devin was definitely not casual. And the thought had her accepting that some things were definitely worth the risk, no matter how scary.

Longing to call him just to hear his voice, she hesitated. Appearing too needy was not attractive and besides, it was only five in the morning. Instead, she filled her go-cup with more coffee and headed to the station.

She had worn Google to a nub when John appeared at eight. He glanced at her computer and sat down. "Find anything useful?"

"We need to check out the state office in Nashville and the schools where Nora worked and Evan's old office. Also, anyone else we can find who might have known them then."

"That's a lot of years ago," John huffed in frustration.

Laura cut her gaze to him. "You have any other suggestions?"

"Psychic network? No, that won't work. You know why?" He didn't wait for a reply. "They're out of business. One thing always bothered me. They went bankrupt. Shouldn't they have known they were in trouble?"

Laura stifled a smile. "I'm feeling generous this morning, so I'll give you a choice."

"I hate just sitting at my desk," he declared.

"Who doesn't. But okay. Take the day and drive to Nashville. See if anyone remembers Nora. Meanwhile, I'm going to dig into Natalie's history and then see what I can find out about the trust fund set up to pay for her. I need to get a warrant, but hopefully the judge will cut me some slack and not make me wait."

***

Watching as John strode away, Devin took a breath and approached Laura's desk. Looking around to ensure no one was watching, he bent to her ear. "If I don't see you soon, I am going to burst into flames and you will be responsible."

He straightened and angled his head, delighted to see the color rise to her cheeks.

"I see, Detective, and I do understand as I feel exactly the same way." Her tone was professional, but she ran her tongue along her upper lip. His body immediately reacted and he cleared his throat.

"We are still on for dinner tonight, right." He raised an eyebrow.

"And dessert," she responded, this time purposefully running her tongue along her bottom lip. Devin was afraid he would embarrass himself right then and there.

"How's your case coming?" he asked, desperate to change the subject.

Laura inhaled and Devin bit the inside of his cheek when her action lifted her breasts. He could almost taste them and… he had to stop this. He was like an out-of-control teenager who had just discovered what girls could offer. But after living for so long in the dating desert it was—an oasis?

"I am frustrated," she declared.

Who isn't? he almost blurted out. Luckily, she continued.

"These people appear to be as normal as they come. No vices, no nefarious activities, their social life revolved around their church. They'd been married forever without a breath of scandal—so far. But, I might have something in the wife's past prove interesting."

"Keep digging," he suggested. "There is always a motive. You know that. Even if it's apparently random."

"So far there doesn't seem to be anything random about this crime. This was personal. And yet, no family other than the daughter with a strong alibi and the dead wife's sister tucked away in a care home. That's the part that's so frustrating."

"Sorry," he commiserated.

"How's yours going?"

"Same. Can't find a motive that sticks. I still think it's going to be someone she knew."

Laura nodded. "It usually is."

"See you later," he said, wishing the hours would fly by, but he knew better. He walked away humming "I Feel Good" and grinning to himself.

***

Natalie Elizabeth Kessler had been thrown out of kindergarten for sticking another child in the face with a pencil. Who gets thrown out of kindergarten? And apparently her life went downhill from there. After her third private school requested she never return, her parents hired a tutor for a year or so and finally, at the ripe old age of eight, Natalie was sent to live in a special home for unruly children. A very expensive proposition at the time, but apparently not a problem for the Kesslers. After that, it was one facility after another. It was clear Natalie was never going to be able to live without supervision. She definitely had some violent tendencies, but it was hard to get hold of an axe and go around chopping up people when you were locked in and guarded all the time.

Her twin, Nora, did not seem to have any of the same aggressive inclinations. She graduated from high school and then she disappeared off the face of the earth for a year.

Real estate records in Nashville confirmed the old family address and reinforced the idea that both Nora and Natalie came from wealth. And yes, both Kesslers died a year apart years ago: she from cancer and he from complications from pneumonia. Other than that, Laura was left with very little to piece together a theory.

The Kesslers had twins, and as cliché as it was, one was good and the other evil. Not technically evil, but certainly mentally ill, Natalie was locked away at the age of eight and apparently forgotten. The thought gave Laura chills. No matter how flawed your child, how could you just abandon her? But then, Laura's mother was around as she grew up and Laura would no doubt have been better off if she hadn't been.

Then there was Nora. The 'good' daughter. At least until she finished high school. And what if she had enough of her parents and struck out on her own? Or if her parents had enough of being parents and made her life miserable? As a rich kid, she probably didn't have too many work skills, but she could have found a friend to stay with and odd jobs that paid cash. Or she could have stayed at home until she got pregnant by Evan and she was definitely the good girl no more. According to Alexandra, her parents disavowed all knowledge of Nora then and she had no choice but to make it on her own.

Did she tell Evan about the baby right away? Or keep it to herself? In which case, did he decide to marry her because he found out? DNA testing wasn't prevalent then, so maybe he thought Alexandra wasn't his. What changed his mind? And was any of this helpful in finding out who killed them?

So Laura still needed a motive. Opportunity was always available one way or another, but taking human lives, and so brutally, required something more than a passing whim. She listed the four 'L's" in her head: Love, Lust, Loathing and Loot.

Love included things like mercy killing, so that was out. Lust? Hardly. Loathing? Maybe? But there didn't seem anything or anyone in their lives that would provoke that kind of vicious response. And last, but not least... money. But the Whitings were not wealthy people and Evan's life insurance would only cover funeral expenses.

Laura closed her eyes and dropped her chin to her chest. What was she missing?

***

Glancing at the clock, Laura packed up her things and headed home. Devin was picking her up at seven and she wanted to take a bath and put on fresh makeup. Just the thought of the man sent tingles up her spine. What was she? A teenager? But the feelings those young girls had talked about—was she finally experiencing them? The racing heart, the heated anticipation, the constant awareness of her nether region... all there. Which meant her romantic experiences had been stunted until now. She'd never had any role models for loving. Her father was absent and her mother was a narcissist and her experience with marriage was—pathetic.

Cara's words echoed again: 'enjoy it'. And Laura had every intention of just that, so when the doorbell rang, she stood back and called out to him that the door was open. When he walked in and closed the door, he seemed puzzled until she dropped her dress to the floor. There was nothing to conceal her body now since she hadn't bothered with underwear.

His sharp intake of breath and his immediate physical reaction, which she couldn't help but notice, convinced her she had made the right choice. He didn't move for what seemed an eternity, but looked at her as if he had never seen anything so miraculous. Her insides filled with light. Moving up to her and, stretching out his hands, he stroked her sides with incredible tenderness, raising goose bumps, then inched closer and went to his knees. His tongue found her core with unerring accuracy and she latched onto his shoulders to keep from buckling as the inferno focused her entire body on the small nub between her legs. She was firing into the universe in a million stars, then slowly, very slowly, easing back.

Now it was her turn to sink to her knees, then lay back and stretch out, the foyer carpet pleasantly scratching the flesh of her back. Her only thought was giving him the same ecstasy and loving caresses he had given her. His clothes were gone and he pressed into her with agonizing slowness, deeper and deeper, melting into her body until they were bound in the eternal link. And then he moved, in and out, pulling her with him into an alternate cosmos where the only meaning was pleasure, all else left behind. The fire took her again and she called his name as he tensed, pushed forward, and moaned his release.

They lay there, together, limbs entangled, and drifted to nowhere in particular, the rhythmic thwap, thwap of the overhead fan cooling their damp skin. Suddenly, his stomach growled and brought them back to reality.

Pressing her lips together to keep from laughing, Laura lifted up on an elbow and smiled at him. "This doesn't get you out of taking me to dinner," she said, lifting her chin arrogantly.

"Well, I was thinking of pasta when I arrived, but you tasted so much better, I almost forgot."

They managed to sort through their clothes and dress, then headed out the door and into his car.

"We could do take-out. In bed," he suggested, leering. "Or on the floor. Like a floor picnic only naked."

"We could. But I'd like to spend some time with your brain."

"I usually take it with me to bed. But then, not with you. With you, all intellect seems to center below the waist."

"Very funny. Please can I pick your brain?"

"Boring, but okay. Your case got you?"

"Yeah. I'm hoping a good cold case guy might have some insights. Do you know one?"

"I could make some calls," he teased. "Talk to me. Or better yet, let's get a glass of wine and some food and then maybe I can concentrate. That greeting of yours caught me a little off balance."

"In a bad way?" Laura hadn't really ever been the aggressive type sexually and she had to wonder if she'd come on too strong.

He snorted. "Hardly. If you do that more often, though, I might have to show up every night."

Unsure if that was terrifying or thrilling, Laura opted for pleasantly unnerving. This man actually liked her and enjoyed her company. And the feeling was more than mutual. Was there a future here? Because she fervently hoped so. In her secret soul, she hoped it would go on forever, banishing the fear.

A while later, sitting with some drinks and fresh Italian bread, Devin reached over and took her hand. He tilted his head and grinned. "We'd better talk business or I'll keep remembering what you have on under that dress and we'll have to leave before we get our dinner."

"I have nothing."

He grinned at the double entendre. "I know. I saw, remember?"

"On the case, I mean. Two dead violently. A daughter with no apparent motive. No exes. The only relative is a crazy aunt committed to a home for the difficult." She made air quotes to emphasize the last word. "Grandparents deceased. Quiet dull lives, with the only social interaction at church. And… no similar murders in this area ever."

"Random?"

"The vics apparently let the perp in since the alarm was turned off and there was no sign of forced entry. They were getting ready for bed, so they were in pajamas."

"Money?"

"None to speak of. The house had a reverse mortgage. There was a 10K life insurance policy." She chewed her lip. "Here's the odd thing. The murders themselves were brutal. Personal. Full of rage." Laura blew out a breath. "I'm stumped."

"Wow," he exclaimed.

"Oh, one other thing that makes no sense. The neighbor says the daughter was spying on her parents from the street for a month before the murders. She saw Alexandra three or four times, watching through the window."

"So maybe the daughter suspected them of something?" His tone wasn't convincing.

"As I said, makes no sense to me."

"There has to be something in their past. Coming back to haunt them."

"Agreed. The wife did have a lapse in her history which we're checking on, but that was more than twenty-five years ago. That's a long time to hold a grudge if there was something there."

"How old is the daughter?" he asked, leaning in now.

"Twenty-six."

"So maybe something happened that had to do with the daughter's birth. Like the real father?"

"Nope. The other vic, the husband, was the real father. At least, he's the one listed on the birth certificate."

"Man, you could get a flat forehead from banging against this wall."

"Don't I know it."

They finished dinner and went back to his house. Laura had been completely satisfied by the night spent with him, except for the work part. He was as stuck as she was for answers. But it had to be there. Elusive, yes. But it was there. She just had to find it.

In the meantime, she was in a lovely house with a delicious man and she wasn't about to waste it. In fact, she made a point of not wasting it all night long.

***

Settling into her desk the next morning, she looked up when John approached, his expression unreadable.

"Which means you are not excited?" she asked.

"No one remembered her," he stated flatly. "In point of fact, it was nearly thirty years ago. But I verified Nora did work there for a little more than a year as a file clerk." He huffed out a breath. "Where was the internet when you need it?"

Laura snorted. "Yeah, doing things the old-fashioned way sucks. If it makes you feel any better, I haven't got anything else either." She huffed a sigh. "But I did get access to Natalie's financials, and I have an appointment with the banker in charge of her trust tomorrow. There might be something there."

"Maybe we should just hope for a magician to appear and wave his wand."

"John, we're missing something important. I can feel it niggling away at me."

"Yes, but what?"

Laura rolled her eyes. "If I knew..." She shook her head. "Let's just go over what we have again and maybe, just maybe, something will click."

But after going nowhere with the work all day, she called Jocelyn and Cara and arranged to meet them for a drink. There was a cozy bar tucked back in a strip mall on the west side of town that actually had some good bands playing. The music was usually jazz or the blues, which meant it was a perfect accompaniment to good conversation.

Jocelyn was waiting at the door when Laura walked in. Waving when she saw Laura, her little-girl-lost look was replaced by a warm smile.

"I'm so glad you came," Laura greeted her. "Cara will be here soon." Laura leaned in. "She's always late. But don't tell her I told you."

"I heard that," Cara said from behind them. "I was early and went to the bathroom."

"You were early? Someone call 911."

Cara gave her a feigned hurt and they edged into the place to find a table in the corner. The music wouldn't be starting for about an hour, so they had time to visit and talk. Laura made the introductions, and they were soon chatting away like old friends.

"So Jocelyn, I don't know anything about you," Laura said.

"And my life is so exciting," she said, rolling her eyes.

"Me, too," Cara chimed in. "Now our friend Laura here…"

"Really?" Jocelyn raised an eyebrow.

Laura took a deep breath. "I don't want to jinx it, but if he meets my mother…"

"Oh hell, girlfriend," Cara interrupted, "no one would think anything but that you're a saint. Seriously."

Jocelyn nodded in agreement. "When people come to live where I work, one of two things happens: they get meaner or they get nicer."

"And anyone who's ever met Laura's mother knows which one she is."

"My mother likes *you*, Cara," Laura stated without rancor.

"Your mother is one angry woman who picks her easiest target, which is you," Cara responded. "But you'd think she'd be smart enough to be nice to the people in charge of her care."

Jocelyn laughed at that. "It's never that way." She turned to Laura. "Do you hear her voice in your head?"

Laura was surprised. "How did you know?"

Jocelyn shrugged. "It's like that kernel of self-doubt that plagues all women. Our mother's voices."

"So what do we do about it?" Cara asked.

Jocelyn smiled. "Consider the source and move on. Every time I hear my mother telling me I should have had better aspirations than being a nurse, I turn it around in my head and I think about all the people I've helped, all the ones who depend on me now, and I make that voice louder. But it takes practice."

"Okay, let's move on to sexier topics. See that guy over there?" Cara pointed to a tall, dark-haired man sitting at the bar, staring into space.

"The one with too much baggage?" Laura asked.

"How do you do that?" Cara responded. She turned to Jocelyn. "I swear, she's a witch. She can read minds."

"No," Laura scoffed. "I'm a detective. Just look at the expression on his face."

Both women glanced in the direction Laura was looking, trying to appear casual. They both turned back and nodded.

"Okay," Jocelyn said, indicating another man, this one of average height, wearing glasses.

"Dull and boring," Laura said.

"Why? Because of the glasses?" Jocelyn prodded her.

"No. Because he seems stunned by all the activity."

"Okay—one more," Cara grinned. "Over there. That one."

Laura suppressed a smile. "Serial killer."

Both women jumped at that, horrified. "How can you tell?" asked Cara.

"We should call someone," Jocelyn enjoined.

Now Laura laughed out loud. "That's my partner, John. He hangs out here too sometimes."

Both women shot her a dirty look, but relaxed. "He is a cutie," Cara remarked.

"Don't bother. He bats for the other team."

"Damn. Not fair." Cara whined.

John approached the table with a wide smile. "Ladies," he greeted them. Laura introduced them and then John touched Laura's shoulder. "Can I borrow you for a minute?"

Laura excused herself and they walked outside.

"Sorry to interrupt, but something's been bothering me."

"No problem. Tell me."

"Whoever killed this couple was furious with them, right?"

Laura nodded her agreement.

"Or maybe not. Maybe it was set up to look like that."

"Okay…" Laura wasn't sure where he was going with this.

"It appears to be someone they knew, but what if the perp wanted us to think it was a rage killing."

"Okay," Laura repeated, "but why? Which leads us back to motive."

"So whoever the perp is wants us to go with 'loathing'. But what if it's 'loot'?"

Laura chewed her lower lip. "A modest house and a ten thousand dollar life insurance policy just doesn't strike me as worth the risk. Unless there's other money we know nothing about."

"Like another life insurance policy?"

Laura nodded. "Yes, like another life insurance policy." Her brow furrowed. "There was no evidence of any other policy in the Whitings' paperwork or records. But that doesn't necessarily mean anything. The good news is those companies don't just pay out automatically. Someone has to claim it." Laura's slow smile lit her face. "And in the case of murder, the company would contact us. Which is a hell of a lot easier than trying to find which company wrote the policy." Laura patted John on the back. "Good thinking. I'm proud of you."

Now it was John's turn to grin, but he quickly sobered. "But also more waiting." He blinked several times. "Thanks for listening. Go back to your friends."

"Good work," she called after him as he walked away.

Chapter Seven

When Laura was alerted this morning a woman had been murdered and she was told the identity of the victim, it didn't come as a complete shock. What did come as a surprise was the murder weapon. Sarah Jane Malone was dirty. Deep down soul dirty. She had worked every angle, twisted every law, and always managed to glide under the radar. It was said that when she smiled, which was rarely, it was only when she was tucking money into her safe deposit box or sending it off to her bank account in the Caymans. Or screwing someone over big-time. She had no friends, no known associates, obviously trusting no one who could turn on her and play her the way she played everyone else.

Sarah Jane's reputation had preceded her and the police had been trying to catch her in one of her nefarious ventures for years. Her 'modeling agency' featured women and men who offered more than just a pretty face for the right price, but knowing it and proving it were miles apart. There were also stories of illegal adoptions and missing children, also without substantive proof. Laura was certain Sarah Jane could satisfy any vice for the right price, but she had been Teflon until now.

The building that housed Sarah Jane's office was

very upscale, all done in metal and black and white. The receptionist's desk stretched across the lobby, but whoever manned it was notably absent. Laura was stunned to see there were no cameras anywhere and no bank of monitors behind the desk.

John met her at the front entrance. "There are no cameras," John stated, equally as surprised as Laura.

"Frustrating. Clearly the clientele here requires discretion. Is there another way in?"

"Back service entrance. It is locked with a code and a security guard has to approve every delivery. I already talked to him and got a list."

"Wow. Impressive," Laura grinned at him.

He shrugged nonchalantly. "Just trying to keep up," he returned.

"Blow smoke somewhere else," she retorted. "Have you been upstairs?"

"Waiting for you. CSI is already there."

"Can you make sure we have a list of everyone who works in this building?"

Nodding, he hustled off to find the security guard.

Attesting to the vic's vanity, and in direct contrast to what was left of her on the floor, photographs of Sarah Jane in various glamorous poses decorated her plushily overdone office. Laura had no doubt much of Sarah Jane's profits were spent on plastic surgeons. She wondered if the coroner would be able to find a real person under all that medical enhancement. Or what was left of one.

Sarah Jane's mutilated body had been cut to pieces with what was most certainly an axe. Her limbs were positioned in such a way that she looked like a broken puppet. Blood spatter was everywhere and pooling under the various body parts. The scene was so horrendously gory as to be almost surreal. The expression on the corpse's face was the same rictus of horror as the Whitings' had been. She clearly did not expect her visitor to slash her to pieces.

Looking around the room, Laura noticed two partially full cocktail glasses. Sitting on the coffee table that squatted in front of the white leather couch, which was now polka-dotted with red bits, they, too, reflected the remains of the violence. So Sarah Jane had offered a drink? Did she not notice her guest carried a weapon? Unless the perp had hidden it somewhere accessible while they exchanged casual conversation. Was it possible the perp had left some fingerprints? Or was that too much to hope for?

Looking around, Laura noticed the murder weapon wasn't on obvious display this time. Did the killer take it when she left? And yes, she was still convinced it was a female.

Marian Vanhouten strode in, dressed in PPE, complete with a cap covering her grey curls. "Whew. Another one?" She directed this to no one in particular. "Who am I, Humpty Dumpty?"

"A little late to try and put her back together, don't you think?" Laura asked.

"Good one. You're getting the hang of the black humor thing," Marian tossed back. "Are we looking at a serial? Because if I get any more of these, I'm going to just go ahead and sell my bone saw."

Without waiting for an answer, she went to work. After a few minutes, she looked up. "Based on morbidity, I'd say she was killed between midnight and..." she glanced at her watch..."eight a.m. I can get you something a little more definitive after the autopsy."

The question was—how was this woman related to the Whitings? Since there was little doubt the murders were linked. An axe was a rare murder weapon and similar murders like this so close together made the connection obvious. Marian had asked if this was the work of a serial killer. Possibly, but this didn't seem like it: the Whitings were a couple, Sarah Jane was alone.

Although serial killers do have a set M.O., their victims have similarities, rather than links. These vics were definitely tied together somehow, but the connection wasn't obvious yet. And the rage made it personal. Again. Which took the wind out of the 'loot' motive.

Just as Marian finished her preliminary assessment and the CSI team was covering the corpse, the janitor who discovered the body emerged from the men's room. Pale as a ghost, he was a man of about thirty, but the broken veins on his nose and his frail body and rounded stomach left no doubt he was a candidate for AA. His hands were shaking and he swallowed convulsively.

"Mr. Watson." Laura approached him. Looking at her with rheumy eyes, the man sank into a chair in the corner of the office space.

"Can you tell me what you saw?" Laura asked.

He leapt up, waving his hand backward at her as he raced back to the men's room again.

John had just come into the room and handed her a list of names. Stepping over to the body, he angled his head and one of the EMT's lifted the sheet. John blew out a breath and moved back to Laura.

"Do you think…?" he ventured.

"No doubt," she returned.

"How do you do that?" he asked, pulling his eyebrows together in question.

Laura shrugged. "Pretty obvious, don't you think?"

John glanced around the room, looking at the uniforms and CSI staff, and making Laura smile. "He isn't here," she stated.

"Who?" he asked innocently, but he dropped his head and suddenly found the floor fascinating.

"Oh, please. Sanchez is definitely a cutie. And useful. He definitely has a working knowledge of camping equipment. But there's no weapon here."

When John looked puzzled, she reminded him it was Sanchez who identified the type of axe at the Whiting scene. "But I'm guessing your idea of camping is when there's no room service." She didn't wait for the response she was sure was coming. "Can we turn from your social aspirations and concentrate?" She shot him a look that said she had no more interest in discussing his personal life. She hoped that would put him at ease about it.

Strangely, he seemed to miss her joke entirely. Frowning, he looked at her with a narrowed gaze, his cheeks flushed. "How did you know?" he asked, his voice quavering.

Now it was her turn to lean in. "Everyone knows," she whispered back.

"They do?" This was clearly a revelation he was not prepared for. "How long has everyone known?"

"You work with a bunch of detectives." She shrugged. "No one cares. Just do your work and don't worry about it."

"Okay." Exhaling, he sounded slightly relieved, but his tension didn't dissipate.

"Can we actually do some work now? Because I have a feeling this case is going to be a bitch."

"Yes, ma'am. Sorry." He looked around the room again, this time with his head in the game.

"What do you see?" Laura asked pointedly.

"Rage again. Unbelievable rage," John stated, shaking his head. "Like the Whitings, this was very personal. It also kills my money as motive theory. But I cannot imagine the connection, can you? It was common knowledge this woman was a conduit for black market everything, from sex slaves to adoptions. But that makes no sense. Alexandra Whiting wasn't adopted. I checked her birth certificate when I was doing my research. And the Whitings were certainly not the type for illicit sex."

"Or were they? Can we be completely sure we know what went on in their house when no one was looking?" Laura pressed.

"Wouldn't there have been evidence of some kind? We searched that house. Mrs. Whiting wore granny panties and there wasn't a handcuff or a dirty magazine or movie or porn on their computer or anywhere else."

"Granny panties?" Laura asked, trying to hide her amusement.

"You know." He put his fingers together, palms up, at his waist. "Definitely not sexy."

"Curiouser and curiouser. Let's hope forensics can give us something."

The janitor re-appeared and sat back down. He didn't look any better than he had a few minutes ago, his complexion a gray-green.

"Mr. Watson," Laura began again. "I can imagine

how upsetting this is for you. Can you tell me what you saw?"

He swallowed hard again. "I was just c-coming in to clean, as usual, and I s-saw her. I think I b-b-blacked out for a few minutes, b-b-but then I called 911," he stammered.

"What time was that?" John asked.

"I came in at five. My usual time."

"Did you see anyone here? Anything strange?" Laura pressed.

He shook his head. "Nothing but..." He pointed to the mound on the floor and any color left in his face drained away.

"Do you know if the building has cameras?" John asked.

"No. The tenants here like their privacy," Watson said. "Too bad, I guess."

"Well, thank you." Laura handed him a card. "Please call if you think of anything. Anything at all."

He nodded and Laura was certain the man would probably go on a bender. Hell, she couldn't blame him.

She edged over to the desk and eyed a laptop. John was already holding an evidence bag before she could ask. Tess, their techie genius, would be able to crack it and, hopefully, there would be something to help.

There was a small bathroom adjacent to the office and a member of the CSI team was emerging from it holding a large evidence bag. Laura recognized the man and greeted him.

"Hey, Chuck. Whatcha got?"

He held up the bag. "A towel. Still wet. There's a shower in there and I'm guessing the perp cleaned up afterward. But we're still going to swab it, of course."

"Did you find the murder weapon?"

"No. We're still looking, but it isn't obvious if it's here at all," he answered.

Laura nodded. "Thanks." That would mean more DNA from the towel if they could recover anything, and assure the same perp committed both crimes. Laura didn't have any doubts, but you couldn't prosecute on a hunch. And where was the axe? Why was it left at the first scene and taken from here?

"What now?" John asked.

"We get to the office early and leave no stone unturned. There is an obvious connection between these murders and finding it just might lead us in the right direction."

***

"What do you think?" Captain Donner asked Laura first thing the next morning.

"Very personal. There's no doubt in my mind this is connected to the Whitings. We just have to do a little more legwork to find the link."

"Do you need help?" Donner held up a hand before she could protest. "Let me re-phrase. Would you like some help?"

She smiled. The man showed her so much respect it was almost embarrassing. He had nurtured her career over time and was clearly pleased with all her successes, giving her more and more latitude in the cases she worked. "Not yet. Not saying no for the future, though."

"Good. Because we are pretty backed up. But don't hesitate if you need something."

"I won't. Thanks. And I'll keep you updated."

"I'm sure you know the press is already all over this. I think you're going to have to make a statement before the whole city imagines it's at risk for being axed to death."

Laura heaved a sigh. "I haven't checked my messages yet, but I'm not surprised. Sarah Jane was that elusive criminal that fascinated everyone. And then to be so brutally murdered, along with a well-respected couple—hell, I can't blame the press for being excited."

"Do you want to make a statement?" he asked.

"No, but I will. I'll make it as innocuous as I can. The last thing we need now is the outpouring of confessions and false leads. Or panic."

Laura was turning to go when Donner loudly cleared his throat and she faced him. "Good news or bad?" she asked.

He smiled and shook his head. "Both."

"Go on," she encouraged.

"I've been promoted to Deputy Police Chief."

"That's great. Congratulations." She hesitated. "But I will miss having you as my boss." She sucked in her lower lip. "And I think I already know the bad news. Crap."

"She isn't as bad as everyone thinks. And how did you know it was Shelly? That weird psychic thing of yours?"

"I just happen to pay attention. And listen. Shelly Goodman is the obvious choice. Between us, everyone knows she's been angling for captain since she was a street cop. And she was no bargain then, except to anyone who could help her."

"Well I'm not just going to let you twist in the wind. The transition doesn't happen for a few weeks and I'll still be around making sure you can do your job."

Relief eased Laura's tension, but with the thought of Shelly Goodman taking over, the stress was only going to increase.

***

Devin missed her and it had only been a few hours since he'd passed her desk and grinned at her. She had blushed and grinned back. Good sign. They had planned to go to dinner again tonight, but the captain had called her into his office. He was sure it was about the murder of Sarah Jane.

Disappointment was an understatement, but he knew she had no choice except to work late. And then she had to go before the cameras and issue a press release that said very little except 'don't panic, people, an axe-wielding Michael Myers is not coming for you.'

Laura promised to call Devin when she could. He decided to grab some food and keep working. If he went home, he would only imagine Laura in his bed, naked, and the time would drag and his body would ache.

Devin was getting nowhere on his primary case and his frustration was irritating. His instinct told him it had to be the husband, or someone close to the vic, but after poring over all the evidence, he could find nothing to back up that theory. This was one of those cases that was going to be solved with luck or probably not at all. Devin didn't accept the latter. There always an answer and he would go over the evidence again and again until he found it. Just like the case Laura was working on.

He sat back in his chair and took a bite of the fast food hamburger. Chewing slowly, he thought about the information he had. What Devin needed was motive. All the transcripts from interviews revealed the victim to be well-liked, with nothing that would suggest retribution or revenge. Money?

Deep in thought, he startled when his cell phone rang. When he saw who was calling, his insides lit up. "Hey, beautiful," he said.

"Devin, I am so sorry about tonight. But I have another homicide that I'm convinced is related to the Whitings."

"Have you eaten?" he asked.

"No time. I'll catch something on the way home."

His expectations dropped like a hammer. Maybe her interest was waning?

"Yes," she said before he could ask. "Tomorrow."

The woman was uncanny. She knew what he was going to ask before he could voice it. But then, he figured he was about as subtle as a brick wall. *Was his insecurity showing?*

"Get some rest," he said, masking his disappointment as best he could.

Sitting back in his chair, his thoughts slogged back to Jillian. Although he tried to put on the 'tough guy' front, when she left, it tore him apart. Disappeared without even the respect to face him, talk it out, try to resolve issues. It probably would have had the same result, but at least he would have had some warning. Like Jim's death. Abrupt, miserable, emotionally ripping. Could he have done something for Jim? How did he not see these things coming? Jim's pain, Jillian's unhappiness?

If this thing with Laura was going to go anywhere, he had to hone his instincts, watch for signs of trouble. Then, if something was going to happen, he could 'gird his loins'. He actually loved that expression and just thinking it made him laugh. Was it all about his loins? And would girding them help clarify anything?

***

Laura couldn't sleep. She gave up the fight before the sun had peeked above the horizon. Getting up, she jumped in the shower, hoping the warm water would soothe her thoughts. Her mind was whirling with possibilities and nothing made any sense. She needed to lay it all out and stare at it awhile. Not wanting to take the time to make coffee, she pulled up to the drive-thru and ordered two cups, then headed to the station. She needed to get to the white board in the conference room and see if she could make sense of anything to do with these cases. And she had to come up with another statement for the press. And she was not looking forward to reporting to her new captain. Donner had been incredibly supportive. He had trusted her and she knew Shelly Goodman would be a micromanager. It was her way of proving she was in charge and getting even for the past.

The two had some unpleasant history. They had worked a case together a few years ago and Shelly had declared to the press she had a person-of-interest. Who didn't exist. When asked to produce the evidence, Shelly had shifted the blame to Laura, which further complicated the situation. When Laura was the one who actually solved the case, Shelly held a grudge.

113

In working a difficult case, what Laura didn't need were more problems and interference. Or having to explain her every move and take direction from someone who didn't know the job as well as Laura did.

Sipping the warm brew, she filled out more notes and pasted them up, then squinted at what she had so far. Her eyes focused on the information, taking it in bit by bit.

An older couple, clean as glass, butchered. A daughter and a volatile aunt who was locked up. A criminal who skirted the law year after year and had more vanity than Narcissus, also cut to pieces. What could they have in common? And the couple's daughter who was allegedly watching her parents surreptitiously for at least a month before the murders. Maybe the couple had some dealings with Sarah Jane? And, if so, what kind of dealings? But that made no sense. It wasn't as if they traveled in the same circles. The computer from Sarah Jane's office might reveal something, but no security cameras in and around her office was so frustrating and just waiting was painful.

Her ruminations were interrupted by footsteps in the hallway outside the room. Turning, she was delighted to see Devin standing at the door, grinning at her. Her heart jumped a little in reaction to the swirling in her stomach.

"Good morning." He took a step into the room. "No one else is in yet, so is it okay if I just kiss you. Just once?"

She closed the gap and wrapped her arms around his neck, their lips melting together as if they had been designed that way.

"Good morning," she breathed as she took a step

back. "You're going to ruin my concentration." A crease appeared between her eyes. "How did you know I was here?"

"Just a hunch. You don't strike me as the casual type, on any level." He winked at her and she grinned. "And a new murder? Can't take the chance that one might get cold."

"Are you going to continue to distract me or are you going to help?" she demanded, feigning irritation.

"If you promise we can continue this later," he said suggestively, and her body reacted instantly.

"I hope so."

He smiled, then turned serious. "Then tell me what you have."

"The vics couldn't be more different. But it was the same kind of murder weapon, and it is damned unusual, so I know they're connected."

"What about the daughter? And her weird behavior?" Devin asked.

"I'm going back to see her this morning. As soon as John gets in." Laura shook her head in frustration. "What about you? Discover anything new on your case?"

"Maybe." He didn't sound convincing.

"Which means… ?"

"I need to interview the children. They're older now and might offer a new perspective."

"Makes sense." She smiled. "Yes, I would."

He raised an eyebrow. "How did you know… ?"

"That you were going to suggest we get together right after work? Just a hunch. "

"Isn't it annoying?" John asked from the doorway. "She does it to me all the time. I think she should go and join the psychic network."

115

"Oh, you'd miss me too much if I left," she returned.

Devin headed for the door, extending his thumb and pinky and lifting his hand to his ear. "Call me," he mouthed. She nodded and turned to John. "Ready to go back to school?" she asked.

"Church, school—always an adventure."

Chapter Eight

It took them the better part of an hour to get out of the station. Captain Shelly wanted every detail of the cases, questioning every conclusion, every result and making it clear she was not happy with their progress.

"When are you going to have some persons-of-interest?" Shelly asked, her tone harsh.

"We're thinking the daughter is the most likely suspect now. We just need to make the connection between the vics." Laura responded.

"Do you need me to bring in some... help?" The way she asked that and the way Donner had asked the same question was night and day. Donner seemed genuinely interested in advancing the case, while Shelly was more interested in making sure they stayed in their place with her in charge. Laura gave the same response.

"We're good for now. If our leads end up in dead ends, we'll certainly ask for assistance."

Shelly blew out a breath, showing her disgust. "Don't wait too long."

It was a huge relief to both John and Laura to slip into Laura's car and drive away. This new captain was not going to make life easy.

"What is her problem?" John asked.

"She thinks I made her look bad on a case we worked together."

"And did you?" he asked, raising an eyebrow.

"It wasn't a contest. I mean, she was in a hurry to act like we solved the thing before we actually did and she blames me."

"So now she's going to get even?"

"God, I hope not."

Not surprised that Alexandra wasn't at work, Laura was certain they would find her at home. She and John approached the small house and she had to smile. Painted the same pale stucco color and flanked by two small oak trees, it was a mini version of the parents' house. She exchanged a look with John, knowing he had noted the similarities as well.

"This isn't a woman who hated her parents, is it?" he commented.

"Hard to know. She might just want to outdo them."

John rang the bell and Alexandra answered, her eyes red rimmed, dark purple smudges under her eyes telling of lack of sleep.

"Detectives," she greeted them. "I hope you have news," she said as she ushered them inside the house.

The difference in the décor, however, was strikingly dissimilar to her parents' house. The big screen TV dominating the living room was clearly an expensive model. The furniture was leather and the rug in front of the sofa had to have cost a fortune. Alexandra directed them to the couch and she took a chair opposite.

"Ms. Whiting, some new information has come to light and we have a few questions."

Alexandra wrinkled her brow. "Okay," she responded, her tone tentative.

"I need to ask where you were between midnight and this morning."

"I was here in bed asleep. You can ask Jeff."

"And he is… where?"

"At work. But you can check. Why would you even ask me that?" Suddenly, her eyes widened. And her mouth opened. "There's been another one?"

"I'm afraid so."

"Like my parents?" Alexandra pressed her palms into her cheeks and swiped at her eyes. "Oh my God."

"Why were you spying on your parents?" Laura asked quietly, working to keep accusation from her voice.

"What?" The other woman's eyes widened. She seemed genuinely surprised by the question.

"You were seen," John said, "watching them from your car and looking into their windows."

Alexandra's eyes widened. "Are you joking?"

"Do we look like we're joking?" Laura retorted.

Alexandra shook her head. "My parents were the most boring people on the planet. Their lives were dull, their activities banal. Don't misunderstand me. I loved my parents, but you could watch them all day and not see anything particularly interesting. Watching grass grow is more exciting. So I don't know what you heard or what someone thought they saw, but I had no desire whatever to watch Mom and Dad."

"Then, do you have any idea who it might be?" Laura said, trying to keep the sarcasm out of her tone. "Because the witness was certain it was you."

Alexandra shrugged. "I have no clue. But whoever

119

supposedly saw me was mistaken. Besides, I don't have the most exciting existence either. I work, I come home, I hang out with my boyfriend. I visited my folks once a week, sometimes with Jeff, but usually without him. I didn't want them to get suspicious."

"That you were living together?" John pressed.

"They wouldn't have approved. They were very old-fashioned."

"Do you have any idea who might have wanted to spy on them?" Laura pressed.

"Seriously, whoever was seen—well, they had to be watching someone else."

"Have you ever heard of a Sarah Jane Malone?" Laura asked.

Alexandra shook her head, but there was a flash in her eyes for a split second and she hesitated slightly before answering. "No, I don't know her." And there was something in her tone that lacked credibility.

"Are you sure you never heard the name before?" John prodded.

Alexandra shrugged. "Doesn't sound familiar." She leaned forward. "Does she have some connection to my parents' case?"

Laura realized this was going nowhere, so she stood. "Thanks for your time. Sorry to have bothered you."

John stood next to Laura and together they walked toward the front door.

"Do you think it was the killer?" Alexandra asked. "That watched them, I mean."

"Well, it's definitely suspicious." Laura answered, turning back. She didn't want to commit to any opinion. "We'll continue to try and identify who and why. That I can promise."

"Detectives," Alexandra said, her tone plaintive. "Please find out who did this."

John angled his head to Laura. "She's the best. If it can be solved, she'll do it."

Laura was a little embarrassed by the compliment. "I promise we will do everything we can."

Ruminating as they walked to the car, Laura was irritated. She took the driver's seat and chewed on the inside of her cheek as John slid in. Fastening his seat belt, he looked over at Laura.

"You don't believe her, do you?"

"I don't know, which is why I'm so frustrated. What do you think?"

"I believe her—I think."

So," Laura exhaled, "then if it wasn't the daughter, we allegedly have a female perp who spied on the couple for a month or so before the murders. Similar enough in looks to be mistaken for the daughter. And a seemingly totally unrelated vic that died in the same brutal way, which must connect them."

"Then we have to figure out the answers," John stated.

"Or at least uncover more questions."

***

Feeling like he'd wasted a day, Devin glanced at the clock. Six p.m. Meeting Laura in an hour, his pulse bumped up in anticipation. He had lined up appointments with RaeAnn Smalley's now grown children for tomorrow. Maybe they would provide some clues since nothing else was particularly promising so far.

He and Laura had decided that he would come to

her place and he would bring take-out. She had denigrated her skills in the kitchen. But then, with her schedule, it was enough she had time to eat. And other things, which he was grateful for. His groin tightened at the image of her naked body stretched out on the bed, inviting him in to taste the wonders of life. Shaking off the thoughts, he realized he didn't know what kind of Japanese food she liked, so he opted for a variety.

"Come in," she called out. "It's open."

Peering around a corner, she verified it was him and scurried back into what he assumed was the bedroom. "Running a little behind. Be right there. Make yourself at home."

Dropping the bag of food on the kitchen counter, he noted the dirty cups in the sink keeping company with a few unwashed dishes and silverware. Neat she wasn't. But hell, if that was his only complaint, he could definitely let it slide. He wandered into the living room. Wooden end tables and an old chest that served as a coffee table flanked a well-worn leather couch which squatted across from an older TV. Bookshelves lined the side walls, groaning with their cache of books. The titles ranged from Jane Austin classics to tomes on the psychology of serial killers and everything in between. The walls were bare and no family pictures were evident.

Returning to the kitchen and opening a few cabinet doors and drawers, he located two plates and silverware. He gave up on finding napkins, opting for paper towels, then pulled down two wineglasses that boasted a coating of dust. Quickly rinsing and drying them, he poured the wine he had brought.

Laura took that moment to appear and his breath

caught. She was wearing a very slim black dress that clung to all the right places.

"You look amazing," he breathed.

"You clean up pretty nice yourself," she responded.

He handed her a glass of wine and leaned in to touch her lips with his. Like fighting an irresistible force, he made himself pull back and touch his glass to hers.

"To a wonderful evening," he said.

She smiled and it turned his insides to mush. "Shall we eat? I'm starving."

So was he, but he was convinced they weren't picturing the same kind of nourishment.

As they ate the delicious food, he decided to talk shop to keep his mind off the tantalizing dip between her breasts that peeked out and made his mouth water.

"How's it going?" he ventured.

"Slow. And confusing. So the neighbor tells me the daughter is spying on her parents, but the daughter denies it. She basically said it would be more exciting to watch paint dry."

"Do you believe her?" he asked.

"About the boring part? And the spying, too. I do. But then, who was outside their house? The killer? And if we go on that assumption, then the perp is a young woman with a vendetta of some kind. But that makes no sense. Mr. Whiting assessed real estate, the wife was a part-time elementary school teacher. What—did she take away someone's toy. Did he undervalue a house? And the third vic—what's her connection?"

"Talk about needing to think outside the box," he commiserated. "Hey, maybe the daughter had a clone."

Laura pressed her lips together and sighed. "Helpful. So, how about you?"

"I'm at a dead end, too, so far. No pun."

Laura held up a piece of sushi between her chopsticks and offered it to him. He licked his lips and moved forward so she could slide the food into his mouth, never taking his gaze from hers. Swallowing, he stood, took her hands and lifted her against him, knowing his erection was screaming his desire.

Holding tight to him, she walked backward down the hallway into the bedroom. The bed was a surprise. They hadn't made it this far the last time. The antique brass head and foot board were polished to a high gleam that reflected the flickering candles on the bedside table and antique oak dresser. The comforter was a beautiful, obviously hand-made quilt and a few pillows in various shades of blues and yellows cozied up at the top.

Easing against the edge of the bed, he reached down and lifted the slim black dress over her head. The barely there black lace bra and panties caused an even more immediate reaction in his already responding groin. But this time, he wanted to savor every part of her slowly. Starting at her throat, he gently kissed the soft skin and swirled his tongue back and forth. Moving down, he stroked her collarbone, then brought his hands together to travel downward still to her bra. Reaching behind her, he undid the snaps and freed her full breasts. In the dim light, her skin was iridescent and it took everything in him to keep going slowly. Bending, he took her left nipple in his mouth and suckled, bit lightly, and cupped her with his hand. Then he gave attention to the right breast. From her moaning response and attempts to tear his clothes off, his body started to burn, his erection ready to tear through his zipper. He knew that anticipation would only heighten the experience, so still he held back.

Slipping to his knees, he pulled her panties down with his teeth and thrust his tongue into the sweet spot between her thighs. She gasped and fell back onto the bed, but he had been prepared. His hands held her buttocks and lifted her hips so he could keep tasting her now soaking wet center. Taking her hard nub between his teeth, he used the tip of his tongue to drive her higher and higher until she cried out her release.

Falling back, gasping, she reached for him, as if insatiable desire was driving her on. So turned on now his thoughts were mush, he pulled off his pants and drove into her, deep into the ecstasy of her cocoon. His cock vibrated, but he didn't want this to end quickly so he stilled and absorbed her essence through his skin. Somewhat controlled, he moved again, very slowly and with purpose, savoring every moment of ecstasy. Overpowered by need, he thrust faster and faster until blinding lightning filled his brain and his body exploded.

Collapsing on top of her, he was suffused with such joy it was hard to fathom. Sex had always been good, sometimes great even, but it had never been like this. This was all encompassing, all powerful, so much more than just a mating ritual. If he made love to this woman every minute of every day from now on, he would still never have enough of her.

Mentally exhaling, he knew he was in so deep he would never find his way out. Reality battled with fear, but he forced himself to concentrate on the now. If this was all there was, he would savor it. If it was snatched away later, he would remember this feeling, this moment and hold onto it. This memory would be his forever.

He was drifting into the netherworld of sleep when her voice brought him back.

"It had to be someone they knew. Someone they trusted. It had to be their daughter, but I don't think it was." She was sitting up.

It took him a second or two to make sense of her words. Just floating down from the most mind-blowing sex of his life, and the recognition of his feelings for this woman, his brain was not in functional mode. He shook off the fog and forced himself to focus, still reluctant to move into a work thought process. "Do you really want to talk about it now?"

She laughed. "I guess I could let it go for tonight."

"How about if I try and take your mind off work—again." A little disappointed that she had not had her thoughts melted along with his, he was determined to make her forget everything in the world but him. His fingers skated down her thigh and between her legs, finding her sweet spot. From her answering moan, her job was disappearing and he hoped she didn't see his satisfied smile.

Chapter Nine

It was a transition Laura hadn't had to make before. Even when she was getting married, her mind stayed clear, her focus laser. But this was different. This was unnerving, unlike any feeling she'd ever experienced. It came with the whole fairy tale: butterflies in her stomach, smiling for no reason, missing him when he wasn't with her. *This is ridiculous,* she chided herself. *You barely know this man.* But deep down, she knew that wasn't true. Her body knew him, her bones, every part of her knew him. And it wasn't just the sex, although until now she hadn't known passion like this even existed.

She had taken the time to visit her mother last night and strangely, just knowing she was meeting Devin right afterward eased the negative emotions that plagued her after each visit. Dementia had robbed her mother of her power. Now that Laura controlled her mother's life, there was no revenge pleasure. There was just karmic obligation. And of course, all those old, bad feelings.

In the past, for as long as Laura could remember, Clair Chandler had run Laura's life down to the minute. If she was five minutes early getting home, it was considered late and there was never any respite unless all the chores were done. As she grew older, Laura knew that her mother was a miserable drunk who demanded control and craved male attention. Maybe that's why Laura had never spent much time in pursuit of men. Her marriage had been an impulse, so unlike her, and she paid the price in angst and legal fees. But until Devin, she never felt she ever needed a man. Now, it seemed, she more than desired one.

After Devin left this morning, she had taken a luxurious few minutes to stretch like a satisfied cat. Her pillow still smelled like him: clean and fresh, like the ocean, only with a masculine undertone that made her body ache with want.

Her thoughts were interrupted as the resident techie scooted up to her desk. Tess held a sheaf of papers, shaking her head. The girl was young, but her computer macho was unmatched. Give her a laptop and she could uncover the minutia without breaking a sweat. Hopefully, Tess had come up with something, since so far there was nothing to latch onto with this case.

"You don't look very satisfied," Laura commented. "So unlike you."

Tess dropped her shoulders and clutched the papers tighter, her myriad of bracelets rattling. "It's all in code." She thrust the bundle forward.

Laura leaned closer to take it, frowning. "That's never stopped you before."

"Not computer code." Tess sounded disgusted. "These are lists with numbers and letters and more numbers. They were in a special document. The rest of the laptop content was just some saved pictures of beautiful men and women, fashion, that kind of stuff. Nothing sexual, nothing financial, which suggests another computer somewhere or something." Tess huffed. "Even criminals need to keep records, don't they? But I couldn't find anything else and these letters and numbers just don't seem enough. As I said, they're more like a list. No pattern, no consistency."

Laura grinned. "Tess, you are brilliant!"

Tess's brows came together in confusion. "I just said I didn't find anything else."

"I don't need to know about her income or her sexual history. I already know it was dirty. I need to know about her clients. And I have a feeling those codes will tell us a lot as soon as we can figure them out."

Tess shrugged. "Okay, well, if you're happy. Oh, by the way, I'm already running a program to try and decode it. If there's a pattern, I will find it."

"Of course you will. You are the best. Thanks."

As Tess walked away, Laura spread the sheets across her desk. Tess was right. Numbers, letters, numbers. Knowing that Sarah Jane had to be pretty smart, Laura still hoped the arrangement here was not so obscure as to be indecipherable. If anyone could find a way to make sense of this, Tess could.

Later, Laura was still staring at the paper and sipping now cold coffee when John slid into the chair beside her desk. "What'd she get?" he asked, clearly referring to Tess.

"Coded entries. Which I am convinced relates to the vic's business interests. Tess is working it now."

"Do you think it'll connect to the Whitings?"

"No way of knowing. There has to be some link and we just have to find it." Laura heaved a sigh of frustration.

"So—just curious. Are we working late?" John asked.

"Why? Is your social life interfering with your work schedule?" Laura teased. "Because far be it for me to cramp your style."

He responded with a huge grin, then stood. "Thanks. Meanwhile, I have some more research to follow up on."

"Glad to see you're still interested in your job," she teased. "Oh, and give my regards to Sanchez."

John leaned in. "He has a first name."

She lifted an eyebrow. "Does he?"

John took a step away and looked back at her over his shoulder. "Randy."

"Have fun."

John raised an eyebrow, grinned, and hurried away.

Well, Laura decided, if he could have a date, so could she. She wasn't going to get anywhere tonight. She was desperate for a clue or at least more information, but she would have to be patient. *Patient? Was that really a thing?*

She picked up her phone. *"Are you interested in easing my frustration?"* she texted Devin.

That depends. Personal or official? He added a smiley face.

Yes.

I might be available. Dinner first or dessert?

Can we have dessert once before dinner and once after?

You are a brazen hussy.

Hussy? Seriously?

Meet you in the parking lot in ten. He added another smiley face.

When she strode across the lot a few minutes later, her heart thumped against her chest. This man was

130

driving her out of her mind. She spotted him in the driver's seat of his car and she slid in next to him. Without a word, he put the car in drive and drove to the edge of the lot where a clump of trees obscured any visibility. He put the car in park, turned off the engine and leaned across, unzipping her pants, pulling them down along with her underpants and slipped his tongue into the heat between her legs.

She nearly came off the seat as his mouth teased and stroked her, the unrelenting fire building toward an explosion. She was on the verge and he reached up to squeeze one nipple, then the other, never ceasing his relentless assault on her hot throbbing core. The release was so intense, she screamed, then bit her lip.

"No one can hear us or see us," he mumbled against her.

Right at that moment, Laura couldn't really have cared less if there was an audience applauding outside the car. All she wanted, desperately, was to feel him inside her. She awkwardly pulled one leg out of her pants, unhooked his belt and unzipped him. His hard penis pulsated under her hand and she straddled him, avoiding the steering wheel as much as possible and pulling him inside her. She threw her head back in exquisite pleasure as she managed to rise and fall, each time driving him deeper, her insides clenching against the sheer ecstasy, awash with sensation.

Some part of her logic kicked in just as she sensed him about to reach his climax and she slid up and away just as he tensed and groaned his release.

Exhaling, he grinned sheepishly, the moonlight seeping in the front window highlighting his handsome features. "At least one of us has some brain power."

"I guess I took you by surprise," she responded, grinning back.

"Woman, you are going to be the death of me. I am never careless."

Laura shrugged. "Well I never have sex in the station parking lot. You do know we're in midtown, right?"

His mood shifted and he took her face gently between his hands. "This isn't just sex," he said, his eyes narrowed. "You have to know that."

"I know. It isn't for me, either, which is what scares the crap out of me."

"Join the club. So what should we do about it?" he asked, his tone gentle.

"I have no idea."

***

They spent the night together at Laura's house, dozing and making love and dozing. Sleeping beside him was a unique experience for her. Devin made her feel safe, protected and—loved. But that was silly. They had only known each other a short time. But she knew in her bones that if she let it, this could go on forever. Again, terrifying. Laura knew so little about love. Her mother had certainly not taught her. And her invisible father hadn't. It was like she had stumbled into a foreign place and yet knew she was home. Could she trust her instincts? As a detective, they served her well, but they were not so reliable in her personal life. Hence, her terrible mistake of a marriage. But that was the thing about experience. If you were paying attention, you learned and didn't make the same errors in judgment again.

Devin was nothing like her ex. He was everything

he should be. She considered the pre-emptive first strike here, but that would so obviously be cutting off her nose… This was something she had to trust or she knew she would regret it forever.

She lifted up on her elbow and watched him. His chest rose and fell in the depth of his slumber and he seemed so at peace. Suddenly, his breath quickened and his head rolled from side to side. He cried out. "No! No! Don't do this. Don't go, dammit." His eyes opened wide and he blinked, then looked directly into Laura's eyes, unseeing.

All she could think was he was begging a love not to leave him. She knew him so little, after all. Was he mourning a past relationship? Was she merely rebound for him? The thought cracked her heart and green venom nearly choked her.

Devin cocked his head at her and reached out to catch a tear as it traced down her cheek. "What is it?" He was clearly awake now. "What's wrong?"

Taking a deep breath, she pulled the sheet up over her breasts, unwilling to be vulnerable. "Who was she?" she whispered.

"She?" Shaking his head, he was clearly struggling.

"The one who left you," Laura stated flatly, moving away from him.

"Another nightmare." He nodded in understanding, then reached out to hold her hand. Feeling the warmth of him, she was desperate to respond, but she was not going to open herself up to being ripped apart.

Taking a deep breath, he rubbed the sleep from his eyes. "My partner, Jim. He didn't show up for work one day and I went to his house." His voice cracked. I tried to save him, but there was nothing I could do…"

Laura pressed her hand to her mouth, torn by his confession and embarrassed at her conclusion. "I am so sorry." She inched closer to him and the sheet fell away, but she didn't notice. "How did it happen?"

"He OD'd. I should have known, recognized what was going on. But I was stupid and he died."

"It wasn't your fault."

"Not a day passes that I don't want to kick myself for not picking up on his problem. But then, we were obviously not as close as I thought." He inhaled sharply. "All Jim heard was the irresistible call of all that heroin. What he didn't know was that his last score was laced with undiluted fentanyl. Jim, along with another seventeen addicts, died that week. We caught the supplier and he's up on murder charges."

"When was this?" she asked, feeling his pain.

"A year ago."

"So that's why you work the cold cases."

He nodded.

The words 'I love you' nearly slipped out her mouth. It was probably instigated by empathy for his pain, and luckily logic took over before she spoke. She knew she just wasn't ready. Instead, she wrapped her arms around him, buried her head against his neck and held on for dear life.

***

Sipping her coffee in the conference room the next morning, Laura stifled a grin as John bounced into the room. "How was your date?"

"I thought we didn't talk about our personal lives," he retorted, but his smile told her.

"We don't. But I'm glad it was good." And she was. John was a great guy and he deserved a happy personal life. "Now, can we get to work?"

"Okay, boss. Where do we go from here?"

Laura blew out a breath of frustration. Then chewed her lower lip. "There has to be some connection between the vics. Let's try brainstorming it."

"Evan Whiting sold Malone some house insurance?" John suggested.

Laura shook her head. "He was an assessor, not a salesman. But that doesn't really work anyway."

"Okay, how about they were all involved in some shady business deal? No, that doesn't make sense either."

"Why do people kill?" Laura asked.

"Money, revenge. Oh and sex."

"So we need something that affected the perp. Money doesn't work since the Whitings didn't really have any. Sex?"

"Not so much," John returned.

"You're right. The Whitings weren't exactly the passionate types and Malone was a cold-hearted businesswoman."

"That leaves revenge."

"Okay," Laura agreed. "So what did the Whitings and Malone do to the perp that made her mad enough to kill? And not just kill. Tear them all apart."

Quiet settled between them as they each tried to work out the possibilities. A moment later, Devin stuck his head in the door. "I think the new wife did it."

Laura and John both stared at him. "There was no new wife," Laura stated, a little annoyed.

Devin grinned and shook his head. "Sorry to

interrupt. I was just really pleased about this. The new wife in my case."

Actually happy for the respite, Laura waved him in. "How did you come to that?"

Devin slid into the chair next to Laura and reached over to her coffee cup. Lifting it, he took a swallow and set it back down. The gesture was so intimate, it made her insides tingle. She glanced over to see if John noticed, but he was looking at some notes.

"Well, I interviewed the children and they both agreed their stepmother spent money like water. There was never enough. The husband was very successful, but he also paid an exorbitant amount of alimony to the ex. So, if the new wife could get rid of that alimony obligation, she would have so much more money to spend."

"Didn't you tell me they had airtight alibis?" Laura asked.

"They did. But I come to find out she has a cousin with a very long rap sheet. I'm about to check out his alibi and his bank account. And hers."

"Wow," Laura nodded. She turned to John. "Money."

"And it's in the family. Which accounts for most of all murders," John added.

"Exactly." Devin stood. "Well, I'm off to check out my theory. How are you guys doing?"

"No family except the daughter with an alibi and the wife's sister who is under lock and key. No money, at least on the couple's end."

"Sex?" Devin asked, dropping his head and suppressing a grin.

"Nope," John responded. "Doesn't work."

"Revenge then," Devin stated.

"Agreed," Laura answered. "But for what?" She shook her head. "You go and solve yours, then maybe apply your brain to ours."

Devin grinned. "I only do cold cases."

"The way we're going, this is going to qualify," Laura sighed.

Chapter Ten

Devin was grinning like a Cheshire cat. Solved was his favorite word and soon the perp on his cold case and her nasty cousin would be facing trial for conspiracy to murder and murder one, respectively. Laura sat across the dinner table in Devin's house, sharing in his victory. She had brought a nice bottle of pinot noir and it tasted like success.

"I know how great you must feel," she said happily.

"I do. But it was mostly just luck."

"And talent," she supplied, lifting her glass in a toast.

He wagged his head from side to side with pride. "Okay, if you insist."

"So are you interested in working on mine?" Laura raised an eyebrow.

"Honey, I will work on your anything," he returned, grinning.

"Okay. Two squeaky clean people and a woman involved in all manner of dirt. What do they have in common?"

Devin thought about it a moment. "No one is that pure. We all have secrets, some worse than others. So, maybe, in the past, they had a connection that bound them together." He bit down on his back teeth in thought. "Maybe the wife was a hooker and worked for the other vic."

From her expression Devin knew he had hit on something. Her mouth dropped open and then she smiled. "No visible means of support could also mean Nora worked for cash. Oh my God. That's it! She worked for Sarah Jane."

Laura jumped up from the table, swept around to him and kissed him on the lips, hard. "You are a genius!"

"Okay, I can accept that," he grinned.

Laura grabbed her phone and hit a key. "John, it's me. Nora worked for Sarah Jane. It has to be. That's the connection. Now prove me right." And she hung up, her smile lighting her face, her exuberance contagious.

"How shall we celebrate?" Devin asked, grinning.

Sitting back down, she smiled. "It's a little soon for that, don't you think?"

"No, I don't. If we don't celebrate the small things, we'll never feel we've accomplished anything. Because the big things come with their own reward."

"Makes sense. Okay." She frowned. "Wait, we're already celebrating your win."

Good move, Devin. Now you have to come up with something.

"I know. How about we share a decadent dessert?"

Looking at him sideways, she tilted her head. "How decadent?"

"Death by chocolate cake."

"And where would we get that?" she asked coyly.

"In my refrigerator?" It wasn't really a question. Standing, he went into the kitchen and returned a few minutes later with one plate, two forks and a ridiculously large slice of cake. "Anyone for a food coma?"

"More like a sugar high. What will we do with all that excess energy, to say nothing of the calories?"

"Eat fast and we'll figure it out." *God, he loved this woman.* He inhaled sharply at the thought.

"Are you all right?" Concern edged her tone.

Clearing his throat, he nodded. "I just realized something important and it caught me off guard."

"About the case?"

"No. About you."

She bit her lip. "What about me?"

"Laura Chandler. Detective Laura Chandler?"

"Yes?" She was clearly confused now.

"I think I might be falling for you." As soon as he spoke the words, he knew he had never said anything more right in his life. "I know it's fast. Really fast, but…"

"Are you sure it's not just the chocolate talking?"

"I'm sure."

"Or the wine?"

"Oh, I'm sure."

She inhaled. Hearing him say those words was a confirmation for her. A cloud dissipated and the sun peeked through. It was a lovely feeling. "Good, because Devin Andrews, I'm falling for you, too."

***

Laura lifted on her elbow and looked over at Devin. It had become her new favorite pastime. In sleep, he looked so much younger, all the lines softened, and she realized asleep or awake, he was still the most beautiful man she had ever seen. And he loved her. And she loved him back. Wow. Just wow.

Laura wasn't the sentimental type. She didn't cry at movies or melt when she saw a baby. She didn't believe in fairy tales or Cupid and his silly arrows.

She'd only known him weeks and yet it was if they had always been together. Was this what people meant when they talked about soul-mates? Crazy. Did this mean she'd have to rethink some attitudes? Maybe. But then, her profession dictated flexibility. If you went into a case with preconceived notions, you were generally so wrong.

This was the kind of thing that happened to Cara, who fell in love every time the wind blew some new man's cologne in her direction. It didn't ever happen to stable, no nonsense Laura. She shook her head. Life was either lessons or adventures and this was going to be both.

Blinking, she realized he was staring at her. "Good morning, beautiful," he greeted her.

"Good morning. Coffee? Oh wait, this is your house. You have to make it." Did she sound edgy?

"Are you okay?"

"Devin, about last night…"

His face fell. "Which part?"

"I'm so confused."

"Well, you're the female and I'm the male and we…"

"Not that part, smartass."

"I get it. But, I guess for me, this is what it is. And I want to grab on with both hands. Because I'm pretty sure this is the best thing that's ever happened to me." He tilted his head and smiled at her.

141

She curled up and snuggled against him. "Me, too." Talk about mixed emotions. She leaned over and gave him a sweet kiss on the mouth. "But I need to get to work. Thanks to you, I have a lead and I need to milk it."

Jumping up, she headed to the shower, stepping out a few minutes later to a cup of steaming coffee on the counter. More and more perfect.

As she dressed, she went over the new possibilities of the case in her head. If Nora worked for Sarah Jane, it had to have been for cash. But, since Sarah Jane was into so much that was ugly, Nora's job could have been as a hooker or an administrative assistant. If Tess could find a way to decipher the codes, maybe they could find out. But did it really matter? It might if Nora had secrets someone didn't want to get out. But, it had been more than twenty-five years. Why now?

One thing Laura was convinced of: that had to be the connection between Nora and Sarah Jane. It might also help to explain why Evan had waited two years to marry Nora. If she was turning tricks, he might have doubted the paternity. Or, if Nora had a steady stream of income, maybe she never told Evan she was expecting. Maybe they had separated and been re-introduced later? But that really didn't matter either, did it?

There was a huge key missing here and it had to do with the intervening years. But what?

***

Laura and John had spent the entire day looking for that missing key. The code Sarah Jane had used was not so much complex as personal. There seemed to be a pattern of initials and numbers, but it wasn't as simple as it first appeared: 117syha, 335jshoc, 347nkoc, etc. The code breaking program hadn't been helpful so far and the only thing Tess had to report was she was certain this wasn't a true cipher.

"What does that mean?" John asked.

"It means there doesn't appear to be a substitution. Ciphers set up a system of different letters or numbers. For example 'a' really means 'b' or '1' really means 'c'. If you can figure out the substitutions, you can crack the code. But this one is straightforward. So, 117 could be January 17. Or November 7. The initials could belong to a person. And the last letter could be a designation. So syha could be, for example, Sally Yost Holden and the 'a' could be administration," Tess explained.

"That's actually really helpful," Laura said. "Thanks!"

"You're welcome," Tess replied, clearly pleased with the praise. "I don't know if I can get you any more than that.

"I don't think we need more, but keep at it just in case. And Tess, good work."

Laura turned to John. "Let's see if we can find the initials 'nk'."

They started at the beginning and there it was at the top of a column. '412nakb'.

What was Nora's middle name?" Laura asked.

John grinned. "Alice." And the 'b'—my guess is bookkeeper. What do you think?"

"As good a guess as any. So, going with that, Nora started working for Sarah Jane on April 12th. Or maybe that date had some other significance."

"But we can't prove it for certain…" John said, his exasperation showing.

"But do we really need to know for certain?" Laura said. "If we go on the assumption that we're right, it makes the gap of time in Nora's history no longer a mystery. It would account for her income and the fact that she had no records during that time." Laura chewed her lower lip. "And it would account for why Sarah Jane would help her out if she was pregnant. It wouldn't have affected Nora's work if she kept the books. And if Sarah Jane paid her in cash—no records."

"Okay. Now what?" he asked.

"We have to find out what happened more than twenty-five years ago that would account for these brutal murders. If something happened back then, why wait so long to get revenge?"

John closed his eyes. "Maybe Nora cooked the books."

"Possible, But I don't think anyone would wait so long to do something about that. And wouldn't Sarah Jane be the one to exact revenge?" Inhaling, she tapped the desk. "We need to talk to Alexandra again. She knows more than she's telling us." Laura chewed her lower lip. "Do you remember when we asked her about Sarah Jane? There was something—a reaction for just a split second—that made me wonder if she was lying. Now, I'm convinced there's more there."

"Okay, but it's late."

Laura glanced at her watch. "How about first thing in the morning?"

"Sure," John grinned. "I have a date anyway."

"How's that going?" she asked absently.

"Fast. But is that wrong?"

He had her attention. *Fast.* "Nothing wrong with fast if it's right." Was she speaking to John or herself?

144

Packing up her things, she tried to focus on seeing Devin later and not on the task at hand. Time to visit her mom and as much as she didn't look forward to it, she knew she had no choice. And there was the possibility of gaining some insight into Natalie Kessler.

Pulling up to the home a few minutes later, she hurried inside, determined to do her duty, and get out as quickly as possible. Jocelyn was at the nurses' station and that always made this easier.

"Hey, Laura," the nurse greeted her. "I sure enjoyed the other night. I haven't had a girls' night in forever."

"Me, too. Let's do it again soon. And how is your favorite patient today?" Laura asked, sarcasm dripping.

Jocelyn grinned and Laura just shook her head.

"How lovely for you." Laura could definitely sympathize.

Laura made her way to her mother's room. Clair was sitting up in a chair, patting the bedsheet. "It's snowing," she said to no one in particular. Not for the first time, Laura thought dementia was a strange disease. Her mother was perfectly cognizant one minute and the next, she was having lunch with her mother who'd been dead for forty years.

"Hello, Mother."

Clair turned and looked at her with a blank expression, then seemingly, recognition dawned. "You have some nerve. It's not enough you stole my husband, you bitch. Now you show up here. To do what? Gloat?"

"I'm your daughter Laura." Her tone was quiet, patient.

"My daughter is a loser. I think she takes drugs. Did you know that?"

145

Laura ignored that. "How are you?"

"Like you care. Get out. GET OUT!"

Jocelyn was at the door holding a syringe before Laura could retreat.

"A little valium will take the edge off. The doctor ordered it to quiet her if it was necessary." Jocelyn managed to stick the needle in before Clair could react and fight it. Clair let out a scream that rocked the walls, then yawned and sank down into her chair, and it didn't take much longer until she was as docile as a kitten.

Laura closed her eyes in embarrassment. "I'm sorry."

Jocelyn smiled. "It happens. Don't worry about it. But we've learned to stop the escalation as quickly as possible. And it's the only excitement we get around here."

Laura nodded, hoping that no matter how old or sick she ever became, she would at least be manageable without sedation. Not so with her mother. Sadness welled deep inside. She had always tried to love her mother, to have her mother love her, but some things just weren't possible.

"Any info on Natalie Kessler yet?" she asked.

"Nothing new. The staff is just paid to watch her and medicate her if she gets—upset. Been that way for years. She only speaks nonsense most of the time, but if I'd spent my life medicated, I'd probably be the same way. But I'll keep my eyes and ears open."

"Thanks."

Jocelyn shrugged. "I never knew police work was so boring," she teased.

"And don't forget about all the glorious paperwork."

"Wow. And I thought my job lacked thrills."

"It's kind of like flying a plane. Boring most of the time and suddenly pure adrenaline."

Jocelyn tilted her head. "Is that why you do it? The adrenaline rush?"

"I'd like to think I have higher motives. But, you never know," Laura said, wondering if something was going to show up one of these days to break this case and bring on that rush. Wouldn't that be great?

Chapter Eleven

"Devin, it's Momma. I haven't heard from you in days and I worry. So please call me."

Devin clicked off the voicemail. Guilt seeped into his heart. She was right. He had been so caught up in the new work and more, the new… love. Was it too soon to bring Laura home to dinner? He knew his mother; she would gush and fuss and ask a hundred questions and embarrass him, but then, he hadn't ever brought anyone home before. Jillian always had some excuse to avoid a visit, so his knowledge was based on his poor brother's experience. When Roy had brought Glenda home, it had been hilarious. But then, Devin hadn't been on the receiving end. And amazingly, Glenda had married Roy anyway and they were about to have their third baby. Laura was a detective. That meant she was tough, right. But was she tough enough to stand up to his mother's third degree? He had to smile at the images the thought conjured.

"Hey, Momma. Sorry. New job. Just been busy." He knew that wouldn't fly, but he gave it a shot anyway.

"Too busy for your momma?" There was the blade. Was she going deeper? "Too important now since you're a detective and your father was only a beat cop?" And the twist.

"Momma, you know better than that. How is Dad?"

"Retired. That sums it up. He's bored and driving me crazy. When are you coming for dinner?"

"I was thinking about the weekend. Would that be okay?"

"Of course it will be okay. As if you have to ask."

"Well…"

"… you want to bring a friend?" She was going for restraint, but he could hear the excitement in her voice.

He nearly snorted. Just like Laura. How do some women do that? "I was thinking about it."

"That would be nice. Since, you never even got Jillian to come to our home."

"Which should have told me something right there," Devin responded.

"So tell me… what's her name. What does she do? Where did you meet her? And don't tell me in a bar. I know I'm old-fashioned, but…"

"Whoa. She's a detective and her name is Laura." He had to stifle the sigh at the sound of her name. Man, he had it bad.

"Sunday? After church?" she suggested. "You go to church anymore?"

He ignored the jab. "Like one o'clock?"

"Sure. You do remember the address, right, since it's been so long." She shoots, she scores.

"Love you, Momma. See you Sunday."

"Love you, too, baby."

And that was the easy part. Now he had to ask Laura and prepare her.

***

"Guess who just called in?" John asked, first thing the next morning, his face alight with excitement.

149

"The perp to confess?" Laura returned, not in the mood for games.

"Atlantic Insurance. Their adjuster wants a copy of the report on the Whitings' murders before they release the payout."

He had Laura's full attention now. "How much?"

"One hundred thousand. And there's more. The current beneficiary is…"

"… none other than our Alexandra." It wasn't a question.

"Yep," John went on. "And it was taken out three years ago."

"Was there a beneficiary named after Alexandra?" Laura asked.

"The payout would go to Evan's estate if his daughter and wife pre-deceased him. It's complicated, but apparently Nora's parents were very wealthy and their money was held in trust for Natalie. Any money from the Whitings would go into that fund as well if there were no other living relatives. After that, it was designated to go to charity."

"Who bought the policy?" Laura asked.

"Apparently Evan Whiting. But since he was under sixty and the payout couldn't happen for two years, no physical was required. The premiums were paid every month on time with money orders."

"That's interesting. Pretty hard to trace a money order. So, anyone could have taken out that policy in his name." Laura chewed her lower lip.

"And guess who claimed it? Since life insurance doesn't automatically just pay out." He smiled, the cat that ate the canary.

"Let me guess. Alexandra Whiting."

"In the meantime, I did a little more deep diving on Alexandra and Jeff Hines and it seems her boyfriend has a little problem with online gambling." John looked pleased with his discovery.

"Also interesting."

Her computer binged an incoming message. She read for a minute and shook her head. "It appears the DNA on both those towels from the crime scenes match Alexandra, as well."

"Ding, ding, ding. I think we have a winner."

Laura held up her hand. "Pretty circumstantial. Any novice defense lawyer could invalidate the DNA. It was her parents' house and she visited all the time." She cleared her throat. "And a hundred thousand dollars—is that really worth killing over?" She chewed the inside of her cheek. "There is always the temptation of jumping to conclusions. What we think and what can be proven can be two different things."

"Are we going back to talk to Alexandra now?" John asked.

"I think we should do more than that. Let's invite her for afternoon tea. I like the idea of getting her out of her element with no chance of interference by the boyfriend. But see if there's any more you can find out first about either Jeff or Alexandra. The more information we have, the better our leverage."

As John walked away, Laura's phone rang. Cara. "Have you got time for lunch?"

"I can make time. It sounds important."

"Could be. Noon at the café?"

Laura hated to take time for lunch, but John was on research and her friend needed her. An hour wouldn't stop the world. And it would take John at least that long to check out more details on Alexandra and Jeff. Then they could go and pick up Alexandra.

Just as Laura was headed out the door, Devin met her in the reception area.

"Can I ask you something?" He seemed nervous and that set off some alarms.

"Is something wrong?"

He licked his lips and swallowed. "What are you doing Sunday for lunch?"

She angled her head. "What's going on?"

"I was wondering… would you have lunch with me?"

Now she was confused. "Of course. What's going on?" she repeated.

"Lunch… at my folks' house?"

Laura's heart skipped a beat and she blinked. Now it was her turn to swallow. "You want me to meet your parents?"

He inhaled and straightened his spine. "You aren't scared, are you?" he said, obviously trying to lighten the mood. "Tough detective and all."

Laura lifted her chin. "No I'm not scared. I just thought…"

He shrugged, then met her gaze directly. "I know. But life is short," he reminded her.

"I would love to meet your parents." That was the next step she hadn't expected so soon, but he was right, life was short. So why wouldn't her heart rate slow down?

"Okay. Good. See you later." He winked and walked away.

Everything about this man was delicious. She remembered a line from *Auntie Mame*—"Life is a

banquet and most poor suckers are starving to death."
Well, she decided she no longer wanted to go hungry.

***

The café was their favorite lunch spot and Laura
realized it had been too long since she'd taken the time
for a lunch break with her bestie.

They ordered and sipped water with lemon in
silence for about a minute before Cara couldn't stand it.
"I think I met my newest ex-husband."

Laura smiled. "And what makes this one ring
worthy?"

Cara leaned in. "OMG. Laura, he's just too perfect.
Which is why I wanted to talk to you." She gave a happy
little shrug. "I'm hoping…

"… that if I run a background check I won't find
anything."

"Sometimes that psychic thing you do is just
creepy."

"Sometimes things are just obvious," Laura
huffed.

"So will you? I know you're not supposed to and I
don't want to get you in any trouble, but he's…"

"… too perfect." And they both laughed.

"What's his name?"

Cara smiled "Tom Dawson." She slid over a piece
of paper. "Here's everything you should need."

The waitress delivered their salads and had just
walked away when Cara leaned in again, going on and
on about all of Tom's great qualities: handsome, good
job, lots of money, nice house. Laura had to agree he
sounded great.

Finally, Cara ran out of steam and took a sip of water. "And now it's your turn. What's up with the detective?"

"Devin?"

"Yeah. Devin. Love his name. It's a bad boy name."

Laura laughed. "Hardly. He's as good as they come, but…"

"But?" Cara lifted her eyebrows.

"He wants me to meet his parents." Even the thought was disconcerting.

"Pretty fast. But hell when you know, you know, right?"

Now it was Laura's turn to lean in. "Cara, I don't know anything about parents."

"You know mine. You've known them since fifth grade."

Laura thought about that. Cara's parents were like a couple out of a sixties sit-com. They were devoted to each other and to their children. And they had enough love that it extended to Laura. They were well aware of her situation and they did what they could to give Laura some stability and encouragement. Laura could still taste the ham and cheese sandwiches on homemade bread that Cara's mother would make every Saturday. It was a special treat to have someone else make lunch. Laura's mother didn't cook at all, so Laura was responsible for all the meals from the time she was twelve. She vowed that when she grew up, she wouldn't cook and she had kept that promise to herself.

"That's different. Your parents are different. You know what I mean."

"I do and Mom asked me the other day when you

154

were coming for a visit." Cara's parents had moved to Florida and were always asking Cara and Laura to come down.

"This one I'm working on is a bad case. Maybe after I solve it."

"We could go with our new boyfriends," Cara suggested with a twinkle in her eye.

"Oh, yeah, your mom and dad would love that. If I recall, they're still pretty old-fashioned when it comes to that stuff. They'd make us sleep in separate bedrooms." Laura shook her head, grinning.

Cara shrugged again. "Maybe it's time to drag them kicking and screaming into the twenty-first century."

"You go right ahead. Let me know how it goes." Laura swallowed. "Speaking of... what if they care that I'm not Black?"

"Do you care?" Cara asked pointedly.

Laura mouth dropped open. "Of course not."

"Why?"

"I care about Devin. Period."

"Well, if he's not concerned about them meeting you, why should you be? But... who are you? It's not like you to worry so much."

"He has me off-balance. He's like no other man I've ever met."

Cara blew out a breath, then smiled, but didn't say anything. They had been friends long enough that words weren't necessary.

They finished lunch and Cara talked more about Tom. "I just hope he's everything he appears to be."

Laura snorted. "Boy, can I relate."

Cara said she'd text Laura all she had on Tom and

then reassured Laura about the upcoming meeting with Devin's family. "Just remember how my parents love you and go with that."

Being around Cara always made Laura feel better and now that there were new leads on the murders, life was getting better and better. And, of course, Devin. As long as she could pass the parents' test.

***

John was waiting when she got back from lunch. "The policy was taken out online. It was on Evan with Nora as the first beneficiary and then Alexandra. So it wouldn't look suspicious. No one would expect a double murder when they were taking out a policy, right. Except the perp. In this day and age, it's just too easy to impersonate someone. So if Alexandra's boyfriend had the right information, he could take out the policy without raising an eyebrow."

"Good job. But again, unless we can prove it…" Laura shook her head.

"So now what?"

"We finesse. Alexandra may be smart, but I doubt she's street savvy. Let's try good cop, bad cop."

"Can I be the bad cop?" John asked earnestly.

"With that baby face, I think not."

He feigned a pout and she cracked up. "Okay you can try."

"Really? I'll be hateful, honest."

Laura stifled a laugh.

They drove together to Alexandra's house and when she appeared at the door they asked her to come down to the station.

"Don't you think it's enough she lost her parents? You have to keep harassing her?" A voice rang out behind Alexandra. Stepping into view was Jeff Hines, her boyfriend, his posture defensive, his fists tight at his sides.

"Mr. Hines, Ms. Whitings parents were indeed brutally murdered and we are doing everything we can to try and find the perpetrator of these crimes. We are hoping Alexandra can help."

"So ask her here," he said flatly. "You have no right to have her go with you."

"We have specific procedures to follow. We need her to come down to the station," John replied. His calm but decisive tone let Laura know he was going to be good at being the bad cop.

"I'm calling a lawyer," Jeff declared, and Alexandra paled.

"Am I being accused of something?" she asked, her voice shaky. Tears ran down her cheeks and Jeff glared at John and Laura.

"Now look what you've done," he growled.

"You are not being accused of anything at this time," Laura said.

"What does that mean?" Alexandra squeaked.

Jeff immediately stepped up and wrapped his arms around her from behind. "I'm going with her."

"That would be your choice, but you'll have to follow in your own vehicle," John stated.

Turning to Alexandra, Jeff took her face in his hands. "I'm going to be right behind you. But I am calling my lawyer, okay?" He leaned in close to her ear. "Don't say anything."

Alexandra nodded, but didn't seem mollified.

Clearly reluctantly, she walked between John and Laura to their car. As they drove to the police station, Alexandra was silent, just as instructed. They escorted her inside and into an interrogation room. She sat at the old, dented metal table, the ring used to hook handcuffs standing at attention, taunting her. And then Laura and John left the room. Jeff sat in the waiting area, tapping his foot in impatience. They ignored him.

It was standard procedure for detectives to let the suspect stew for a while. Let the person sit and wonder and worry and soften up. Laura and John each went to check for messages and took some time reviewing what evidence they had. After about forty-five minutes, they met at the room door and entered. Laura sat while John stood over Alexandra. She appeared absolutely terrified. Tears had washed her face and left streaks of mascara on her cheeks.

"Tell us about Sarah Jane Malone," Laura said quietly.

Alexandra's eyes widened so they nearly ate her face. "I… I don't know her."

Now it was John's turn. "I thought you told us before you never heard of her."

Alexandra dropped her head and inhaled. Then she shook her head. "I think I'll wait for my lawyer."

"Bad move," John said. "If you cooperate, it will go so much easier for you."

"But… but I didn't do anything." She hiccupped and the tears started anew. "My mother and father were killed. Why are you doing this?"

"How does one hundred thousand dollars sound for a reason," John pressed. "Just for starters."

Alexandra looked up, bewildered. "What?"

"Did you think we wouldn't find out?" John demanded, his voice raised.

"Find out? I don't understand." Alexandra sounded so sincere, Laura almost wanted to believe her. But she had learned it was too easy to get suckered by good acting.

Laura leaned across the table. "Look, my partner is just asking for a reason. We're guessing that the policy had something to do with Jeff, but we still are wondering about your connection to Sarah Jane."

"What policy? And I never met Sarah Jane."

"But you knew about her," Laura said quietly. "Your mother told you about her? How she helped her out."

"I never met her. But I know it was hard for her. For Mom. A single parent and having my twin sister die. Sarah Jane was her friend. It was only later I found out she wasn't such a nice person."

A twin sister? Who died? John and Laura exchanged a look. "When did your sister die?"

"Right after we were born. Mom said it was really hard for her, as I said, and Daddy wasn't there, so Sarah Jane helped her. Mom's family had thrown her out when they found out she was pregnant, so she had no one else." She heaved a sigh. "That's all I know."

"Where was your father?" Laura prodded.

"Away at school. He didn't know about me, us, until he came back home. He told mom he couldn't stop thinking about her and then, when he found out she had me, he married her."

That answered some history questions about Nora, but still didn't provide a motive for why the three were killed.

"And the policy?" John reminded her, none to kindly.

"What policy?" Alexandra asked, her voice strained. "I don't know anything about a life insurance policy."

"Please stop treating us like we're stupid. You claimed that policy. We were contacted by the insurance company," Laura said, none too kindly.

"Your father apparently took out a life insurance policy three years ago. To the tune of one hundred thousand dollars. Conveniently, the company didn't ask for a physical since he was well under sixty with no pre-existing conditions. With your mother dead too, you are now the beneficiary," John explained, glaring at her. She fidgeted under his stare. "And, although you say you know nothing about it, the company reported you just claimed the payout."

Alexandra looked shocked. "I did no such thing. She heaved a sigh, clearly weighing her options. "Oh, wait—that policy? I guess I forgot."

"Forgot?" John snapped. "How convenient. You didn't remember asking for a hundred thousand dollars?"

"I wasn't trying to hide anything. I just forgot. I've been so upset. I was just trying to take care of business. It's pretty overwhelming, you know." She leaned across the table. "And Jeff is trying to help me, but mostly he just makes things harder."

So now they had confirmation on the history about Nora. But still didn't provide a motive for why the three were killed.

A knock on the door interrupted them. They both stepped out of the room, leaving Alexandra to continue to sweat. A tall, thin older man wearing a rumpled brown suit stood tapping his foot. He angled his head to the room. "My client in there?"

"And you are?" John asked.

"David Paulson, Ms. Whitings' attorney. I hope you haven't been violating her rights by questioning her before I arrived," he sneered, chewing on gum and cracking it.

"She is not under arrest and she hasn't been charged with any crime at this point," Laura stated calmly. What Paulson lacked in class he made up for in his unctuous manners.

He pushed forward and John opened the door. Turning back to them, he said," I need some time with my client."

John nodded and closed the door behind him and he and Laura went back to her desk to wait the requisite few minutes.

Returning, they knocked and entered the room. Paulson and Alexandra were sitting close together, but she didn't look comforted. Her lips were white lines.

Paulson spoke first. "I believe you were asking my client about a life insurance policy her father took out. Unless you have proof it was not a legitimate transaction, I suggest you either charge her or let her leave.

"And one more thing. I believe you are investigating the death of her parents and one other woman. Is that correct?"

Laura frowned, but didn't answer.

"And they were all killed with an axe, correct?"

Again, Laura just waited. Paulson looked so smug, Laura had to resist the urge to bitch slap him.

"Well, my client couldn't have been the perpetrator then. It is physically impossible." He sat back and crossed his arms in front of his chest.

This time, Laura raised an eyebrow. "Do tell."

"She damaged her right rotator cuff fairly significantly a few months ago when she fell off a ladder. She couldn't possibly have raised her arm high enough to use the weapon in question."

That struck like a bomb, but Laura forced herself not to react. "Can you prove that?"

His smile was irritating. "Of course. We can get you the report from the doctor who examined her after the injury." His smile widened. "We are leaving now."

Both Laura and John knew they didn't have enough to hold her, which was infuriating. Just when they thought she was trapped, she managed to wiggle her way out. Reluctantly, Laura stepped up. "You are free to go, Ms. Whiting. But we ask you to please not leave town."

A little color returned to Alexandra's cheeks as she stood, then directed her gaze to Laura. "I didn't kill my parents." She sounded vulnerable and pathetic, but Laura wasn't buying it.

Paulson stood then and took her arm. "Let's go."

But Laura was pleased they had some new leads to follow. Alexandra had definitely connected Nora and Sarah Jane and according to Alexandra, there had been a twin who apparently died. John had pulled the birth certificate on Alexandra, and now needed to dig deeper to find the one for her twin, as well as the death certificate. They also wanted more information on the insurance policy. The company would gladly comply if there was a possibility of saving a one hundred thousand dollar payout. And Alexandra had initially denied claiming it. The 'why' of that was obvious. It would make Alexandra look guilty. It was possible she knew that and merely panicked. Possible. Still nothing definitive but better than nothing.

As promised, Laura took a few minutes to run a background check on Cara's new boyfriend and the man came up clean, except for five parking tickets. She picked up her cell, called Cara and left a message.

Chapter Twelve

Laura was sweating. She had changed her clothes five times, finally settling on a pale green silky blouse and black slacks. A gold chain and some dangly gold earrings and she was ready. Well, maybe not ready, but as good as it was going to get. A drop of sweat inched between her breasts and she glared at herself in the mirror. "Suck it up, Buttercup."

The knock on the door meant it was time and she let Devin in as she ran to the kitchen to retrieve the bouquet she had bought for his mother.

"You look great," he exclaimed when she returned to the living room. He grinned. "They're going to love you."

She inhaled and exhaled through her nose. *Was it too late to come up with a good excuse?* "If you say so."

Devin's parents' house was in a lovely subdivision with well-kept lawns and mid-sized houses. Theirs was an older brick home with a porch and lots of flowers. They started up the walk and Laura hesitated. Devin just shook his head. "It's lunch, not a firing squad."

She inhaled again. "You're right. Just a little nervous."

As they walked up to the front door, Laura hesitated. "Is it going to bother them…"

She didn't get to finish her sentence before the front door was flung open and Devin's mother, his white mother, wrapped her arms around him. Laura had expected both of Devin's parents would be Black and she had been concerned her color might be a concern for them. But that was an unnecessary worry. Now her anxiety was whether she could get them to like her.

His mother was a tall, thin woman. Her hair was very short which accentuated the finely wrought bones in her face. Laura could see where he got his good looks. Releasing her son, she turned to Laura. "You must be Laura. You're so pretty."

Laura blushed. "Thank you."

"I'm Betty. Come in, come in."

Laura extended the flowers and Betty took them in one hand and stepped up to give Laura a hug. It was so welcoming, emotions threatened, but the butterflies in her stomach stopped fluttering.

"These are beautiful and so thoughtful. Lunch is almost ready. Devin, get Laura something to drink."

Laura was introduced to Devin's father, James, his brother, Roy and Roy's wife Glenda, who gave her a broad, welcoming smile. Some of the flutters quieted.

They sat in the comfortable living room and exchanged small talk while Laura wandered into the kitchen to offer help.

"I'm good here but we could take a minute or two to get acquainted."

"Sure, I'd like that."

"Devin tells me you're a detective, like him."

"I am."

"I always wondered… is it hard?"

Laura was confused. "Is what hard?"

"Doing what you do. Seeing what you see. My husband and sons seem to take it in stride and you know how men are. They don't like to show weakness. But it has to wear on you."

Laura inhaled deeply and chewed her lower lip. "I'm working a case now. The victims... well, what happened to them was unimaginable. But I learned a long time ago that you have to treat it objectively as a case to be solved, to compartmentalize. A surgeon friend of mine once described it this way. He operated on children. But in his mind, he operated on a body part until the surgery was over. He said if he thought about cutting on a child, he couldn't do it, so instead he repaired damage. Once the child recovered, in his mind it was a child again that he made better. Does that explain it?"

Betty thought about that, then nodded. "That makes sense." She cocked her head to the side. "Do you love my son?"

Laura was a little taken aback by the question, but Betty didn't give her a chance to answer. "Because he's never brought anyone home before. So I'm hoping you feel about him the way he evidently feels about you."

No reason to be coy with this woman. "Yes. Yes, I do."

"Good. Now, can you help me get these plates to the table?"

***

Watching Laura interact with his family was a whole new experience for Devin. His father and brother regaled them all with embarrassing stories about him as a child and the food was, of course, everything it always was: hearty, wholesome, comforting and so good. He wondered, briefly, if Laura would take some cooking advice from his momma, since she seemed to pride herself on her lack of skill in the kitchen, but he knew better than to ask. Especially now. She was so beautiful, smart, and she was charming the socks off his family.

"Tell everyone about your case," Laura prompted. "How you figured it out."

She was bragging for Devin and he preened just a little. "The current wife did it because the husband was paying too much alimony to his ex." He shrugged.

Laura leaned in. "Devin minimizes it. But it had gone cold and he solved it."

Devin just smiled.

"What about you, Glenda?" Laura asked. Glenda was a beautiful woman in her thirties with short dark hair who was obviously madly in love with her husband if the way she looked at him was any indication.

"I'm a CPA. Which means all the money in our house is mine." She grinned at Roy, who nodded, resignation in his expression.

"Don't let her humility fool you," Roy interjected. "She's more than just a CPA. She's a forensic accountant. And she is a tiger."

Glenda dropped her head, but she was smiling.

"Impressive. And Roy?" Laura turned to the man who was a little older and almost as handsome as his brother Devin.

"He works for IA, but we forgive him," James teased.

"Without internal affairs, there would be chaos," Roy returned. Glenda took his arm and leaned against him supportively, but he just shook his head. He had obviously taken abuse for this choice for a while, and it clearly no longer stung. James rolled his eyes, but didn't disagree with his son. Then James turned his attention to Laura.

"How about you?" he asked.

"Homicide. And I have one going now that's giving me a flat forehead."

Roy laughed. "From hitting walls."

"Yep," she responded, grinning.

"Can we help?" James asked.

"He's retired, and he misses it," Betty put in.

"I was just a beat cop, not a detective."

"You were a sergeant," Devin said. "Don't diminish that. And a training officer. You taught a lot of cops to be good cops."

James rolled his eyes again. "I want to hear about Laura's case."

"Pretty brutal killings. Three. A couple and another woman. The woman was dirty, but the couple weren't. Just made the connection, though."

"You're working on the Lizzie Borden case?" Roy asked, a little awed.

She shook her head. "Why does the press feel the need to name these things?" Laura asked to no one in particular.

"So we can keep them straight," Roy said.

"So what was the connection?" James pressed.

"It seems the wife worked for Sarah Jane years ago. Still working on the motive, though."

"Persons of interest?" Roy asked.

"Not that make sense. It's pretty complicated. There is the daughter, who looks good for it, but there also might be a twin sister who supposedly died at birth."

"Interesting. Well, if you need to bounce some ideas, I'm here," James offered.

"Me, too," Roy chimed in.

"And I think I'll just take you up on that," she grinned. "Just as soon as I find the right questions to ask."

***

"I told you they'd love you," Devin affirmed as they parked in front of Laura's house.

"Your family is so great. They welcomed me so warmly. I don't know why I was nervous."

"Big tough detective afraid of a few grown-ups," Devin teased.

"You better be nice or I'll call your mother."

"Oh, no," he feigned a cry. "Anything but that." And they both laughed.

They spent the night making love slowly, sweetly, lovingly. Laura wondered if it could always be this way. A shelter from the storm. Devin's mother had asked how she did it, seeing the human tragedy day after day. And her answer was accurate. She had resented her upbringing, but it had taught her skills she called on every day: resilience, toughness, compassion from a distance. But Devin was teaching her the meaning of love and it was incredible. She so wanted to trust it, to know in her bones it wouldn't just disappear one day. She didn't believe in blind faith, but so far he proved to her every day he was going to be there for her and it made her so much stronger and more hopeful.

The buzzing of her cell pried Laura's eyes open. She fumbled on the nightstand until she managed to grip the dreaded noisemaker. A groan from beside her reminded Laura of the night before and she grinned in memory. Too bad she couldn't stay like this forever.

It was still dark outside and a glance at her clock told her it was six a.m. "Yes?" she whispered into the phone, as if the ringing wouldn't have disturbed Devin. Raising his head, he blinked at her and she mouthed 'work'. He dropped back to the pillow and rolled towards her, waiting.

It was her new captain, which immediately set her hair on end. The woman's voice was—the only way to describe it was metal on metal. Unless she was talking to a potential benefactor.

"Detective, there's been another murder, same MO," Shelly said without preamble, then rattled off an address. "How long will it take you to get there?"

"I'll be there in fifteen," Laura said, hanging up and jumping out of bed. Another murder in an upscale neighborhood.

"What's wrong?" Devin asked, sleep making his voice even deeper.

"Another body. Gotta go."

She slapped some water on her face, ran a comb through her hair and pulled on a pair of slacks and a shirt. She leaned over and kissed him on the mouth, then hurried from the room. "Coffee's in the kitchen," she called behind her.

"You made coffee?" he returned, clearly shocked.

"No, it's in the kitchen. I gotta go," she repeated, trying not to laugh out loud.

***

Laura didn't have time to ponder all the revelations of the night before. There was another body and it was obviously connected to the other vics. Was this a serial killer? Or was it possible one perp hated four people enough to butcher them?

She raced to the address the captain had given her and wasn't surprised to see the uniforms and ambulance already on scene. John pulled up right behind her and together, flashing their badges, they approached the house. The lawn was very green in the early morning light, decorated with diamond drops of dew. The home itself was painted bright yellow, three stories and obviously more expensive than its neighbors. The definition of conspicuous consumption, the owners were making a statement and they would not be ignored.

Officer Sanchez was already on scene and the look he and John exchanged made it clear things were going well between them. "Just like the last," he said to John.

"Later?" John mouthed and Sanchez smiled.

John caught Laura watching and pulled his shoulders back.

She gave him a quick nod. "Hey, what you do on your time is your business. And, as I've said before, he is such a cutie."

John just smiled and seemed pleased. Good to have something nice before viewing carnage. Not that it took away the horror.

Laura and John donned their PPE and strode into the living room where a very attractive woman dressed in jogging clothes sat on a leather couch. Her long blond hair was pulled up in a ponytail and her makeup was perfect. Or had been before it started running down her face.

An officer was attempting to both comfort her and get some information as she sobbed loudly in apparent grief. The uniform tilted her head to indicate the vic was further back in the house. They angled back down the hallway and into the state-of-the-art kitchen. Gleaming stainless steel appliances were spattered with red. In front of the sink, lying in a pool of congealing blood, parts of the latest vic lay twisted on the floor. He looked more like a broken puppet than a human. The instrument of his destruction was pretty obvious.

Marian Vanhouten was kneeling next to the corpse. "If someone wants to start a trend, could it be something like decorated tennis shoes or small purses?" She stood and rolled her shoulders back. "This is just plain hideous."

Again, the weapon was nowhere in evidence and Laura doubted it would turn up at the scene. Why would the killer have left the axe at the first scene and taken it away at the last two?

"Serial?" John asked Laura quietly.

"God, I hope not," Marian interjected. "I don't know about you guys, but I've had enough of this mess."

Laura nodded her agreement. "Haven't we all. Now we need to figure out how this one connects to the others." She knew she was stating the obvious. "We need to stop her."

"Her?" Marian asked, then frowned in concentration. "Yes, that makes sense. I can see a woman doing this." She turned to Laura. "I don't expect any surprises, but I'll be in touch." And she strode away.

The CSI team was numbering and photographing, so Laura and John stood back. Up close and personal wasn't necessary just now. Instead, they returned to the living room and, immediately, the officer sitting next to the woman stood.

"Detectives, I'm Officer Walsh. The vic was Rusty Leach. This is his wife," she said, indicating the crying woman still seated. Moving a few steps away and lowering her voice, Walsh checked her notes and briefed them.

"She went running this morning, which she did every morning, and came back to discover her husband. The neighbors heard her screaming and one of them called 911. Then she apparently passed out. The EMTs revived her and that's all I have."

"Thanks, Officer Walsh. That helps."

Walsh walked away and John smiled. "You are always so nice to the uniforms."

"Because I remember being one." She walked back to the wife.

"Mrs. Leach, I am so sorry for your loss," Laura started.

"Loss? Loss? This wasn't a loss. It was hideous. How could anyone do such a thing? It isn't human." By the end of the sentence her voice had risen to a shriek.

Just then, the gurney bearing what was left of her husband was wheeled by. Mrs. Leach let out a keening sound that made the hair on Laura's neck stand up. The sound ended with a deep moan.

"You're right." Laura's tone was soothing. "And that's why we need as much information as you can provide so we can find out who did this."

Just then, a CSI strode into the room, headed for

the front door. He held a large evidence bag, and John immediately stood and approached him before he could leave. John was back a moment later and his expression told Laura the contents of the bag was a wet towel from a bathroom. Laura nodded and turned her attention back to the wife.

"Mrs. Leach, you said you were out running. Did anyone see you?" Laura's conversational tone was meant to put the woman at ease, but it seemed to have the opposite effect. Mrs. Leach jumped up, her eyes wide.

"How dare you?"

"I'm sorry, but it is standard procedure to find out where anyone who was close to the victim was at the time of the murder. No one is accusing you of anything," Laura assured her. *Yet.*

Mollified, the woman regained her seat. "Yes, the neighbor at the end of the street, Ally Wallace, runs with me every morning at 4:30. We both love the quiet and she has to be at her job early, so it works out. She can tell you I was with her the whole time." Laura knew the time of death would determine if this alibi would stick. But again, with this M.O., there had to be a connection with the other vics. Unless it was a copycat. "The Lizzie Borden Murders" were headline-making and this could be a way to kill her husband and pass the blame. It was possible this woman murdered her husband, showered, and then went out with her friend to establish her alibi, the grief being nothing more than an Oscar-worthy performance.

"Mrs. Leach, did your husband have any enemies?" John asked.

"My name is Eva. And my husband dedicated his

life to caring for people. Who could hate him for that?" the woman shrieked, clearly incensed by the question.

Laura looked around, taking in the extravagant decorations. "What did he do? For a living?"

"He was a registered nurse at Commonwealth Hospital."

"Excuse me? Did you say a nurse?" John asked, raising an eyebrow.

Mrs. Leach snorted and waved her hand around the room. "Oh, this? He had a trust fund. But he worked as a nurse because he loved it. And he was one of just a few male nurse-midwives."

Laura tucked that away. Something about this seemed very important.

"We're going to need a DNA sample from you to rule you out," Laura ventured, prepared for the onslaught of anger. "And fingerprints."

"Oh, of course," Eva replied meekly. Not what Laura expected. John handed over a swab vial and a fingerprint kit. Laura collected the samples and properly stored the evidence in her bag.

"Do you have a security system?" John asked.

"Yes, we do, but I never set the alarm when I go running." Eva shook her head, then a thought brightened her expression. "But there is a camera at the front and back door. Follow me."

John and Laura followed her upstairs into an office. It, too, like the rest of the house, was overdecorated with a faux antique rolltop desk and three overstuffed chairs. A computer perched in the middle of the desk and Eva punched up a program. She fast forwarded it to four a.m. They watched Eva leave the house through the front door and a few minutes later, a figure stepped out from the bushes next to the house. Eva let out a gasp. It seemed obvious she had no idea someone was waiting outside. Based on the stature, it was a woman. She was dressed in dark clothes with a hoodie that covered her face, but she was carrying something that appeared to be an axe. Twenty-two minutes later, the figure re-appeared coming out of the house and slipped away into the darkness.

"Can we get a copy of this?" Laura asked.

"Of course." Eva put in a zip drive and transferred the file, then handed it to Laura. Tears sprung anew from her eyes. "Please find out who killed my husband. I really did love him."

"Is there someplace you could stay? Someone we can call for you?" John asked.

"My sister will be here in a few minutes. I can stay with her and her husband."

"We'll need a number where we can reach you," John said.

"Okay." She rattled off her cell phone number and John wrote it in his notebook.

"Is it all right if we walk around the house?" Laura asked.

Eva nodded, then suddenly sank into herself on the couch. If she wasn't grieving and suffering from shock, she was a damned good actress.

John and Laura toured the home. It was huge and every room was so over-decorated it made Laura's eyes ache. Pink and gold and hanging chandeliers and nothing particularly tasteful. Just extravagant and no doubt expensive. John counted six bedrooms and eight bathrooms, including an en-suite master bath that was made of marble and gold. The tub was as big as Laura's living room. There was a big screen TV mounted above it. Candles were everywhere, along with a full bar and a wine fridge along one wall. This was a couple who indulged their pleasures.

"That must be some trust fund," John commented. "Let's see if she'll share without a warrant."

John went to talk to Eva while Laura continued the tour. She wandered into a room that was decorated like a library but probably served as an office. On the massive dark mahogany desk, a calendar lay open. Laura leafed through and found it. An entry from three weeks ago.

A meeting with SJ. Paydirt! Talk about lucky breaks. She pulled out her phone and took a picture, her thoughts whirling. Trust fund my ass, she thought. This guy was in cahoots with Sarah Jane and that's where all the money came from. Of course, they needed to follow up on the trust fund angle, but this explained a lot. Especially if they could get Eva to confirm the association.

Excitement vibrated like buzzing bees and she had to take several deep breaths to control the blood pulsing through her. She ambled back to the living room, where John was sitting with Eva, whose gaze was on the floor. She was nodding.

When John saw Laura, he stood and moved over to her. "She said the bank has all that information. She never got involved in the finances. But she said we could talk to them. She'll see to it we get permission to look into their accounts."

"Okay." Laura licked her lips. "Watch this trick," she said, and stepped over to Eva.

"So, Eva, can you tell me how often your husband met with Sarah Jane Malone and what their association was?"

Out of her peripheral vision, Laura saw John subtly react, but she ignored it. She hadn't had a chance to fill him in about the calendar, but he was savvy enough to not say anything.

"Sarah Jane? Sarah Jane? Oh yes, that was one of his investors. He was going to start a home care business to help the elderly. He was such a good man." Another tear slipped out and ran down her cheek.

"One of his investors?" Laura pressed.

Eva shrugged. "That's all I know. They'd been friends a long time. Years." Then her eyes widened and her voice rose. "You aren't suggesting there was anything between them, are you? Because my husband would never cheat on me."

"No, no," Laura soothed. "Nothing like that. Did you know her?"

"No. I told you, I didn't get involved in my husband's business affairs."

"Did you know she was murdered." Laura hesitated, letting that sink in. "In the same way your husband was. As were two more people."

Eva gasped. "Oh my God. No!" Now the tears came in earnest again.

Laura sat beside her and waited for the waterworks to slow. "Do you have any idea why anyone would want them all dead?"

Eva shook her head. "So terrible. So terrible. How could anyone hate people so much?"

"Good question. We're intending to find the answer."

Eva nodded. "How can I help?"

Back to basics. "Can you show us where your husband kept his financial records."

Chapter Thirteen

Goodman was waiting for them when they got back to the station. "Serial?"

"Possibly, but not in the traditional sense," Laura answered. "These people were all connected, and the killings are full of rage and definitely personal. We just need to keep at it to find the link which will lead us to the perp."

"Do you want help?" It was not a question. Shelly had already asked this before the latest murder, but this time Laura reconsidered. If Laura didn't cooperate, Shelly would insist anyway.

"Have you got anyone to spare?"

"How about the cold case guy?" John suggested and Laura choked on her coffee. "I heard he just finished a case."

"It's okay with me," Shelly affirmed. "Just solve this. Yesterday."

As she walked away, Laura turned to John, her mouth open. "Seriously?"

"It's obvious you guys spend all your free time together. Why not make it count?"

Laura couldn't argue with the logic. Shaking her head, she picked up her cell.

Devin showed up a scant minute later and they all

walked into the conference room. "Bring me up to speed." He stated, barely concealing his grin.

"… how Leach fits in," Laura concluded.

"You said he was a nurse, right? At Commonwealth?" Devin asked.

"Yes," John answered, tapping at his laptop, then looking up. "He worked in neo-natal But, he was also a nurse midwife."

"Men do that?" Devin asked.

"They do. There just aren't very many of them."

"And where was Alexandra born?"

More tapping. John nodded. "At home. I can't believe I didn't write that down before."

"Probably because it didn't seem relevant before," Laura said, letting him off the hook. "But what have we learned?" She said it nicely but it made the point.

"No detail too small."

"Right."

"And Alexandra said she had a sister that died. A twin?" Devin pressed.

Again, John was tapping away. He stopped and then restarted. This time when he looked up, confusion was etched between his brows. "There was only one baby born to Nora Kessler that day based on filed birth certificates."

"Now why would Alexandra lie about that?" John asked no one in particular.

"Or did her mother lie to her? But what would be the point in that?" Devin asked.

"We need to talk to her anyway," Laura said. "So let's go."

"I can see if I can find anything more about Rusty Leach," Devin offered.

"Everything from his home office is in that pile," John said, pointing. "We'll check back in a while."

Laura resisted the urge to kiss him goodbye, then inwardly laughed at herself. *Who are you? Cara had been right to ask. This man changed things.*

Just as they got in the car, Laura's cell rang.

"Hey, Cara. What's up?"

"You didn't get back to me on that little matter we discussed."

"That was why my message said you should call me back, silly. He's good."

"Yay."

Laura heard her heave a huge sigh of relief. "So will you and Devin have dinner with us next week?"

Laura hesitated. This case was a mother, but sometimes a quick break was just the thing to refresh the brain cells. "I'll ask him, but I'm sure the answer will be yes. Where and when?"

"Tuesday night. The Chop House at seven?"

Laura almost laughed out loud at the name. How appropriate. Sick gallows humor. But without it, homicide detectives wouldn't survive. "Sure. See you then. And I'm looking forward to meeting Tom."

***

Alexandra was back at work and paled when Laura and John entered her office. She gestured they should sit in the guest chairs, but her body was so tense it sang.

"Do I need my lawyer again," she asked, her tone stiff and her expression wary.

"Why did you tell us you had a twin that died?" John asked without preamble.

Confusion caused her brows to come together. "Because that's what my mother told me."

"And the twin supposedly died right after you were born?" John pressed.

"Yes. Mom named her Alana. Why are you asking me this?"

"We are searching for a birth record and a death certificate for a twin sister, but so far we haven't been able to locate either."

Alexandra made a sound from the back of her throat. "Well, that's crazy. That isn't something my mother would make up."

"Are you aware that your Aunt Natalie is seriously mentally ill?" Laura raised an eyebrow.

"Yes, I did know that. But that's all I know about her."

"Is it possible your mother had some problems with mental illness as well?" Laura ventured.

"What kind of a question is that?" she demanded, her eyes wide with anger.

"Could your twin sister have been some delusion of your mother's?" This from John.

"You people are unbelievable. If you spent as much time searching for whoever killed my parents..." She straightened in her chair and raised her chin. "I have her baby bracelet. Alana's. At my house. In my jewelry box. Hers and mine with our names. Made of tiny beads. I can show you. My mom had them made just before we were born." A sob caught in her throat. "Why are you people tormenting me?"

"We're investigating some murders. No one is trying to torment you. But we are determined to find the truth here," Laura explained calmly. "You have your sister's baby bracelet?"

"Yes, and why would anyone have made that if she didn't exist. What is wrong with you?"

Neither Laura nor John responded to that.

"My entire world has been turned upside down," Alexandra sobbed.

"We were wondering about your boyfriend's gambling problem," John said.

Alexandra's back stiffened even more. "He's in recovery. He hasn't touched the online sites in months now."

"And the debt he accumulated?" Laura prodded.

"He's paying it off. He took out a loan. You can check. And he goes to Gamblers Anonymous meetings every week. You can check that, too," Alexandra repeated. "Can you please go now."

"One more question. Do you know a man named Rusty Leach?" John asked.

"Should I?"

Her reaction showed nothing.

"We'll be in touch," John said as a parting shot.

Getting into the car, Laura's head was spinning. "Do you believe her? About the sister?"

"I don't know. I suppose it's possible. You?"

"If it's true, someone messed with the birth records."

"But why?" John asked.

"Think about it. If you were Sarah Jane and you worked with a neo-natal nurse who was also a nurse midwife…" Laura started.

"… and I wanted to sell babies on the black market… babies that wouldn't be missed…"

"Exactly," Laura affirmed. "There's a huge amount of money to be made. Babies can go for upwards of one-hundred-thousand."

"Which ties all the murders together. But then who is the perp?"

"Someone who is pretty pissed off," Laura responded.

"But so many years later?"

"What if the perp didn't find out until recently?" Laura posed.

"So you're saying it's maybe the dead twin who isn't dead?"

"Which means the DNA would match Alexandra. But the fingerprints wouldn't."

"What?" John asked. "I thought identical twins were identical."

"Their DNA matches. There are exceptions to that, but on average, pairs of twins have genomes that only differ by an average of 5.2 mutations that occur early in development, according to a new study," Laura quoted. "Not that we have the sophisticated equipment to determine this DNA differential. But their fingerprints are never an exact match."

"How do you know that?" John was clearly impressed.

Laura raised an eyebrow. "Google. Actually, I looked it up for something else, but I'm glad I did."

"So, if the girls were identical, we would need fingerprints to tell them apart."

"Exactly. The perp didn't seem to care about leaving DNA, but so far there are no unique fingerprints left at the scenes." Laura chewed the inside of her cheek.

"I'll check on the gambling thing. But right about now it seems to me that life insurance policy is the only motive we have."

"Who inherits if Alexandra is convicted of murder?" It was not a question. "The next of kin."

Laura shook her head. "So you're thinking, if there actually is a twin and she is the perp, she was setting Alexandra up to take the fall. But that would mean she was planning this for at least three years."

"Well, it's possible, right? If the twin was angry at the parents and the facilitators, then it makes sense she would resent her twin sister Alexandra. Maybe she thinks Alexandra got the life she deserved. Having her take the blame for the murders would certainly punish her. And there would be a hundred-thousand-dollar bonus."

"Logical. If we go on the supposition there actually is a twin," Laura remarked.

Just then her cell phone rang. It was Jocelyn and Laura sighed. A problem with her mother was not what she needed right now.

"Hey, Jocelyn. What happened?"

"You need to come over here right now." Her voice was up several octaves with urgency.

"My mother?"

Jocelyn snorted. "Oh, no. She's fine. Just hurry."

Laura drove at breakneck speed, and they reached the nursing home in record time. They raced inside, going to the nurses' station where Jocelyn usually sat. Another nurse directed them to the area that housed Natalie Kessler.

Maneuvering their way through the crowd at Natalie's door was not easy amid the chaos. Orderlies and nurses were desperately trying to corral some of the residents away from the room. Several other orderlies were standing around Natalie's bed. The woman herself looked delighted, a huge smile on her face. Next to her, on the bed, was a box, the rectangular kind flowers come in. Nestled among the sheets of tissue paper, complete with blood and whatever else it had acquired during its work, was an axe. It looked to be the same kind as the one at the Whitings. A tray with what was probably the remains of dinner lay spread over the floor, a mix of gravy and peas and meat and pudding someone had skidded on.

Laura stepped around the mess on the floor and sidled up to Natalie. "Hello, Natalie."

The woman's face lit up. "You came back. You said you would and you pinky swore and here you are."

"Yes, here I am." Laura pulled a chair up to the bed, on the opposite side of the axe. "Natalie, can you tell me if you had any other visitors today?"

"It's a big day." Natalie slammed both hands down onto the mattress, which made the axe jump. A collective gasp went out from the crowd. Natalie clapped her hands together, like a child receiving a much wanted present. She smiled at Laura. "You know, I never have visitors. And two today." She shook her head in disbelief.

"Who else came to see you, Natalie?" Laura asked.

"My niece. I have a niece. I didn't know. Her name is…?"

"Alexandra?" Laura prompted.

"No, that wasn't it. Alana. Yes, that was it. Pretty girl. Looks like me. She didn't stay long, but she brought me a present. Or I think it was for me. I'm not sure. Because what would I do with a dirty axe?"

"Did she say anything to you?"

"She said she was sorry, but everything would be okay and I shouldn't worry." She cocked her head.

"Why would I worry?" Now she took a deep breath and smiled. "She said she would come back. She pinky swore, too, so I know she will." Natalie hesitated. "You will, too, right?"

"I will. Pinky swear." Laura stood and moved over to John as Jocelyn stepped up to them. John closed his mouth long enough to be introduced. Laura knew what he was thinking, since she was thinking the same thing: what the hell was going on here?

"That's how Tricia found her a little while ago. She screamed and the whole place reacted. I called you right away," Jocelyn said.

"Tricia?" Laura asked.

"Another one of the nurses, assigned to this section. Specifically to keep an eye on Natalie." Jocelyn pointed her out and Laura and John approached her. She was a young thing, probably newly minted from school, and she had a look on her face that communicated this was not what she bargained for when she took this job. She stared unmoving at Natalie.

"Tricia," Laura said, and the sound of Tricia's name shook her from her gawking. Turning her head slowly, it took her a moment to focus on Laura.

"Y... yes."

"Can you tell us what happened?"

She just shook her head.

John stepped closer. "Hi. I'm John. I know this is quite a shock, Tricia, but we need to know what you saw when you came into this room before. Can you help us?"

Laura was impressed by the calm tenor of his voice. It was soothing and reassuring. John seemed to reach the girl and she nodded.

"I just left Natalie for a minute. To get her dinner.

The kitchen staff was short-handed, so I wanted to help. I was only gone for maybe a minute or two and when I came back, she was just sitting there, grinning, like something out of a horror movie."

"Did anyone touch anything?" Laura asked.

"I don't think so," Tricia responded. "I screamed and people came running. But Natalie wasn't moving, so we were a little afraid to approach her. We figured you guys would want us to leave it."

John quickly donned a pair of gloves and stepped up to the far side of the bed. Very slowly, so as not to alarm Natalie, he reached for the box and picked it up. Natalie's head turned and her gaze followed him as he moved away and exited the room. Natalie just smiled triumphantly as if she had just accomplished something wonderful.

"So this was a taunt." Laura said to herself, swallowing her frustration. She turned to Jocelyn. "I'm going to need the camera footage from the front entrance."

"Of course." Jocelyn turned to leave and hesitated. "So much for security at the front. And the constant supervision." The disgust in her tone was obvious.

"You know, the receptionist never pays any attention to me when I visit. If you have the door code, I guess it's not worth her time to peel her attention off her phone. In fact, when I flashed my badge the other day, she acted as if she'd never seen me before."

"I know. We've complained about her, but she's related to one of the owners. A niece or something," Jocelyn replied, the disgust evident in her tone.

"I'm going to need to talk to her," Laura stated. "Is there an office I can use to interview the staff?"

Allison Merriweather appeared at the door to

Natalie's room. "What happened here? I was in a meeting and I just got back." She directed her attention to Laura.

"You can use her office," Jocelyn said. "Can't she, Ms. Merriweather? To interview staff."

"Umm, sure. But will someone please fill me in?"

Just as Laura pivoted to follow Merriweather to her office, something caught her eye. She grabbed John's arm and he turned to see what had her attention. On the bedside table, a framed picture of the Whitings with Alexandra stared back at them. Laura stepped over to Tricia and pointed.

"Was this here before?"

Tricia cocked her head and bit her lower lip. "No. I don't remember it. In fact, Natalie never had anything personal here. This is definitely new. Do you think the person who left the… you know… left this, too?"

Laura didn't answer her. Instead, she angled her head to John. "Oh yeah, definitely a taunt."

The receptionist was incongruously named Sage. She was sucking on a lollipop, getting more and more on Laura's nerves. The girl's gaze kept dropping to her phone until, after another minute, Laura had enough. She reached over and snatched the phone away and put it on the desk. Before Sage could protest, Laura picked up the wastebasket and held it up under Sage's mouth. Sage looked at her like she was crazy.

"The candy. Now." It was her 'don't screw with me' detective voice and very effective. Sage spit out the offending substance and sat up straight. Still sullen, she was at least looking at Laura now.

"Do you ever pay any attention to who comes and goes?" Laura asked, her tone hard.

Sage shrugged. "If they have the code, why bother? I'm there for questions and to sign in visitors."

"And how do you know who the visitors are if you never look up from your phone."

Sage rolled her eyes. "I do my job."

"Do you? Then can you tell me how someone walked in here this afternoon with a large box and walked right into Natalie Kessler's secluded section without being questioned?"

Sage shrugged again. "She probably had the code."

"Which is, I'm sure, top secret, right?"

Sage glared at her. "Look, I didn't do anything wrong. Big deal. Someone got in with a box. No one was hurt, were they? It was probably just a prank."

"I see you're taking this very seriously. So, how does this sound. Accessory to murder after the fact? That's about a ten- to twenty-year sentence."

Laura said this very matter-of-factly and it took a moment for it to sink in. Then, Sage gasped. "You can't do that."

"Can't I? Well, if the weapon we confiscated—from that box— was the one used in at least two—count them—two murders, and you let someone bring that weapon into one of the residents…"

Sage finally had the good grace to pale. "Okay, okay. I might have seen something. But it just looked like flowers. That's what flowers come in, right? A young woman I didn't recognize came in before. She was wearing a hoodie and I didn't get a good look at her face. But she seemed young. And she was just making a delivery."

"Hair color?" Laura prompted.

"Blond, I think. But she didn't stop at the desk, so I didn't pay much attention."

Really? "And what time did she come in?"

"I'm not sure."

"What time did she leave?" Laura was holding her frustration in check, but it wasn't easy.

Sage gave her a sheepish head shake. "She was a delivery person. I don't really have to deal with them unless they have a problem."

"And what if it was a resident trying to sneak out?" Laura suggested.

"Oh, I'm sure I would have noticed."

"I'm sure," Laura retorted, not bothering to cover the sarcasm.

She and John spent the next several hours interviewing residents and staff. No one had paid much attention to the girl in the hoodie. People came and went here all day every day. But the description Sage had given, such as it was, would fit with Alexandra. Except Laura and John were with Alexandra when this woman showed up with the murder weapon.

They had also reviewed the footage from the front desk surveillance camera and were given a copy. And yes, a slender woman with a lock of blond hair peeking out from her hoodie strode in this afternoon, carrying a long rectangular box. Detailed analysis would confirm if what she was holding matched what was left with Natalie, but Laura was sure what the conclusion would be.

Laura and John both knew it could be the murder weapon from the last two killings since no axe was recovered from those scenes. The lab would determine if the blood on the blade was even human, and if it matched the last two victims, but there was no doubt the killer was taunting them, daring them to find her. Or to point a finger at Alexandra. Which would explain why no weapon was left behind at either of the last two murders.

"Well, there's no doubt now about the family connection," Laura stated as they were leaving. "That axe and that photograph was left with Natalie to confirm it. For some reason, the killer doesn't want us going off in the wrong direction."

"Is it possible Alexandra was the one who hired a look alike to deflect suspicion?" John asked, getting into the passenger side of the car.

Laura shook her head. "She couldn't know in advance we would be interviewing her at the same time." Laura rubbed her neck, trying to release that ever-present knot. "Or it's possible she really does have a twin she believed died." Laura chewed her lower lip. It was so outrageous to think it might be the evil sister. It was Sherlock Holmes who said, 'once you eliminate the impossible, whatever remains, no matter how improbable, must be the truth'. "So let's go on the assumption that Nora did have twins. We can assume that Sarah Jane, her friend"—Laura air-quoted the word friend—"was present at the home birth. A home birth attended by none other than Rusty Leach. So say they spirited away one of the babies and told Nora the baby had died. Nora would have no reason to doubt them."

John nodded, digesting this. "So, they sell the second baby and Nora never even suspects."

"Sure. If you can't screw over your friends…" Laura shook her head. "But say the baby grows up and finds out she was sold. She would blame her biological mother and the other two people who were instrumental in her being taken." Laura concluded.

"So you're saying Alexandra's twin is a homicidal maniac." John said. "Which, based on Natalie, is not so farfetched."

"There's no scientific evidence that really supports that mental illness is genetic, you know. If the woman who left the axe with Natalie wasn't Alexandra, who was with us, who was it? The only way to know for certain is to find out if a twin exists and, if so, what happened to make her a vicious killer who needed to exact revenge." She heaved a breath and poked at the relentless knot in her neck.

"Talk about a needle in a haystack. There wouldn't be any real adoption records." John was stating the obvious. "Where do we start?"

"There would have to be a birth certificate. Falsified, but one that exists. We start there." John was right. It was a needle in a haystack. But it was a needle where nothing existed before.

Chapter Fourteen

Laura was dreaming. Someone with large hands was massaging her neck. Those pesky knots were loosening and she dared not move for fear the incredible motion would stop.

Reluctantly, sleep ebbed away and Laura recognized the feel of those hands.

"You fell asleep at your desk," Devin said.

"No. Don't stop. I'm still asleep and dreaming this lovely dream."

He laughed. "I can do a better job if you're lying down," he teased.

Shaking the last vestiges of sleep from her exhausted body, she looked around. "What time is it?"

"Past midnight. I take it you've been at this all night?"

Sinking into a chair next to her desk, Devin looked at her expectantly. She filled him in as he sat quietly listening.

"I sent John home a while ago to get some rest." She rolled her shoulders and stretched.

"What about you? No, never mind. Did you find anything?"

Laura gave an unladylike snort. "Do you know how many birth certificates are filed in an average year in this city?"

"Thousands?"

Laura nodded. "Luckily, they're broken down by ethnicity. There are other delineations, as well, but for all we know, Sarah Jane lied about the mother's age and other data. But they're also broken down by home births. Which helps. They wouldn't dare have claimed a hospital birth."

"How many does that leave?"

"Well, obviously eliminating the males, we started with twenty-two thousand. We can't be sure of the date of birth since that could easily have been falsified. But we're hoping the certificate was filed within a week or so either before or after. That narrows it down to three-thousand."

Devin's nostrils narrowed. "Wow."

"Well, this is a crap shoot, after all. If it was easy, anyone could do it." Laura's attempt at humor lightened the mood. "The good news is Tess is running a check looking for certificates signed by Rusty Leach.

"I'm also cross referencing with death certificates signed by him. If they wanted to cover their tracks, they might have filed the actual death certificate and then filed another birth certificate. Twenty-five odd years ago, records weren't as accurate as they are today." She took a deep breath. "I'm hoping I can find something that jumps out."

"I have faith in you."

"Have you found anything helpful?" she asked.

"As a matter of fact, it turns out that Jeff isn't the only one with debt. Alexandra has some serious credit card issues. To the tune of thousands."

"Okay, but most people in America have that."

"Yes, but her parents' credit cards were also

195

maxed. With things like a big screen TV and fancy clothes and jewelry."

"Hang on." Laura rifled through her desk and came up with a manilla folder, which she opened and scanned.

"None of which was apparent at their house. They were simple people. John went through that house with a fine-tooth comb and wrote down a preliminary inventory. There was no safe, their closets were definitely not full and their TV was the old-fashioned kind." She hesitated. "I do remember a big screen TV when I interviewed her at her house. And her clothes weren't from a thrift store."

"Which strikes me that maybe their daughter was using their cards to improve her lifestyle."

"Well, I think we should ask, don't you?"

"Yes, but first you need food and sleep and I have appointed myself in charge of both," Devin declared.

"And some love?"

He grinned. "Always."

***

Watching Laura chow down on the fast-food hamburger made Devin grin. "Hungry?"

"Starving. I didn't realize how hungry I was." She took another huge bite and groaned in pleasure. "Nothing better than this kind of food after midnight."

"Agreed. Can I have a French fry?"

"You're driving," she mock whined, then leaned over to him with a handful. He had to admit they were absolutely delicious.

He pulled up to his house a few minutes later and

they got out, Laura grasping the bag of food as if she feared someone would snatch it out of her reach.

"Don't worry. There are three orders of fries in there and another hamburger," he teased.

"Really? You are a good man."

"Follow me and I'll show you how good."

Still chewing, she walked behind him into the house, and he guided her to the couch. Striding into the master bedroom, he called out, "Don't eat yourself sick now."

"I won't," she mumbled through a mouthful.

He turned on the taps in the bathtub and filled it with hot, steaming water. Adding a generous portion of bath salts and oils he had bought the other day for just such an opportunity, he strode back into the living room. Taking her hand, he waited while she ate a few more fries, then led her into the bathroom.

She tilted her head at him, letting him take complete control, which he knew wasn't so easy for her. Unbuttoning her blouse, he slid it off her shoulders, letting it drop to the floor. Her bra was next, and he had to control himself when he saw her magnificent breasts. She was smiling, as if knowing what power she had over him. If only she knew how much.

Unzipping her skirt, he slid it along with her panties to the floor and had to restrain himself from tasting her. Instead, he took her hand and led her to the tub. She sank neck deep into the water and her sigh of pleasure rippled through him.

Taking a washcloth, he lathered it and ran it over her shoulders and neck. Rinsing the soap away, he kissed her on the collarbone. Reaching for a cup, he filled it and poured water into her hair until it was fully wet, then added shampoo and massaged her scalp. Her eyes were closed, her expression one of complete and utter pleasure and relaxation.

He rinsed her hair and continued washing her body until he reached down between her legs. Her hips lifted and it was almost more than he could bear. His erection was pressing so hard against his zipper, he was afraid it would leave marks.

Exercising Herculean control, he reached for a towel and lifting her by the elbow, helped her from the tub and patted her skin dry. Leading the way into the bedroom, he quickly lost his clothes and together they intertwined on the bed. Her skin was silk and velvet, the space between her legs an irresistible secret he could not wait to explore again. There would never be enough for him. He knew he would want her like this every day of his life. The thought was exciting and calming and made him smile.

Her fingers sought his hardness and wrapped around his shaft. Thinking he might just explode into a thousand pieces, he fought to hold it together until he was certain she was satisfied. Kissing her breasts, he sucked the nipples until the taut tips tormented him. Licking and kissing his way down her body, he gently spread her legs and let his tongue find the tight nub. She bucked against him as she cried out his name, her body shuddering with her release. He tore open the foil packet and put on the condom, then slipped inside her and the world disappeared All that existed was the joining of their bodies and the waves of heat building to the heavens.

***

Laura woke the next morning to the enticing scent of fresh brewed coffee. The bed was still warm where Devin had slept, and she rubbed the sheet. She had never wanted to need anyone before, but she knew she couldn't lie to herself about Devin. He had crawled into her soul and she actually liked it. Would revelations never cease?

Appearing in the bedroom doorway with two steaming cups of the reviving brew, he was smiling. She leaned up on an elbow and tilted her head. "Is this the honeymoon phase or will it always be like this?"

Handing her a cup, he sat on the edge of the bed, his expression serious. "I was engaged. Years ago. One day, she sent me a text and I never saw her again."

Laura snorted. "Her loss."

"I think she couldn't live with a cop. She had higher aspirations."

"Ain't no cure for stupid."

He laughed.

"I'll bet she kept the ring, though."

"How did you know that?" His hand went to his chest.

"Her kind always do. No sense of honor." Taking a sip of coffee, she groaned with pleasure. "Definitely her loss."

He kissed her and shook his head. "I am one lucky man."

"So, will you have dinner with me and my friend Cara and her new boyfriend Tuesday?"

"Sure," he said, smiling. "Where are we going?"

Laura pressed her palm to her lips to stifle her laugh. "The Chop House."

Now it was his turn to snort. "Seriously?"

"Cara doesn't know about the case."

They were mixing their lives and it didn't make Laura the least bit apprehensive. In fact, it felt right. Which did make her a little apprehensive.

"So, since today is Sunday, and you definitely need a mental health day, there's an art show downtown in the park there."

"That sounds great. Is it near the Greenline?"

"As a matter of fact, it is. Want to ride bikes?"

Perfect man! "Yes. Do you ride a lot?"

"Whenever I can. We can swing by your place and pick up yours. And if we find something to buy, we can go back and get it later."

"Let me just clean up and check in with John."

***

An hour later, Laura had changed her clothes and they were breezing down the Greenline, the shaded air a welcome relief from the coming onslaught of heat and humidity. Parking their bikes near the entrance to the street art show, they walked hand in hand up and down, perusing and commenting on the pieces as they went. When Devin stopped to admire a specific piece, Laura tried to see it through his eyes. She had never spent much time experiencing the arts, her life requiring pragmatism rather than experience. Like everything else to do with Devin, this was a whole new world and she relished it.

He strode up to one booth and greeted the artist.

"Kenny, this is my friend Laura. Laura, Kenny. I have several pieces of his and I see…" He stepped over to a large canvas of blues and yellows. It reminded

Laura of spring and energy and joy. "… my newest acquisition." He turned to Kenny. "We rode our bikes. Can you hold it for me and I'll pick it up at your place tomorrow?"

Kenny grinned. "Of course. How can I deny my biggest fan anything? And this way I can still show it for the rest of the day."

"Thanks. See you tomorrow." He turned to Laura. "What did you think of it?"

"I love it. It's so… happy."

"I agree. Nice to have that to look at after a day of murder and mayhem."

"I never thought of it that way, but you're so right. I only ever depended on mindless TV and a glass of wine."

"Until you met me," he said, nodding. "Right?"

"I have to admit you have changed my life for the better in so many ways."

They rode back to Devin's house later, tired, full of food sampled from the vendors at the show, and relaxed.

As he opened the door, they both sensed something amiss. The door wasn't locked. Laura reached for her gun, but she had left it at home. Glancing at Devin, she realized he, too, was unarmed. Mistake. But there were two of them.

Slowly, soundlessly, slipping into the hallway with Devin in the lead, he stopped short when they reached the living room.

"Hello, darling," a woman's voice rang out. "Did you miss me?"

Laura stepped forward to get a better look, pressing against Devin's back and straining to see over his shoulder. The woman was gorgeous. Long dark hair fell in perfect curls to her shoulders. Bright blue eyes were highlighted with long dark eyelashes and her skin was peach perfect. Devin didn't have to tell her who this was. She could tell the way his spine stiffened and his entire demeanor changed.

"What are you doing here, Jillian?" he asked. His spine had straightened and his jaw was clenched.

"Devin, this is my house, too." She turned to Laura. "He bought it for me. For us." The woman batted her eyes and Laura's bile rose.

"Why don't I just let you two talk," Laura suggested, hoping Devin would disagree.

"Good idea," Jillian responded.

Trying her best to appear calm, although the green-eyed monster was taking large bites from her, Laura pivoted to the door. Before she could reach it, Devin took hold of her arm. "You don't need to go." *You're right, she needs to go.*

"We'll talk later," she said, dismissing him. Her first reaction was rage, which distilled down to annoyance, fueled by doubt. But she was certain he hadn't invited the woman. So why was she here? Devin had loved Jillian once, loved her enough to propose. Would he succumb to her charms again?

Laura had followed Devin home in her car when they went to pick up her bike, so the bicycle was her only transportation and her house was miles away. But the ride would do her good as she again teeter-tottered between anger and resentment and jealousy and hurt. Jillian was gorgeous. How could she compete with that if Jillian was willing to come back to Devin? Would he take her back? She had hurt him, but if Jillian said all the right things, would he forgive her? And the biggest, most overpowering question of all: could Laura trust him?

It was a fact that sometimes the past could come back and bite you in the ass. Should you be judged by that? She wondered how she would feel if Devin judged her by her mother. Or the lack of feeling she had for the woman who had made her so miserable all her life. Would Devin think Laura heartless? Or would he weigh the facts?

By the time she got home, she was soaked in sweat and tied up in knots. Her legs were rubbery, more from the upset than the exercise, and she just wanted to go to bed and sleep.

So, of course, her cell phone rang. If it was Devin, should she answer? Or let him worry? But she didn't recognize the number.

"Hello?"

The woman on the other end was whispering and sounded panic-stricken. "Detective Chandler. She's here."

"Alexandra? Who is there?"

"Alana. I told her I had to pee so I could call you. Please hurry." And the call ended.

Without bothering to clean up, Laura stowed her bike and ran down to her car. She called John to meet her and raced to Alexandra's house. She was slumped on the front porch, Jeff hovering over her. A quick assessment said no blood had been shed and Alexandra was just very upset.

Laura hurried up the walk and Alexandra raised her gaze, then shook her tear-stained face. Kneeling down to eye level, Laura touched Alexandra's shoulder. "Can you tell me what happened?"

"Can we get her inside?" Jeff demanded. "That other woman, the one who looks like Alex, just threatened her life."

"You saw her?" Laura asked him.

"Of course I saw her," he snarled.

He half lifted, half carried Alexandra into the living room and eased her onto the sofa.

"Where did she go?" Laura asked.

"I have no idea. She just took off," Jeff responded.

"In a car? On foot?"

"She ran." Jeff lifted Alexandra and led her inside to the couch. He disappeared into the kitchen and returned a moment later with a cocktail glass partially filled with a dark amber liquid. "Drink this, honey."

Alexandra's hands were shaking, but she managed to sip the alcohol and then coughed.

John appeared at the front door and walked in. He gave Laura a questioning look, but she just gave a tiny shrug and sat down across from Alexandra. John took the chair next to Laura's.

"Can you tell us what happened?" Laura repeated.

Jeff sat next to Alexandra and rubbed her back in a calming motion. "It's okay, honey. Tell them."

Alexandra nodded. "There was a knock at the door. Jeff answered and he gasped, which made me come running." Her voice was erratic from crying, so she cleared her throat. "She pushed her way in. It was like looking in the mirror. She looks just like me." Alexandra pressed her lips together and twisted her hands in her lap.

"Why did she come to see you?" John asked.

"She said she wanted to see my face when she told me everything." A sob choked her.

Laura and John waited for Alexandra to collect herself and continue. "When we were born, Mom kept me and rejected her. She was sold to a very rich woman who wanted a baby. But the woman decided it was way too much work, so she sent her into foster care. She had a terrible life and vowed one day to get even."

Laura digested this. "How would killing your parents and the people who sold her benefit her?"

"She was going to make sure I am blamed for the... you know... deaths."

Laura smiled without humor. "But she waltzed into your aunt's room at the home when you were with us. So all that was for nothing, right?"

"She said no one saw her face there and it could have been anyone. She was upset and she said if I didn't get arrested she would come back and make me pay." Alexandra reached out her hands to Laura. "You'll protect me, won't you? You have to, right? It's your job. You'll find her and stop her?" Her voice was rising close to hysteria.

John turned to Jeff. "You saw her?"

"It was uncanny. I couldn't tell them apart."

"Did anyone else see her?" Laura asked.

"One of the neighbors must have seen her. Of course, they would have thought it was Alexandra," Jeff answered.

"Please, please find her and stop her before she comes back. I'm terrified." Alexandra was weeping full out now.

"How did she find you?" Laura asked.

"I asked her. She said she found a copy of her birth certificate and when she traced the parents listed, they didn't exist. So she took a DNA sample and went on one of those family sites and I was listed." She inhaled another sob. "I never should have been curious about my ancestry. But with so little family…"

"Did she touch anything?" Laura asked.

Alexandra's eyes widened. She turned to Jeff. "Did she?

"No, I don't think so," he responded.

"Why were you on the porch?" Laura asked.

"We were going to go after her, but decided it was too dangerous. So I just called you." Alexandra drew in a deep breath. "I can't believe I had a sister I never knew about. And one that would kill our parents. She must be very angry. Or had a terrible life. Maybe her adoptive parents were really terrible as she said. Or maybe she was just warped. It can happen you know. I wish I knew more about her. Where to find her. I would help more if I could."

Laura and John stood. "We'll do everything we can to locate her. Meanwhile, lock your doors and call us right away if you see her again." Laura's tone was very matter-of-fact and John narrowed his gaze at her.

Walking back to the car, John reached out and touched Laura's arm. "What was that about?"

"What do you think?" she tossed back.

"You first. Please."

"Well, I'm more and more convinced there isn't a twin. It just seems too convenient."

"And I'm more and more convinced there might be one," John responded.

"That's the problem. It absolutely could go either way."

Chapter Fifteen

"What do you want, Jillian?" Devin asked for the third time. She was still very beautiful, but he had noticed a hardness around her mouth and a coldness in her eyes. Why hadn't he seen that before? His insides turned into a swirl of old scars and pain. He had loved her. Or thought he did. Is that what love was? Or was it more like what he was discovering with Laura? Because he would definitely choose the latter.

"Well, since this is our house…"

"… that I bought and paid for," he interrupted.

"I just thought…" she batted her eyes, "… that I might try again. I was foolish and impulsive, and I never should have left."

She stood up and moved very close to him, reaching up to wrap her hands around his neck. His back went rigid of its own accord and he pulled back, disentangling her.

"Jillian, I have no idea why you're here or what you want, but we are done." He said it and he meant it. Deep in his soul. He had burned for her, ached for her, but today, now, she was an unpleasant part of his life best forgotten, or at least pushed into the recesses of old memories. Thinking back now, most of the years with Jillian were about her needs, pleasing her. He was so caught up with his work, drilling down into the dark side, that she was a welcome respite, so he was more grateful than anything. He was truly and finally over her, and he was filled with such relief his knees went momentarily weak.

"Because of that woman you came in with?"

"Laura and I are together, yes, but that isn't the reason you and I are done. I have moved on and I'm happy. I'm sorry you're not." Yes, Laura did make him happy and didn't drain the life from him in the process.

"I missed you."

He glared at her. That wasn't even worthy of a response.

"I saw you guys at the art show before and I realized how much I missed you. How wrong I was to leave. How we belong together."

"So now you want what you think is yours... namely me. Or is it this house?"

She lifted her shoulders, her expression a mask of innocence.

"Did you really think you could just come back whenever it suited you?" He was truly amazed.

"You're mine. We were going to get married. You can't just wipe that away."

He took her arm and led her to the door. "Yes, yes I can. Not good seeing you, Jillian. Now go away."

"You know you don't mean that. I know you were torn up when I left. Jim told me."

The mention of his late partner's name was like a shard of glass to his heart and he froze. "You talked to Jim?"

She nodded. "We were... well, we ... but he loved his drugs more than anything."

"You slept with Jim?" It was everything he could do to keep his mouth from dropping open.

She shrugged. "You and I had broken up and Jim and I ran into each other. It wasn't serious. And besides, I didn't want to get involved with the stuff he was doing."

"Which means?" Devin was beginning to feel a little nauseous.

"Well, you knew he sold the stuff, right? Being a cop and partnered with a straight arrow like you protected him for years."

Devin schooled his features. He wouldn't give her the satisfaction of reacting. Instead, he just shook his head. Reality was sometimes so ugly, but it did put things into perspective. "You know, I can forgive Jim. He had bigger problems and his thought processes were distorted with the addiction. But I didn't need to know you slept with him." He wanted her gone before his emotions threatened to immerse him. "Why did you tell me now? Were you so anxious to hurt me? Why?"

"Oh, darling, I just want to make it better. I wanted you to know how much I truly appreciated you after spending time with Jim." She reached out her hand to stroke his cheek but he stepped back. "Let me take the old hurt away."

"Good-bye, Jillian. Don't come back." He shooed her out the door and closed it and the room went dark. His partner, his friend, had slept with his ex. Dealt drugs behind his back. Used him as a cover. And died a miserable death, which Devin had felt was partially his responsibility. He believed he should have seen the trouble Jim was in. But now, he knew Jim was not what he seemed. He wasn't an innocent caught up in the web of illicit drugs. He was a player. And Devin had never suspected. It never even occurred to him that he and Jillian were sleeping together. How could he have been so stupid? It was a lot to take in.

What Devin wanted was Laura. He needed to talk to her. To reassure himself she was not like Jillian, would never use him for her own purposes. He picked up the phone and dialed, disappointment crushing as it went to voicemail. He couldn't blame her. If he had come home to one of her exes, he would be pretty pissed off, too. But he needed to explain, and he was desperate to finally release the bands of guilt around his chest that had, for so long, pressed the pain into his soul.

His phone rang and he jumped for it, hoping it was Laura. He was greeted by his mother's voice instead.

"Hey, baby. How are you?"

"I'm good. How…

"… What's wrong?" she interrupted.

"Nothing."

"Devin Charles Andrews, do not ever lie to your mother."

"Jillian was here."

His tone was without emotion, unlike his mother's response. "And what in the name of heaven did she want?"

"To ruin my day."

"I hope you sent her away."

"Of course." He hesitated, wondering how much he should reveal. His mother already hated Jillian for the way she treated him. But the newfound knowledge was coiling in his belly like a poisonous snake. He didn't want it to tear him up, but he had no choice.

"She had an affair with Jim before he died." Just saying the words out loud made his bile rise.

"Um huh."

"Did you know?" He tried not to sound accusatory.

"No, but I can say I am certainly not surprised. She always struck me as an opportunist. You're well rid of her. What did she want, anyway?"

What did she want? "I don't know and I don't care." And that was true.

"On a happier note, how is that pretty girlfriend of yours?"

He schooled his tone this time. "Great."

"Good, since you two are invited to dinner next Friday. It's…"

This time it was his turn to interrupt. "… Dad's birthday. I didn't forget. I even bought him a present."

"What?"

He snorted. "You can't keep a secret from him. So don't even bother asking what I got him. You'll see on Friday."

"Love you."

"Love you, Mama."

***

"When you ask a suspect a question, how do you know they're lying?" Laura asked.

"Because they talk too much."

"Exactly. They offer more details than you asked for. Or ramble on with information that is just working to convince us of something."

"You're right. So you think the whole visiting thing is a lie?"

"I don't know. We have to check with the neighbors. If someone else saw her… but then she could have left the house and circled back."

211

"I didn't have a chance to tell you. Tess found the birth certificate for a baby girl born on the same day as Alexandra. But, it wasn't filed by Rusty Leach, which is why it didn't show up right away. Another mid-wife signed off on it. And it was filed under the name of Madison, which was Nora's mother's maiden name."

"We need to talk to that midwife." Laura slid into the driver's seat. "Okay. So there actually might have been a twin." She rubbed the knot in her neck. "I suppose if you were going to steal a baby, you would definitely want a death certificate." She narrowed her eyes. "Can we locate another birth certificate on file that would match the twin? Like a baby born on the same day in the same place?" Her mouth opened. "Or not. If you want to pretend the baby didn't exist, you would only need a birth certificate. A fake one."

"But if the twin really did die at birth, it should be easy to locate the death certificate."

"Again that still opens the possibility that no birth certificate was issued for Alexandra's twin so no death certificate would need to be filed." Laura shook her head. "Tricks within tricks."

"Tess is still checking." John scratched his head.

"Good. But if that other birth certificate was issued for the adoption, would Rusty Leach have signed that one? Probably not, since if there was a problem, it would lead right back to him."

"Everything does point to Alexandra. She has debt, opportunity, and a one-hundred-thousand-dollar motive. And a twin only seen by her, her boyfriend and her crazy aunt." His brow furrowed in concentration. "And twenty-five odd years ago, the records were not as pristine as they are today."

"Don't forget we were with Alexandra when Natalie had her visitor," Laura reminded him, talking out her theory. "But then no one saw her face except Natalie, who apparently had never met Alexandra before. It might have been anyone and Alexandra could have hired a lookalike." Frustration edged her tone. "Something about this case smells bad." It had not been a good day for Laura.

"Let's go talk to the midwife," John suggested. "Her name is Florence Ashton and she still lives in town."

"Good idea."

John had the address, and Laura's cell rang just as they pulled up to Florence's house. It was Devin, but now was not the time to hash this out. Laura had reverted back to her 'job first' mode, setting the emotional part of her life in last place.

***

Florence answered the door and when she saw their badges, she ushered them inside. She was a woman of about seventy with smooth skin and dark grey hair. Her smile was both warm and sad. The inside of her house was small and cozy, and a fat tabby cat rubbed against Laura's legs as they made their way inside.

"Teddy, go eat a mouse or something," Florence directed at the feline, who, of course, ignored her and proceeded to rub against John.

"He's very friendly. Please come in and sit down. I'm guessing you're here about Rusty."

"Bad news travels fast," Laura commented.

"We midwives are a small community and Rusty

213

was one of the few men in the field. I liked him and I was sorry to hear of his passing. I was his mentor, you know."

John and Laura perched on the edge of the striped couch and a whoosh of cat hair moved aside to make way for them.

"Sorry about that," Florence commented. "We don't get many visitors and I have five cats. The others all wait until Teddy approves before they even consider showing their faces." She smiled that sad smile again. "How can I help you?"

"Do you remember a set of twins born twenty-six years ago to a woman named Nora Kessler?" Laura ventured.

Florence dropped her gaze and Teddy jumped into her lap. She stroked him absently. "You know, in my career I've birthed an awful lot of babies. Even twins. Can you give me any more information?"

"One of the twins died," John responded.

"Oh, I would have remembered that. So, no, that didn't happen on any of my cases." She tapped her finger to the corner of her mouth. "I did have a case of twins where one was much smaller and had to go to the hospital, but I'm pretty sure she survived. But that one was only about eight years ago." She looked at Laura. "I've been very lucky in my career. That's why I retired before I started making mistakes."

"Is it possible Rusty signed your name to a birth certificate?" Laura ventured.

Florence tilted her head. "I wouldn't know why. What would be the point?"

That wasn't a no.

Laura stood and John followed suit. "Thank you so

214

much for your time." She handed Florence her card. "If you think of anything that might help, please don't hesitate to call."

"I won't. I hope you find out who did this to Rusty. I always admired him. It takes guts to be one of the few men in a field run by women."

***

"Let's go get some food," Laura suggested. "And ruminate." They had called Tess to track down a woman with the last name of Madison born on the same day as Alexandra Whiting, but they knew it would take time.

"Can I ask you something off subject?" John asked. "It's personal. But there's no one else I can talk to about this."

Laura was pleased he trusted her enough to confide in her about his private life. "You know my philosophy. Rip off the band-aid."

"Do you know what I am going to ask?" He knew the answer and was always surprised when she was one step ahead. It probably didn't strike him as logical.

"Well, let's see. I'm guessing it's going well with Sanchez. Did I mention he's a cutie?" She grinned at John. "And at some point, you might want to take him home."

"They don't know." He dropped his voice.

"I think you'll be surprised. Whether they welcome it or not… only way to find out is… to find out. And whatever it is, you'll deal with it."

Growing very quiet, he stared out the window for a few minutes, then nodded. "You're right. Thanks."

"Now, can we get our minds back to work?"

As if to mock her, her cell rang. She decided to pick up, knowing it was Devin.

"Hey," she said. They definitely needed to sit down and talk to each other about Jillian and the past and yes, even the future. But for now, the case was ever present and took priority and she realized another educated point of view could help.

"We need to talk." He sounded resigned and very sad.

"Is she gone?" Laura asked pointedly.

"Yes."

"Then I think I want you to meet my mother."

"Really?" He sounded relieved this time, but still a little unsure and confused.

"I'll explain later. In the meantime, are you busy?"

"No." Devin responded. She could almost hear the "why".

"Can you meet John and me at the Blues Café?"

"Now? Sure. I'll be there in fifteen."

John and Laura were seated when Devin walked in. He hurried to the table and pulled up a chair. They ordered and waited impatiently for their food so they could get to the real meat.

"We need a tie-breaker," Laura explained. "John thinks there is a twin and I think there isn't one. It just seems too pat. It's easy to blame someone who can't defend themselves or even show up."

They filled him in on all they had and he listened carefully, then blew out a breath. Their food arrived and between bites, Devin asked questions and clarified what he had been told.

"You're right," Devin acknowledged. "It could go either way."

216

"That's the problem," John said.

"What about the Madison baby? You need to track her down and get a DNA sample," he suggested.

"On it," John responded.

"But what do your instincts tell you?" Laura pressed.

"It could go either way," he repeated. "There's the crazy aunt, which opens the possibility that if there is a twin, she could be crazy, too." He held up his hand, palm out. "I know, that's not scientific, but it could happen. And if Alexandra was convicted of killing her parents and there was a twin sister who could prove her relationship to the family with DNA, she could claim the insurance payout, superseding the estate designation," Devin finished.

"Exactly," Laura agreed. "So—to twin or not to twin?"

"I think the real question is—would you kill four people for a hundred thousand dollars? That isn't so much money. But then, I guess it's all relative. No pun."

Chapter Sixteen

With still no answers, they had to wait while Tess tried to track down the Madison baby. If there was a stolen twin, it would have to be her. Unsatisfied, they left the restaurant. John went one way and Laura followed Devin to his car. He slid into the driver's side and she into the passenger seat.

"Before you say anything," Laura said, her hand raised palm out to stop any explanation, "let me just say I know you had nothing to do with Jillian showing up."

"Thank you," he responded, leaning over to kiss her on the lips. Then he sat back, his face a mask of sadness.

"What happened?" Laura asked, this time edging closer to him.

"She just gave me insight I didn't want or need on my late partner, Jim."

"The one who died from an overdose?"

"The one who slept with my ex, dealt drugs and, it turns out, used me as a cover for his activities."

"She told you all that?" Laura was nonplussed.

"She did. It's funny. I have carried the guilt about Jim ever since he died and Jillian just released me. I should feel relieved, but instead I just feel disgusted. Mostly at myself for caring about both of them. And a little sick. I really feel so stupid that I was clueless."

Laura reached over and stroked his cheek. "It's your ability to care that makes me love you."

He reached over and scooped her into a hug. "I thought you'd be pissed." He pulled back and looked at her. "Why weren't you pissed? I would have been."

"You're a detective and you still don't know things are not always as they seem?" Her tone was teasing. "Because I sure do. And you haven't met my mother yet," Laura said, taking a deep breath and rubbing the knot in her neck.

"Point taken. So what was this about meeting your mother?"

Laura dropped her gaze. "I guess I just feel like we shouldn't have any secrets."

Devin drew his brows together. "Do you think I thought you didn't have a mother?" He was teasing, but she didn't smile.

"My mother is not a nice person. She is a mean, spiteful narcissist and you should know what you're getting into."

He pulled her back into his arms. "I won't judge you by your mother if you don't judge me by Jillian."

"No time like the present, I guess." Shivering in unpleasant anticipation, she directed him to the home.

This time, as they walked past the reception desk, the girl sitting there challenged them. They were asked to sign in and say who they were visiting.

"And who says you can't teach an old dog new tricks—or a nursing home," Laura whispered. "Before the axe showed up, they cared less who came and went."

Walking down the hallway, Devin looked into the rooms as they passed. "This is a very sad place."

"It is," Laura agreed. "But sometimes there's no other choice."

"It wasn't a judgment," he responded quickly.

"I didn't take it as one."

Entering her mother's room never got easier. The hits just kept on coming. Clair was awake and sitting up, sipping on a drink. Glaring at her visitors, she scowled.

"Is there a reason there's no bourbon in this?" she demanded. Her gaze went to Devin. "Are you my new nurse? Because I am sure I need a bed bath."

Wanting to melt into the floor with embarrassment, Laura pressed her lips together. "Mother, this is Devin."

Now her mother's glare was focused on Laura. "And who are you?"

"I'm your daughter and this is my boyfriend." Laura kept an even tone.

"Hah. You always tried to steal my boyfriends because you could never get one of your own."

"Okay," Laura exhaled. "I see you're doing well. We need to go."

"As if you care." Clair turned to face the wall and harrumphed her disgust as Laura led Devin back into the hall and down the corridor.

"How long has she been like this?" Devin asked, his tone sympathetic.

Laura smiled without humor. "All my life."

Stroking her arm, he angled closer to her. "I'm sorry."

"Don't be. The point of this visit was to let you know I hope you don't judge me by her actions, any more than I judge you by Jillian's."

He was quiet until they got back to his car. Hesitating to start the engine, he swiveled toward her in his seat. "I love you."

"I love you, too."

"My parents want us to come to dinner next Friday. It's my dad's birthday." He held up his hand, palm out. "And yes, they invited you. They like you."

"I'm glad. I like them, too. And I'd love to spend more time with your family. And, we also have dinner with Cara and her new boyfriend on Tuesday."

"Well, aren't we the social butterflies?" he responded laughing.

***

Monday morning saw Laura and John in Goodman's office again, not giving her the answers she wanted.

"You two are going to have to do better than this. I need an arrest. And soon."

"Agreed," Laura responded. "But right now all we have is circumstantial. We're still waiting for information on the possibility of a twin and a motive that will stick."

"Well get on it or I'll have to find someone who can do a better job."

Exiting her office, they were out of earshot when John shook his head. "Nice. Nothing like a vote of confidence to start your day."

Laura shrugged. "We're doing all that we can. And that's all we can do."

Just then, John's cell rang. He answered and all the color drained from his face. A strange gurgle came from his throat before he said, "Okay. I'll be right there," and hung up.

"What?"

"It's Randy. He's been shot. They're taking him to hospital emergency and he asked the EMTs to call me."

"How bad?"

"I don't know." His expression closed in on itself as he tried not to give in to tears.

"Well, go."

"But—"

"Family first. Now go."

"Thanks," he called over his shoulder as he tore down the hall. "I'll call you."

Laura shuffled back to her office, thoughts of something happening to Devin churning her insides. She plopped into her chair and, as if by the power of wishful thinking, Devin appeared at her desk. Standing, she took his hand and pulled him into the conference room, closed the door and threw her arms around his neck. Holding her, he rubbed her back until she calmed.

"What happened?" he asked.

"Randy's been hurt. John's boyfriend. Shot." Voicing it made it very real and upsetting.

"I am so sorry. How?"

"I don't have any details. John went to Baptist. I just feel terrible for him. They really like each other."

"And were you worried about me?"

She took a step back and looked him right in the eyes. Words didn't need to be exchanged. He just pulled her into his arms again and held her.

Finally, they moved apart. "Can I help with the case more since you're short-handed?"

"Yeah. That'd be great. But I still have nowhere to

go with it. It's all just smoke and mirrors." Laura heaved a sigh.

"Did anyone else see the twin the other day?"

She sank into one of the hard wooden chairs. "Two of the neighbors saw a woman fitting the description running down the street. Apparently she jumped onto a bicycle and took off."

"So there could have been a twin or it could have been Alexandra who rode around the block and slipped in to her house via the back way."

Throwing up her hands, Laura groaned. "Exactly."

"How about we start back at the beginning."

Laura chewed her lower lip. "There is one thing that keeps bothering me. Nora worked at the Department of Vital Records in Nashville for about a year. She was a file clerk. And apparently she was friends with Sarah Jane at that time…"

"File clerk as in birth records?"

"Yes. And twenty odd years ago, nothing was computerized. Everything was paper."

"So you're wondering if Nora played a little fast and loose with the birth records."

"If Sarah Jane was doing illegal adoptions and she had a friend in the filing department…" Laura continued.

"Sadly, I don't see how we can ever find out. Unless…"

"The problem is we can find missing children and maybe, just maybe connect them to different birth certificates, but that would take an army of people. And we still couldn't account for babies that were kidnapped at birth."

"Are you certain Leach was working with Sarah Jane?"

"No doubt in my mind. His trust fund," she air quoted, "is an offshore account that had regular large deposits over the years. And he was so certain he wouldn't get caught, he didn't even bother to try and hide it."

"Do you think his wife knew?"

"Definitely not or she might have been less forthcoming with the financials," Laura responded

"Okay, so we have Leach and Sarah Jane acquiring babies and children, re-filing birth certificates so they couldn't be traced and making a fortune."

"And I have no doubt they had other filing clerks on the payroll." Laura shook her head. "Their possible treachery is mind-boggling."

"So you think Alexandra's twin found out all this and wanted revenge?"

"Alexandra said Alana disappeared and was then abandoned to foster care. That could do it."

"Which reinforces the possibility of a twin," Devin remarked.

Laura inhaled and then exhaled loudly. "Alexandra apparently had a good life. Which doesn't preclude the possibility she's a killer, but what was her motive? We're missing something here. It's all connected somehow."

Suddenly, Devin's eyes widened. "Trust fund."

"Yes, Leach's wife said he had a trust fund."

"Not him. Didn't you tell me Natalie was supported by a trust fund? Worth millions. And that Nora had control of it."

Laura's mouth dropped open. She jumped up, threw her arms around Devin's neck and kissed him soundly on the mouth. "Motive!"

"But which one? Back to—is there a twin?"

Laura dropped her chin to her chest. "One step forward, two steps back."

"That also means that some of the children listed as missing over the years have been adopted, their birth certificates changed to make it legit and we can never give the families who have lost their children closure."

"Sounds like a job for cold-case man."

He shook his head. "That isn't just a job. It's a career."

***

Laura obtained a warrant to look into the Kessler trust fund that supported Natalie. Poring over the documents, it was obvious that Alexandra could now step up and gain control of the fund. Unless she was charged with a capital crime, in which case control went to the next of kin or to the bank which was listed as the back-up trustee.

The trust was now worth over fifteen million dollars. When it had originally been set up, it was only worth one-tenth of that. So, either the Whitings were brilliant at investing or they had used the trust to hide the illegal income. And, since Nora had control, she could draw out the money when and how she saw fit. And why didn't they tap into it? Did they have a crisis of conscience? Were they saving it for their retirement, so they could go off and spend it and no one would notice?

If control passed to Alexandra or her alleged twin, it could certainly support a lavish lifestyle and made for a definite motive to kill. And if Aunt Natalie's

225

circumstances were to be diminished—well, would an axe murderer really be concerned about that?

Now, how to prove there was or wasn't a twin…

Her mind spinning, Laura glanced at the clock and remembered it was Tuesday and she and Devin had planned to go to dinner with Cara and her new boyfriend, Tom. She had just checked in with John, and Randy was out of the ICU. The bullet had hit his spleen, but once the organ was removed and the bleeding stopped, he was on his way to recovery.

John told her Randy had been shot while he was walking out of a gas station restroom, so either he was being followed or some random shooter saw an opportunity to take down a cop and took it. Neither idea was acceptable and she knew the entire department would move heaven and earth to find the perp. But for now, Randy was going to survive and recover, which was great news and a huge relief. Laura had told John to take a few days and stay with his friend.

Hanging up, her thoughts drifted back to the case. She really wanted to figure out a way to know if a twin really existed or not. The Madison lead was still pending. Tess was running facial recognition against driver's licenses, pictures I.D.s and the live surveillance video, even though the latter was brief and difficult to see. As evidence, it might not stand up in court, but it could tell them if there was an Alexandra lookalike. In the meantime, Laura decided she might as well go eat and spend time with Cara.

Just then, as if summoned by magic, Devin appeared at her desk.

"Ready?"

"Yes, I suppose. But if this guy is like any of

Cara's other boyfriends, we're in for an evening of all about him and let's see how fast we can get through this meal."

***

Since it was a Tuesday, the restaurant wasn't very busy and they were shown to a table right away. True to form, Cara was late, but that gave Laura a chance to stroke Devin's thigh.

"If you do that again, we're leaving," he whispered, grinning.

She responded with an innocent rolling of her shoulders just as they were joined by their dinner companions. Tom was a nice-looking man with short hair and a one-day scruff that gave him an air of bad boy. Just Cara's type. Introductions done, they settled in with small talk. Drinks arrived and Laura actually found herself relaxing.

"So Cara tells me you're detectives," Tom said. Laura did not want to talk shop tonight, so her muscles tightened.

"I have a great story about my arrest." Tom was grinning.

That stopped all conversation cold. Laura had run a background and the man had no record.

"Well, it was actually mistaken identity. I used to be an actor and I got hired for one of those reality 'most wanted' type of shows to portray a killer. A few days after it aired, I was getting gas and a police car drove up and pulled me out of the car. I was handcuffed and taken down to the station before they would believe I was an actor and not the actual guy."

227

"What happened after that?" Cara sounded horrified.

"I gave up acting, of course. Even though I was clearly good at it, I figured it was too dangerous. That's why I sell real estate with Cara now."

Laura closed her eyes. Mistaken identity because he looked like someone else. How apropos.

The evening was actually pleasant and Tom turned out to be a really nice guy and Laura was happy for her friend.

As she and Devin were leaving the restaurant, she couldn't shake the story he had told.

"What if Alexandra hired an actress to go to the home and to appear at her house?" Laura ventured. "It would be an easy enough thing to do."

"Don't you think almost everyone knows about these murders? Anyone she might hire would be in danger of being charged with accomplice after the fact."

"Maybe she had something on the other woman. Maybe it was blackmail. You know 'you do this for me and you're off the hook' kind of thing." *Was she grasping at straws?*

"It's possible. This case is like chasing Alice down the rabbit hole. The more information you get, the less sense it makes."

***

Walking into Laura's house, Devin followed her into the kitchen and lifted her up on the counter. Her quizzical look made him smile, but she didn't offer any protest.

"How about some dessert?" he asked.

"Didn't we just share some cheesecake?"

He shook his head. "I'm still craving something sweet." Opening her refrigerator, he pushed some things around until he found what he was hoping for: some jam and some whipped cream. Talk about romance novel cliché. But hell, it worked for him.

Delighted she was wearing a skirt, he pushed it up, exposing her bare thighs and... no underpants. She raised an eyebrow and her smile lit his world.

Keeping his gaze on hers, he opened the jam and stuck his index finger inside, circling the jar. Withdrawing his hand, he very slowly traced the inside of her thigh, stopping just short of her center. When he finished repeating the action on the other leg, she was squirming on the granite surface. Lowering his head, he used just the tip of his tongue to lick away the sticky jelly on both legs, again just moving away before he touched her core.

Straightening and turning his attention to her blouse, he yanked it free from her skirt and unbuttoned it, pulling it from her shoulders and reaching around to unhook her bra. Her breasts were gorgeous, and he cupped them with both hands and buried his head between them. Her skin was silky soft and her fragrance, roses and lavender, surrounded him, filling his senses. Then, he took hold of the whipped cream can and shook it, then squirted the contents over her nipples. He feasted on the sweetness, sucking and teasing until she moaned his name.

Slipping his finger between her legs, he knew she was very ready for him. He pushed off his pants, his stiff erection desperate to sink into her soft, warm cocoon. He eased into her and she threw back her head with obvious pleasure. He knew he could lose himself completely in this woman and the thought no longer scared him.

Wrapping her arms around his neck and pulling him closer, the feel of her fingernails through his shirt, digging in, pulled him to the edge and he pressed into her once more before his release shook him just as she clenched around him.

For a while, they stayed woven together, one flesh, and Devin knew he was tasting heaven.

"Ready for bed?" Laura asked after a while.

Devin smiled. "Is that granite surface getting to you?

"Without the distraction, I notice my behind is getting sore."

"Want me to rub it?" he leered at her.

"Well, get me down from here and we can negotiate."

Chapter Seventeen

Laura was looking forward to tonight. She was very comfortable with Devin's family now and decided to, as Cara had said, 'just enjoy it'. She also wondered if they might have some insights into the 'twin or not' conundrum. After checking with Devin, she selected a bottle of Maker's Mark as a gift, since it was James's favorite. She also bought a bouquet of flowers for Devin's mother.

Betty greeted her with a warm hug and Laura held out the flowers.

"You didn't need to do that." But she was clearly pleased.

"Are you kidding. You're cooking another wonderful meal and you included me. This is the least I can do to show my appreciation."

Betty hugged her son and ushered them into the living room. Glenda stood and moved over to Devin and Laura, giving each of them a warm embrace. Laura's insides turned into mush.

"Happy birthday, Dad," Devin greeted James as Laura held out the bag with the bottle. James's face broke into a grin when he pulled out the liquor.

"Well, let's drink to that!" James responded.

"Hey, Roy. You want to get some glasses?" Devin asked.

Roy gave Laura a quick hug as he hurried into the kitchen. A few minutes later, drinks poured, they all toasted James. Then, since dinner was ready, they sat around the table and proceeded to feast on Betty's roast. Conversation soon turned to Devin and Laura's case. She filled them in on all that had been discovered so far, hoping James and Roy could offer suggestions.

Roy shook his head. "Here's the main problem. It's impossible to prove that something doesn't exist."

"You're right," Laura returned. "Several people claim to have seen the twin sister, but the only ones to clearly see her face were Natalie, Alexandra and her boyfriend. None of whom are reliable witnesses."

"But reliable enough to screw up your case. And make the D.A.'s job difficult at best," James added.

"What about facial rec?" Roy asked.

"Still working on it. Nothing so far."

"And the trust fund angle?" Roy continued.

"Yeah. Fifteen million dollars and the control now goes to the next of kin. So, if Alexandra is convicted, she can't inherit. But her twin could," Devin added.

"What we need is a confession," Laura said.

"Yeah, good luck with that," Roy stated. "All I can say is, I do not envy you."

"How about some cake?" Betty asked.

"Better alert the fire department first with all those candles," Roy teased.

"Still young enough to beat your butt," James returned.

As they were driving home later, Laura leaned closer to Devin. "I love your family."

"And they love you."

"That's so nice. They just accept me."

"Of course. I love you and that's good enough for them. But they also like you because they like you. In fact, I'm beginning to worry they love you more then they love me," he teased.

"I doubt that. But it is so wonderful to have a family like yours."

"They're yours if you want them."

It took a moment for the words to sink in. "Are you saying what I think you're saying?" Her throat was suddenly tight.

"I am," he affirmed.

"Then I do." The weight of that was nearly overwhelming. Laura had promised herself she would never remarry, but this was Devin and he was the love of her life. She wanted to wake up with him every morning, and kiss him goodnight every night. She couldn't imagine her life without him in it. Yes, this was right. And the butterflies took flight.

***

Baby girl Madison, born on the same date as Alexandra Whiting, was now Tara Kellogg. She was married and living in Rutherford, about an hour's drive from Memphis. As soon as the report came in, Laura was ready to hop in her car and drive north. Before she could get out of the station, she was summoned into Goodman's office.

"Well," the captain demanded. "And where is Resciniti?"

"I'm about to check out a lead in Rutherford and John had to go to the hospital. One of his friends was shot. A cop."

Even Shelly Goodman had sympathy for the shooting of another officer. She hesitated a moment. "Okay, so now you're working this case alone?"

"The cold case guy, Andrews, is on board still and right now I'm good."

Shelly lifted her chin. "You do know our job is to solve cases here. Not solving them makes us look bad."

Laura's blood heated close to boiling, but she controlled herself. "I know that. And I promise if I need more help I will not hesitate."

"You have seventy-two hours. And then I call in reinforcements. And probably have to answer why they weren't called in sooner."

"Seventy-two hours. Okay." Laura shifted from foot to foot to dispel the energy urging her to shriek at her captain. It wouldn't help and it would only blow back on her. The self-imposed pressure was more than enough; she didn't need this. But that's the way it worked sometimes.

She slid into her car and checked the GPS. It was an easy drive along mostly country roads and she shouldn't encounter much traffic, so she could concentrate on the case. Laura wasn't sure what answers she'd get from the interview with Tara, but she had to check out every possibility. Clues and answers sometimes came from the strangest places.

The driver's license photo of Tara wasn't the best—were they ever?—but she couldn't see any resemblance to Alexandra. But, they could have been fraternal twins. The DNA hadn't come back yet, so Laura knew a face-to-face was the only way to tie up this loose end.

The Kellogg's house sat at the top of a rise behind

a fence. It was isolated, the nearest house far off on the horizon. Two horses grazed on the side and a barn was visible in the back. The home itself was older, but appeared well-kept.

Laura pulled into the driveway and as she exited her car, the front door opened. A woman in her mid-twenties stood in the doorway, a quizzical look on her face. Laura flashed her badge and the confusion on the other woman's face deepened.

"Can I help you, officer?"

Laura smiled. "I'm looking for Tara Kellogg."

"Yes? Can I help you?" Laura knew instantly this was a dead end. Tara Kellogg's mixed heritage was obvious.

"I was... I was checking on women born on August fifth, twenty-six years ago." This was awkward. Laura couldn't reveal too much information about the case, but the other woman was entitled to an explanation for why the police were showing up at her door.

"That's my birthday." Suspicion narrowed her eyes and Laura didn't blame her.

"I'm working on a case and there was some confusion about birth certificates issued around that date. Specifically by those filed by midwives."

"Okay." Again, the word had several more syllables.

"Were you delivered by a midwife?"

"I was."

"Were your parents present?"

Tara raised an eyebrow. "Well, my mother sure was." She shook her head. "And yes, my father was there, too." Her tone was defensive and the frown lines

235

on her forehead etched deeper. "What is this about?"

Laura had no choice but to explain. "There have been some murders in Memphis and there was the possibility that twins were involved. So I was following up on baby girls born on your birthday."

"And because I'm Black, you suspected I was involved." Now anger replaced confusion.

The reality of her statement was disheartening. "Just the opposite. I'm looking for a Caucasian blond woman."

Tara visibly relaxed. "Well, I hope you find her."

"Thanks." Or if she didn't exist, a confession from Alexandra was probably the only definitive way to solve this. The idea was becoming firmly planted.

***

"What is the plan?" John asked, and even through the phone she could sense he was nervous. "Because I don't want you to do anything alone that might get you into trouble."

Driving back to Memphis, she knew what she had to do next. "I just need to make a stop at the brokerage firm that controls Natalie's trust fund and then talk to Alexandra. Maybe she'll slip with something we can use. And if she is the perp, she's dangerous. Don't forget that. And at this point, I have no doubt she knows she is the prime suspect. I am sure she thinks she is smarter than we are, which I can use to my advantage. And I'm going to see her at her office. A very public place."

"I don't like it," John said.

"We're out of time. Goodman gave me seventy-two hours to come up with a suspect we can indict. Then

I have no doubt she's going to take the case out of our hands. Which would really piss me off after all the time and work we've put in so far."

"I get it. But maybe we could use other eyes on this."

"I don't have a problem with that. I just want to follow what we have without other people second-guessing us."

"Because you think…"

"There's more here than just the murders. I am beginning to wonder if the bigger picture includes missing children and black market adoptions on a much bigger scale than we initially thought." She inhaled. "If Goodman steps in, we'll lose credibility and I'm afraid it will compromise our ability to figure this out."

"You know as well as I do, nothing we have on Alexandra will stand up in court," he reminded her.

"Yeah, her rotator cuff injury really screwed us up." Lightning struck. "Unless I can prove she's ambidextrous."

"Listen, Randy's going to be released tomorrow. Just wait until then so I can back you up."

"You take care of Randy. I'll be fine. But I am glad he's okay. Any idea who's responsible yet?"

"No, but you know every cop with a spare minute is working on it. They'll find the perp."

Hanging up, Laura put her plan in motion. It was so simple. And she just happened to have a stress ball in her bag. She called Devin and had to leave a message.

***

"Hello, Alexandra," Laura greeted her, stepping

into the other woman's office.

Alexandra stood and rested her palms flat on her desk. "Do I need my lawyer?" Her tone was tinged with poison.

"No. We're just still trying to trace your twin."

"And?"

Laura reached into her bag and pulled out the ball. "I just want to test a theory of mine."

She tossed the ball to Alexandra's left side. Without thinking, Alexandra grabbed it with her left hand, turned it over, and stared at it. She lifted her gaze to Laura's, the look full of challenge.

"Well, we now know your injured right shoulder isn't a factor, since you're obviously ambidextrous, so why don't you just tell me the truth."

Alexandra sank into her chair. "I was trying to protect my mother's memory."

"Go on."

"I was adopted. My twin was, too. But then she disappeared."

Laura was completely caught off guard. This was not what she expected. "Your birth certificate contradicts that."

Alexandra looked at her as if she was the most naïve creature in the world. "Do you really believe all those are accurate?"

"Why don't you start from the beginning."

"My mother left home when she had just graduated high school. She had met Sarah Jane Malone and moved in with her. And no, she wasn't thrown out of the house. I suppose the lure of what Sarah Jane had to offer was too much to resist.

"Sarah Jane had other friends, too. Some she

worked, you know, on the streets, and some she placed in jobs at the Bureau of Vital Statistics. So after a while, my mother took one of those jobs and it was up to her to file birth certificates, including switching those supplied to her by Sarah Jane."

"Falsified birth certificates," Laura clarified, more for herself than for Alexandra..

The magnitude of that was mind boggling. She had suspected this, but hearing confirmation made her sick to her stomach. How many children, how many babies delivered by midwives and stolen? And it was so straight-forward, so easy. Just change the birth certificates. How simple and how heinous.

That would also explain why Evan's name was on the birth certificate. Sarah Jane had one of her cronies file it when Nora and Evan married and decided to adopt Alexandra and possibly her twin. Still, was there a twin?

"Yes. Children that disappeared from their homes or just after they were born. A new birth certificate and a new life." She cleared her throat. "I was one of those children. My twin and me."

"So you're saying your mother adopted you and your sister and the records were changed."

"Yes. It was Sarah Jane's insurance that my mother would never reveal anything about the business. But my sister disappeared. I don't know what happened exactly. But, of course, my mother could never file a report. She was terrified her little schemes with Sarah Jane would be exposed. And the rest of what I told you was true. Alana somehow ended up in foster care and had a terrible life. At least that's what she said."

"What happened to your sister's birth certificate.

It's not on file."

"I have no idea. All I can tell you is what my mother told me."

"That's quite a story."

"I know I should have told you sooner. But you didn't believe me about having a twin, so I was afraid to tell you the whole truth."

"I thought you said you were protecting your mother's memory."

"Well, that, too, of course. She changed after she married my dad. Went all holier than thou. Went to church. Loved her neighbors. She was just working out her guilt. I mean, what else could she do? She was as much a part of their schemes as they were. And he went along with her. Too bad they didn't spend as much time with their daughter. I suppose they were worried she might turn out to be a 'sinner', too." She sneered at the word.

Just then, Jeff appeared at the office door. "What now?" he demanded, glaring at Laura.

"I had to tell her the truth," Alexandra stated.

Jeff blinked at this. "The truth?"

"About my mother. And Sarah Jane."

Jeff's eyebrows drew together, but he said nothing.

"And what about Rusty Leach?" Laura asked.

Alexandra shrugged. "You can't just walk in and steal a baby. You need help."

"A midwife to spirit away the newborn and pronounce it dead," Laura responded. "And what about the women who wanted to hold their babies, even though they were supposedly dead?"

"I guess Rusty and Sarah Jane found some way to talk them out of it. I don't know. It wasn't as if I was there." Alexandra sounded defensive now, her voice rising.

"Well that explains a lot." Laura inhaled, then exhaled. "But there is one missing piece here."

"And what would that be?" Jeff snarled at her.

"The little, or not so little, matter of the trust fund. You remember, the fifteen million dollars. I stopped by the brokerage. And apparently it is now under your control."

Alexandra visibly paled and her hands tightened into fists. She glanced up at Jeff.

"Check," he ordered her.

She opened her laptop and tapped away. After a minute, her features softened and she audibly exhaled. "Still in transfer."

Laura's visit with the broker hadn't been completely disappointing. In a case like this, without proof or a specific warrant, they couldn't interfere with the trust fund. But she managed to have them agree to delay the transfer.

She grinned at Laura. "That is my retirement. My parents wanted to be all ethical and wouldn't agree to touch it except for Natalie's care. My mother's parents set it up originally, but the bulk of it came from less than legal means. And my asshole parents decided they were afraid to spend it. They were sure there would be too many questions, and too stupid to figure out a way to avoid an inquiry. So they lived like paupers. What a waste…" She shrugged as if killing them was inconsequential.

"And Sarah Jane and Rusty Leach?" Laura pressed.

Alexandra shrugged. "Collateral damage. It also worked with the fake twin angle and diverted attention away from Aunt Natalie's fund, which as you know is now mine. Too bad you were so smart. A few more days and we would have been free and clear in a no extradition paradise."

The fake twin angle. There it was. And Laura knew Alexandra was only confessing because she was certain Laura could never tell anyone.

Jeff looked directly at Alexandra and raised his eyebrows.

At her nod, he held out his hand to Laura. "I'm gonna need your gun and your cell phone."

Looking at him as if he had three heads, Laura smiled until she saw the revolver in his other hand. It was pointed at her abdomen. There were few worse things than getting shot in the gut. It would be a terrible way to die. She inhaled slowly. Getting upset or responding in any way that would agitate either one of them right now wouldn't help her situation.

"Gun and cell phone," he repeated, his nostrils flaring.

Reluctantly reaching into the holster on her hip, she extracted her gun and handed it to him. He stuffed it into his belt and she could only hope it would discharge. Of course, luck didn't usually go that way.

Then she reached into her bag.

"Slowly," he admonished. "I would hate to shoot you."

"I think that might attract some unwanted attention," Laura countered.

Lifting his chin to Alexandra, she reached behind her and pulled out a pillow. Laura was aware firing a small gun through something like that would definitely deaden the sound. So, they had prepared for this. She should have suspected, since it was pretty clear the woman across the desk and her boyfriend were axe murderers. She, however, had not imagined they were so brazen as to try something in a public place.

A small drop of sweat trickled down between her breasts and her mouth went dry. Her mind, however, was assessing all her options.

Continuing to rummage in her bag, she withdrew her phone and gave it to Jeff. Grabbing her hand, he pulled her thumb to the keypad and pressed, unlocking it. He was looking down at her cell and seeing an opening, and counting on his lack of experience in handling a weapon or holding a hostage, she charged him, knocking him off balance. He was not unprepared. He recovered instantly and slammed his fist into her jaw. Her phone in his hand increased the impact of the blow and sent her reeling.

"Don't make me shoot you," he sneered. "Before I'm ready, that is."

Then, scrolling through her contacts, he stopped at one and started texting. When he finished, he dropped the phone to the floor and stomped on it until it was crushed.

"Now you won't be missed for days," he said, grinning in victory. Waving his gun, he motioned her up.

Laura imagined he had texted John, since they knew he was her partner. But would he believe the message? She hoped not. Her life might depend on it. "No twin, huh?"

"Of course not," Alexandra snorted. "But pretty clever, don't you think? You are supposed to be one of the best and I had you going, didn't I?"

Yes, she did, although Laura was loath to admit it. The perfect plan. Create another possible perp and make certain all the evidence was circumstantial, which meant there was no chance of a conviction. Laura did have to give them credit. It was a brilliant strategy.

"What about me?" Alexandra asked.

"Follow me in her car and then I'll bring you back here. That way you can play the innocent if anyone comes by to check. I'll will meet you later at the house." Then he turned to Laura. "I am going to have my gun trained on you as we walk to your car. One false move and you will regret it. Oh, and leave your bag."

"You'll get caught." Laura tried to sound blasé.

"Maybe, but you won't care since you'll be dead."

Chapter Eighteen

Where the hell was she? Devin was getting frantic. It was past seven and he hadn't heard from her all day. She hadn't shown up at the office after her trip north and when he got to her house, her car was parked outside, but she wasn't home. He drove to his house, poured a scotch and paced, trying her cell again and again. Voicemail. He wanted to throw his phone across the room, as if that might alleviate the gnawing in his gut.

Just then, his phone rang and he snapped it up, hoping it was Laura.

"Hey, Devin, it's John. I'm sorry. I should have called you sooner. But they just released Randy and I was helping him and I just got the message from Laura."

"Where is she?" he barked, pacing back and forth and clutching his cup of coffee.

"Well, first she called me on her way back from Rutherford. The twin thing was a bust. But she said she was stopping by the brokerage firm that controls Natalie's money and then she was going to talk to Alexandra. But then, a while later, I got another message."

"And?"

"She just said she needed to take off for a day or so and get her head clear."

The words sank into him like a brick thrown against his chest. *About me?* Was this another Jillian? Just walk away and leave behind the carnage of a heart chewed up and spit out.

"I'm worried," John said.

"Did she say anything else? How did she sound?"

"It was a text."

That struck Devin as odd, even though that had been Jillian's M.O. He could understand if Laura didn't want to deal with him directly about their relationship, but she and John were knee deep in solving these murders. Even if she wanted to walk away from Devin, he couldn't imagine she would walk away from that. And in her last message to him she said she'd call him later. That she was following a hunch. That didn't sound like someone who was taking off to clear her head. None of this made sense. He hadn't known her that long, but his gut told him she would never do that kind of thing. It wasn't who she was.

"I know, I know," John said before Devin could respond. "I am worried," he repeated. "This isn't something she'd do. Especially now."

"What does that mean?"

"The new captain put a time limit on us to come up with a person of interest and the clock was winding down." John took a deep breath.

"What was her plan?" Forcing himself to remain calm, he hoped John wasn't going to say Laura was doing something that would put her at risk.

"I think she was going to try to get a confession."

"Alone?" Devin's pulse ramped up so high he thought he might have a stroke.

"I know. There's that ridiculous part of her that

forgets she's not invincible. I'm on my way to Alexandra's now."

"Text me the address and I'll meet you there."

***

Her head was pounding and her eyes burned. Slowly blinking them open, a fresh shot of pain riveted through her head. Focusing on staying calm, she looked around but all was near darkness. She was strapped to a chair and her legs were bound at the ankles. Wiggling her limbs, she was tightly secured. But at least there was air to breathe.

Trying her best to remember what happened, she recalled being pushed into the back seat of a car. Jeff had leaned in and stuck the gun against her forehead and instantly she felt the prick of a needle in her neck. The drug hit her hard and quickly, but she still had been conscious enough to remember he had tied her hands with a zip tie he had plucked from his pocket. He had put the gun down, but her body had been too heavy with sedation to resist. She was furious at herself for letting this go so far. Knowing her opportunity would come to fight back, she tried to keep her mind clear. The drug would only last so long.

She knew the car was an older Honda that smelled of cigarette smoke and the filthy seats were covered with torn fabric and sticky. Concentrating on the details was all she could do.

They stopped and Laura recognized her neighborhood, and knew they were at her house. Alexandra had then slipped into the car and they pulled away, stopped again after a while, then the other woman got out and Jeff drove on. So Alexandra had been taken back to the University and Laura's car was now parked at her home. If John and Devin were looking for her, they would see her vehicle and waste precious time trying to find her there. But she slipped into the abyss before she could worry about that or try and determine where Jeff was taking her.

Later, she had been vaguely aware the vehicle was no longer moving.

"Awake?" Jeff had asked as he leaned in next to her and shoved another needle into her arm. Before she could resist, her body had given out on her completely and the blackness overwhelmed her. It made sense a biology professor would have the expertise to concoct injections that would serve his purpose.

She was awake now, groggy and hung over from the effects of whatever he had given her. But she knew she just had to remain calm. Unfortunately, since she had been drugged, she had no idea how long she was out or how far they'd driven. She had no clue where she was, but she had to assume this place was isolated.

Concentrating on her senses, she smelled musty hay and old manure. What she could discern of the enclosure, there was muted light seeping in from over the walls. The chair she was anchored to sat alone in the middle of a rectangular space.

Outside, there was the chirping of crickets and the hoarse crying of frogs. She was in a horse's stall, in a barn, in the country. Obviously isolated, she knew calling out was probably not the best plan. She had to release her arms and get out of here before Jeff came back, but the drugs were still dulling her thought processes. Her hands were still bound with a zip tie, and she knew to tighten the plastic to make it taut enough to break, but her lips and teeth weren't working properly. Damn her uncooperative body. She had no weapon, and it was possible his plan was to abandon her here to die of hunger and thirst. The object was to get her out of the way. What had Jeff said? *Now you won't be missed for days.* And by then, they would have transferred the money from the trust and they'd be long gone.

But she had no intention of staying here. The thought of dying here alone, slowly withering away, was unthinkable. She was Laura Chandler, Detective Laura Chandler. Wasn't that how she had introduced herself to Devin? Devin. How she missed him already. If she were to be found here, she hoped he would never see her body. She wanted him to remember her as she was. Not as some desiccated corpse.

No! Alexandra had revealed a monstrous ring of baby thieves. Perfect for the cold case guy. She would get out of here and they would track down those children. Return them to their rightful families. And see Alexandra and Jeff sent away forever. And then have their own children.

That was her last thought before the drug wrapped its arms around her again and she sank back down into darkness.

***

Knocking hard on Alexandra's closed office door, it took a few moments for it to open.

"What now?" Alexandra demanded, her exasperation clear. "I already spoke with Detective Chandler this afternoon. When will you people stop harassing me and find my twin? Before she kills again."

"Do you know what time Detective Chandler left here?" Devin asked, trying to keep the irritation from his tone.

Alexandra shrugged. "An hour or so ago." Narrowing her eyes, she glared at John. "Why, can't you people keep track of each other? No wonder you can't find my parents' killer."

Devin rolled his shoulders to calm his breathing. He desperately needed to take this woman into custody, but the evidence was still so circumstantial, he was afraid he'd never get a warrant. With no action to take and no specific question to ask, they needed to go.

"Thank you for your time," he said and pivoted. John followed suit.

When they got to Devin's car, John turned to him. "She is guilty as homemade sin."

"Knowing and proving are two different things. For now, we have to find Laura. We just verified her last known stop was at Alexandra's office. I passed her house on the way here and her car is parked in front of her house but she's definitely not there. My gut is telling me she's in trouble."

"I agree."

"Let's go back to the station and find out if either Alexandra or her boyfriend have any property outside of town."

"You think they kidnapped her?" John clearly hadn't considered this.

"If she could axe her parents to death, she's capable of anything. I think Laura confronted them and they wanted to shut her up."

Devin couldn't even entertain the idea they had killed her. The very suggestion made his blood run icy in his veins and he had trouble breathing. He prayed they needed to keep her alive, if only to find out how much she had learned so they could cover their tracks. And as stubborn as he knew her to be, it wouldn't be easy for them. For that, he was grateful.

***

She couldn't think straight. It was like crawling up through a cloud of confusion. Gritting her teeth, she would not succumb. Focusing on something concrete, she pictured Devin's face. What had she been thinking about before she passed out again. Having children—with Devin. She loved him and he loved her and if she got out of here—and she had every intention of doing just that—she would spend the rest of her life showing him how much he meant to her.

Hearing his voice in her head, he told her to fight like hell. Her spine straightened and she blinked, her eyes coated with sand. Swallowing hard, she directed her gaze to her hands. A zip tie. Hell, she learned how to break those her first month in the Academy.

Luckily, her hands were bound in front of her. First she tightened the plastic by grabbing the loose end in her mouth and pulling it as hard as she could. It dug into her flesh, but that was good, since the pain helped her concentration. Then, raising her arms over her head, she brought them down hard toward her abdomen. Too weak. Again, she demanded inside her head. It took five tries before the tie snapped and her hands were free.

Turning her attention to her legs, she realized this would not be so easy. Each leg was bound to the chair with rope covered in duct tape. The wrappings were several layers thick. If she tried to peel them away, it would take too long. What she needed was a tool.

Darkness still permeated the area, but she was used to it now and her vision, though limited, was better than it had been when she first woke up. She scanned the area and there, in the corner, was a gift. A hoof pick peeked out from a pile of moldy hay. She could make that work if only she could manage to get hold of it.

Heart racing, she popped the chair over inch by inch. Sweat ran down her face and burned her eyes and her shirt was soaked with it. She was so thirsty. Schooling her thoughts, she continued her mission.

Finally, the thing was at her feet, and she was able to bend at the waist. Her fingers kissed it, but she couldn't wrap them around it. Rocking the chair, she was careful not to let it go so far that it fell over. Stretching until she thought her insides might burst, it was an agonizing hairs breath away. A groan and—she had it, nearly dropped it, then gripped it hard. Wanting to cry with relief and utter victory, Laura set to work on the tape pinning her right leg.

***

All he could think was how much he loved her, how his life would be bereft without her, how all he wanted to do was wrap her in his arms as he waited for Tess and the other detectives to find any possible location. He hated just waiting, but he didn't want to slow their efforts by interfering.

Finally, Tess came bounding into the room, her breath coming in gasps. "An old farm out beyond Cordova. Listed as owned by Jeff Hines' uncle."

Devin was tearing to the door before she finished. "Text me the address."

"I know, and notify all available," she called after him.

Devin had to find her alive. He drove like a maniac, breaking all speed limits, but he had the portable beacon on top of the roof, making it clear he was on police business. Devin had to keep his mind clear and focused. He had no idea what he would find when he got where he was going, but he wanted to be mentally ready for anything. His over-riding thought was he wanted to kill anyone who tried to hurt Laura, but he knew he had to control himself and remain calm.

***

The tip of the pick was dull, but useful. It was taking an agonizing amount of time, but finally the tape was in shreds and she tore it away. Underneath was a thin white rope tied with a square knot. She was able to defeat that in a minute. Then she started on the other leg.

She had just released the cord on her left leg when she heard a car pull up. She thought about hiding next to the door, but it offered little concealment if he looked inside. Deciding on another tactic, she lifted the chair and replacing it in its original position, grabbed the tape and cords and tucked them behind her. Retrieving the zip tie, she placed it over her wrists, concealing the hoof pick in her hands. It wasn't much of a weapon, but she hoped the element of surprise would give her the opening she needed.

Just settling herself and inhaling deeply to ease her

rapid breathing, she looked up to see Jeff in the stall opening. Holding a gun and muttering to himself, he kept shaking his head.

"She said I have to kill you. I'm not the killer. She is. I don't see why we can't just leave you here until we're gone. It's not as if there's extradition where we're going."

"You're right," Laura soothed. "You don't have to kill me. I'm stuck here. I have no phone, no way to communicate and I'm guessing we're out in the middle of nowhere. I can't stop you." She had to keep him talking.

He was clearly thinking about this. "No, I have to do what she says."

"Why? She'll never know."

"Did you know she was in on it? Stealing the kids. The babies. She stepped in to take her mother's place when Nora went all ethical." Disgust twisted his voice. "Alexandra kept records in case they wanted to turn on her. She never trusted any of them. And she wanted money. That's when the whole idea of claiming the trust fund came to her."

"She murdered her own parents." Laura had no love lost for her own mother, but she couldn't even conceive of killing her, let alone axing her to death.

"They weren't her parents. She told you they adopted her. Weren't you listening?"

"But they took her in and raised her as their own."

"As their own slave. They believed children were to be seen and not heard, and obedient to the point of doing all the chores. You know... spare the rod..." He shook his head. "She truly hated them and their rigid rules."

254

It wasn't a surprise to Laura. And it explained so much. Laura wondered who Alexandra's real parents were and hope they never found out the truth of their missing, or suspected dead, child.

"Alexandra bragged about how she took her time with those two and wove them together so it would look like a crazed animal did the deed. She enjoyed it." He shook his head.

"Why the others? Why kill Sarah Jane and Rusty?" She already had the answer but she had to keep him engaged until she could strike.

"She told you. She needed to tie up loose ends. Once the Whitings were dead, those two were the only ones who could contradict her story about a twin. Pretty clever of her to get rid of them. And the Whitings? They treated Alexandra like a servant, kept her isolated. I'm sure they were worried she might discover she wasn't even their kid. And she did. Once she found out about the fake birth certificates, she did some investigating on her own. And her DNA didn't match either of the Whitings. Little did they know how smart she was. How one day she would turn on all of them."

"And the invented twin?"

"Pretty clever, huh. She even got my sister, Gail, to impersonate her. Of course, Alexandra never told her why, but Gail didn't care as long as she got paid."

"Bottom line? All this for the money?" Laura suspected he wanted to clear his conscience with confession and that was working her advantage. "Or revenge for a bad childhood?"

"She likes expensive things." He shrugged.

"And why would you agree to go along?"

He shrugged. "I needed help and I had no idea how

255

deep she was in when I agreed to go along with her plans. I have this little problem."

"The gambling."

Eyes narrowing, he nodded. "Yeah. I borrowed from some very nasty people and she agreed to help me if I'd return the favor. I promise, I didn't know what she would do to them."

"Why don't you leave her now? It's not as if she can turn you into the police."

He laughed at that. "Leave her? Leave fifteen million dollars and a life in paradise. Are you kidding?"

As he stepped closer, Laura tensed her muscles, gauging the distance. Based on his lack of reaction, he hadn't noticed her legs were free. Time shifted to slow motion as he lifted the gun and aimed at her chest.

Wound up tight and ready, she sprang from the chair, angled to the side to miss the discharge from the gun and, hoof pick extended, head-butted him in the abdomen as she aimed the pick at his temple. Crying out, he fell back as blood spurted from the side of his head. Her knee slammed into his chest, her weight thrown forward, as he lifted the gun and attempted to target her again.

Grabbing his wrist, she twisted as the gun fired. Dirt and dust rained down in a sheet from the roof and nearly blinded her as she wrestled the weapon from his grasp.

"Freeze," she shouted at him, but he threw himself up and tackled her. Falling onto her back, she managed to hang on to the gun. It fired again and he fell on top of her, limp this time. Pumped with adrenaline, she rolled away from him, and skittered backward to get some distance. Expecting him to attack again, she pointed the gun as she got to her feet. A huge hole gaped wide in his back and the ground was saturating with blood.

Hearing a noise at the opening of the barn, she pivoted and steadied the gun. If Alexandra had followed, she was ready.

***

Blood pumping hard, Devin had moved to the outbuilding. Its condition was not much better than the house hovering next to it, but it was upright, some walls were still standing. A gunshot screamed in the quiet and Devin took off at a run. Another shot and by now Devin was at the entrance, frantically searching for Laura.

"Laura?" he cried out.

"Here," she answered, gasping. Seeing Devin, she stood on shaky legs and fell forward into his arms, her knees barely supporting her.

"Oh my God," he breathed. She was covered in blood and his hands shook as he searched her body for wounds. Looking down, she hastened to reassure him.

"The blood's not mine."

Relief bathed him like a balm. She was still gripping the gun and she angled it into the stall.

"Is he dead?" Devin asked.

"I think so."

Devin peered into the dark. Approaching the body on the ground, he kicked at it, but Jeff didn't move. Kneeling down, Devin checked his jugular. No pulse.

Walking back to Laura, he nodded. "Are you all right?"

"I am now. But I'd rather not do that again."

257

"At least you have your sense of humor back."

"Can I borrow your phone?"

He handed her the cell and she called John. "Arrest Alexandra now."

"Where are you? Are you okay?" John was clearly frantic. "I'm almost there."

"I'm fine, but she's guilty. They both confirmed it. I'll explain later. Just get to her and take her into custody before she can destroy any evidence."

"Consider it done."

"Oh and send some units here. Jeff Hines is dead, but we need to secure this as a crime scene."

He and Laura sat on a fallen rock outside to wait for the others to arrive. As they held onto each other, Laura related everything Jeff had told her.

"So the innocent Whitings weren't so innocent after all," he responded.

"But the good news is, Jeff said Alexandra kept records. If we can tap into those, we might just be able to find some missing children and return them to their parents."

"That would be great."

Chapter Nineteen

"It's still all circumstantial," Goodman snapped. "There's no proof she murdered those people."

Devin had driven Laura to the station so she could meet with the captain. "I disagree," Laura responded. "Before he died, Jeff told me Alexandra kept records. There's certainly no tangible proof of a twin and Jeff kidnapped me and tried to kill me."

"I don't like it and the D.A. isn't going to like it. Get those records. We need more."

"In the meantime, John has gone to arrest her."

John appeared at the captain's door. He was out of breath and his expression radiated bad news. "She's gone."

"Gone where?" Goodman demanded. That was obviously rhetorical.

John didn't bother with a response to that. "She left in a hurry. We got her computer and some notes from her desk."

Goodman shook her head and rolled her eyes. "I hope it's worthwhile."

"Could you give us all a break here, Captain," Devin said quietly, controlling the irritation running through him.

"We'll get her. There's an APB out on her and

we've covered all the ways out of town. We'll get her," Laura repeated.

Goodman glared at Laura. "Well, you just shot someone, so you're on administrative leave until further notice."

Stunned, Laura couldn't say anything, but Devin caught her eye and winked at her. Roy, his brother, was in IA and he could see to it the incident was reviewed quickly. And even though she was officially not working, nothing was going to stop her from gathering evidence to put Alexandra away.

Laura, Devin and John went into the conference room and examined all the paper documents as Tess worked to break the password on Alexandra's computer. It didn't take Tess long before they could open a file called 'rewards'. Of course Alexandra would view the additional income that way, with no thought to the lives she and her family and associates had destroyed.

Soon, they had proof positive that babies had been taken and missing children sent to new homes. There were pictures of birth certificates that would lead them to some of the abducted and kidnapped.

"Looks like you have your work cut out for you," Laura said to Devin.

He was grinning. "Nothing like justice to make things better."

"And job security," John added.

"There's no more we can do tonight," Devin said. "Let's get some food and some sleep." He turned to John. "You coming?"

"No, thanks. I need to check on Randy."

"I'm so glad he's recovering," Laura said. "Do they have any idea who shot him?"

John's face twisted in a combination of disgust and sadness. "A thirteen-year-old kid who got hold of his dad's gun and was out with his friends showing off."

"Oh my God," Devin and Laura said together.

"Randy will recover, but I wonder about the kid," John said. "He'll have to live with that."

***

Hamburgers never tasted better. They ate those with fries and washed it down with two glasses each of white wine. That was just before they went to bed and feasted on each other. Even exhausted, Devin knew he could never get enough of her. After today, when he very well could have lost her, he savored every part of her even more. His memory of that fear fueled his passion and Laura's thirst equaled his. Sweaty and worn out, he fell into a deep sleep, only to wake a few hours later. Holding Laura in his arms, he treasured this time and knew he never wanted to let her go. He would have to convince her not to put herself at risk like that ever again. She never should have gone alone to interview Alexandra.

A shuffling noise from the living room startled him. *Damn squirrels. They think the roof is their playground.* Carefully sliding away from Laura, so he wouldn't wake her, he edged his way down the hall. And never saw it coming.

***

"Bitch. Three years. No, longer than that. And you had to go and screw it up for me. It was so brilliant. I know I had you going for a while."

Laura heard the words through the fog of her dreams. Suddenly awake, the shadow over her was a nightmare. Alexandra Whiting was a black hoodie, holding an axe over her shoulder and primed to strike. Her right hand was bound to the bedpost with rope. Damn.

Twice in one day was too much. Heart throwing itself into her chest, Laura was not about to become chopped liver. Almost laughing inwardly at the terrible pun, knowing her thought was due to denial and shock. Devin? Where was Devin? Oh dear Lord, had she hurt him? Was he dead? Rage-fed adrenaline pumped through her veins and she quickly assessed her options.

"Where's Devin?" Keeping the hysteria from her tone was difficult.

Alexandra shook her head. "Where's Jeff?"

"He's dead."

Laura waited for a reaction and was a little unnerved when Alexandra just nodded.

She just had to keep Alexandra talking.

"It was a brilliant plan. I hated to ruin it for you."

"Then why did you?" Alexandra snarled.

"Because you can't just go around killing people."

Alexandra's slow smile revealed sharp white teeth. "But of course you can. People do it all the time. And I had a fifteen million dollar incentive.

"But, since I can no longer get away with being a twin, I decided to steal your identity. Your badge, your I.D., even your driver's license. It won't work for long, but it will get me onto a plane. The money's transferring, so all I have to do is get to it. And now I don't even have to split it with Jeff. Lucky break. I might have had to do away with him, too. He was such a loser."

So that was it. And Alexandra was right. A little hair dye and contact lenses and she could probably pass for Laura. She certainly could once she was away from here, where no one would know the difference. And if no one found Laura's body for a day or so, Alexandra could be long gone.

Laura had really never thought about dying. Not even earlier when Jeff had that gun pointed at her chest. But now… now her time just might be up. Devin could be dead or certainly incapacitated. She had been placed on leave and her phone had been destroyed, so no one would call. And no one would check on them until tomorrow afternoon at the soonest. Plenty of time for Alexandra to dispose of the bodies and get away.

Calm pervaded. So odd. Her heart slowed when it should be pounding and her blood pulsing, but instead she was filled with a terrible resignation. Her life didn't pass before her eyes; her only regret that Devin had been hurt because of her. A single tear slid down her cheek as she watched with horrible fascination as the axe rose and arced toward her.

The screaming report of the gunshot and the blood spurting from Alexandra's chest was surreal. The axe fell, burying itself deep into Laura's left wrist. Alexandra's body dropped beside it with a resounding thump, shaking the bed.

Laura suddenly couldn't catch her breath. Her gaze lifted to see Devin in the doorway, holding his gun in both hands before he, too, collapsed. Blood streamed down his right bicep. He was alive and he had just saved her life. Now, she had to get to him.

Angling her body, and her adrenaline rushing through her veins, she felt for the pen she kept on the bedside table and wiggled it under the bindings, releasing her arm. Dizziness slowed her progress, but she managed to lift her hips and buck Alexandra's body off. Grabbing at the sheet, she wrapped it around her wrist, only slightly aware of the amount of flowing blood.

Racing to Devin, she felt for a pulse. Finding it under her fingers, relief eased some of her panic and she searched his pockets for his phone. Grabbing it, she dialed 911. "Officer down, officer down," she screamed, gave the address and cradled his head in her lap. Applying pressure to the wound, she was relieved to see it didn't appear to be fatal. The blade had sliced down into the shoulder rather than across to the neck. She wished they'd hurry. It was her last thought before she passed out.

***

Awaking in the hospital was an odd sensation and it took Laura a minute to acclimate. Her left wrist felt strange and she noticed it was covered in bandages. Betty, Devin's mother, was hovering over her, speaking quietly.

"Devin?"

Betty stroked her forehead. "He'll be fine. Some rest and rehab and he'll be good as new. Thank heavens that boy has such great reflexes. The doctor said if he hadn't moved when he did, he might have…" Betty choked and her face glistened with tears. "But you're both okay. And you are both going to stay with us so I can make sure you are taken care of."

Hearing those words filled Laura with such emotion, she too broke down and let the tears flow.

"Can I see him?"

"You lost a lot of blood. You're pretty weak. But, if the nurse says it's okay, I will wheel you over to his room."

A while later, Laura was carefully manipulated into a wheelchair and taken to see Devin. His lips were pressed together fighting the pain, but when he saw her, he smiled so broadly her world lit up.

There were no words, so she angled as close to him on the left side as she could and put her head down on his chest, carefully avoiding the swath of bandages over his right shoulder and across his chest. With his left hand, he stroked her hair as she listened to the sound of his heart beating. It was the most beautiful thing she had ever heard.

Epilogue

Two months later

Devin was hard at it already, trying to track down the missing children and babies. Goodman had grudgingly admitted privately they had done a great job at incredible personal risk, but publicly took all the credit. Randy had completely recovered and he and John were going strong and Cara was still dating Tom.

Laura was getting a little antsy. The murders that had come across her desk were fairly simple, and it was easy to make the arrests with enough evidence to successfully prosecute. She was spending her off time these days sorting through her stuff since she and Devin had decided to move in together and she wanted to rent out her house.

Laura was deep in mentally re-decorating when John startled her, appearing at her desk. "The captain wants us."

Reluctantly, she stood and moved with him to the captain's office, wondering what they had done wrong this time.

Goodman stood in front of her desk, her arms crossed over her chest. Laura wished the other woman would just get over it. "A woman was just found dead in her employer's home. The owner is Eleanor Madsen. *The* Eleanor Madsen." She scribbled something and handed it to Laura. "Here's the address. Can you handle it?"

Laura had learned not to rise to this woman's constant insults. It was a game she chose not to play.

"On it," Laura responded.

"And this time, try not to make more headlines than the deceased."

About The Author

Leslie Hachtel's various jobs have included licensed veterinary technician, caterer, horseback riding instructor for the disabled and advertising media buyer, which have all given her a wealth of experiences. However, it has been writing that has consistently been her passion.

She is an Amazon bestselling author who now lives in Florida with her very supportive husband, and her new writing buddy, Josie, the poodle mix.

She loves to hear from readers!

Website: https://www.LeslieHachtel.com/
Facebook: www.facebook.com/lesliehachtelwriter/
Twitter: @lesliehachtel
Blog: LeslieHachtelWriter.wordpress.com
Bookbub: www.bookbub.com/authors/leslie-hachtel

www.ingramcontent.com/pod-product-compliance
Lightning Source LLC
Chambersburg PA
CBHW071122170626
46809CB00002B/469

* 9 7 8 1 7 3 3 7 2 7 8 5 3 *